First Generation

David La Piana

ISBN: 1492965324
ISBN 13: 9781492965329
Library of Congress Control Number: 2013920073
CreateSpace Independent Publishing Platform
North Charleston, South Carolina

To my parents, who did everything they could to help me, and to Mary, Marisa and Tessa, who listen to my stories.

I

The Order-Filler.

I am eight years old and Dad is sitting on the old brown couch in a worn-out sleeveless T-shirt, that big red welt cutting across his left bicep, four smaller welts splayed like fingers in a semi-circle below it. I like to climb in his lap, to run my small hand over the fat, lumpy wheals, feeling their raised smoothness like small riverbed stones. When I ask about them he says he had an accident when he was young. He makes it out to be nothing.

"But it musta hurt, didn'it?"

"Nah, it was a long time ago," he says.

"How long ago?"

"Way back before you was born." Then, looking over at Mom: "Before I even married youse, right Gina?"

"But I bet there was lots a blood."

"Nope, no blood. *Mannagia*! Dontcha got nothin better to do than pesterin yer ol' man?" he says lightly, putting an end to my questions.

Mom listens from her place at the dinette; she keeps at her work, shelling walnuts. "What's on TV?" she asks. "Try Channel Four, maybe they got that new one on with what's his name."

—⁂—

Thinking back on it as an adult now that he's gone, that's how my talks with Dad always went: brief, empty, and cut short by Mom. It made no difference what I tried to talk to him about – his job at the factory, the Dodgers' chances, or those awful scars on his arm – he never had much to say; and, with Mom around, he would not have had a chance to say much if he had wanted to.

Even when I was a little kid he had his life and I had mine. When we were forced into the same space at dinner Mom did most of the talking, like she had to carry both ends of the conversation for us. He just sat and ate and nodded, approving of the food and of her opinions in the same slow motion of his head. With Gramma and Grandpa at the table the conversation flowed back and forth among the three of them in broken Sicilian and English, with seldom a need for either Dad or me to speak at all. He liked it that way.

—⁂—

I am twelve and as I get older, I wonder if a story is being told between the few words of these empty conversations, if some parallel life with real people, real conversations, real connections, is lurking just out of sight but is somehow there, sustaining them. If so, it is my story too but I cannot figure it out. I see it only in small pieces, the way I catch only bits when the grown-ups speak in dialect.

"Eh, how cuma you no eats – *mangia o ti mangia i cani*," Gramma reliably says to me if I do not clean my plate from a second serving of pasta. Eat or the dogs will eat you.

"Mama, he don' like your sauce, *é trop amargu*," says Mom, making a face like she is tasting something really bitter, getting a dig in the unending battle between our two cooks.

"*Porcu miseria!*" Gramma explodes. "Gina, *é* you food taysta lika sheet. *Chista ca,*" she is pointing to the spread before us, "*é buonu*, eh Gianni?" She puts Dad on the spot, trying to make him choose sides, but he will never do that, not in this fight or any other.

"Ma, da *pasta*, it's always good, if you make it, if Gina makes it, it's always good; *é semp' Buonu*," he says, John Russo the diplomat.

Dinner is served as soon as Dad walks in the door. I sit and listen to the talk but the words carry so little meaning they soon float away like the cigarette smoke rising to the ceiling above the dinette. They are similarly insubstantial, smooth and light, with no place offering a meaningful grip. If there is a story being told, I can't grasp it.

"John, wash up, it's on the table," Mom says as he comes home, letting the screen door slam like a gunshot behind him.

She places a platter of steaming pork chops on the dinette. Then, as Dad washes quickly, using Boraxo to get the grime off, we assemble. When he joins us he is still wearing his work boots and paint-spattered pants but has removed his dirty flannel shirt, relaxing in his threadbare, sleeveless undershirt. He smells antiseptically clean from the recent hand scrubbing.

"Dat S.O.B. Addington," Dad sits down, a look of utter disgust on his face. "'Ficiency expert,' dey calls him. Expert, my eye; he don' know his ass from a hole in da ground."

"Mama, give the kid some mashed potatoes, I made 'em with chicken broth instead of milk, I like 'em better like that." Mom says. She acts like Dad has not said a word. She has her priorities, and Dad's constant complaining – right now it is this new boss, in a few minutes it will be the L.A. traffic – does not rate much consideration. He doesn't seem to mind. He feels better just getting his complaints off his chest, launching them into space on a lonely one-way trip.

"Honey – tell Gramma and Grandpa what they made you do at school today. I don't know how the hell they expect these kids to learn all the crap they throw at 'em." In sixth grade Mom is overwhelmed by the New Math. So am I.

"They make us do these problems where we have to find X," It's like Newton explaining gravity. I know it's the best way to ensure they lose interest quickly. "But how am I s'posed to know X? And then they want us to find Y. It don't make no sense, why can't we just use numbers?"

"See, what's all this crap, and why are they making it so hard on him?" Mom asks the table in general, but once I have used words like "problem," and "X," and "Y," they are as lost as I am so the conversation moves on.

I try not to gag when my eye passes the overflowing ashtray that always sits in the middle of the dinette. I look away when they light up, everyone except Gramma, who maintains an old-fashioned lady-like abstinence from alcohol and tobacco. The others blow lungs full of blue smoke upwards, aiming at the overhead light, gray with the years' nicotine. I want to eat fast and get away, to go back outside to the fresh air with my friends. I want to be anywhere but here. I want to get as far away from them, from all of them, as possible.

After dinner he sits in front of the television watching *Bonanza* or *Gunsmoke* or slowly poring over the Teamsters paper, his lips moving to the words of an article on the recent re-election of the same slate that has always run the Local. It is the only thing I ever see him read. He does not really seem to care what is happening in the union. Hell, he doesn't seem to care what is happening in his own little stucco rental. No matter what, he goes to the factory every day and loads endless cases of paint into living-room-size trailers that are then pulled away by big diesels bound for Fontana, Ojai, Hemet, Reseda, or far away San Francisco; exotic names that exist for us only as words from his mouth. He calls himself an Order-Filler; his real title is Shipping Clerk, which sounds a lot better to me.

"It's da same shitty work no matta what you calls it," he says.

He leaves early each morning, earlier than necessary. He goes to the little coffee shop near the Emerson Paint factory in the City of Industry. Guillermo lets him in before opening time because Dad makes the morning pot of coffee, brings the chairs down off of the table tops, and generally helps open the place up. He does this even though it means getting up an hour earlier than necessary because he likes "Chewin' da fat" with the guys. It is hard for me to imagine him gabbing with "the guys" before work. After work he comes home, eats his dinner, and sits on the couch, or in his old vinyl lounger, smoking cigarettes, watching television, and nodding off until bed time.

Next to Dad's chair is an ashtray holder about the height of an end table. It stands on a round, sloping, brass-colored, weighted metal base support-ing a single Corinthian column topped by a concave disk in which an amber glass ashtray rests. It is the only interesting piece of furniture we own. I am fascinated by it, especially by the handle. It arches high over the top, bridging the ashtray itself, and is in the shape of a leaping antelope. When a smolder-ing cigarette sits below it the antelope appears to be jumping through smoke over a flame, like a lion in a circus act. It is a graceful creature, all outstretched limbs and solid flanks, head turned toward you. I often find myself staring at it.

—m—

One night Dad as usual refuses to play catch with me in the yard after dinner in the last of the summer's fading light. Later he half-listens to me talk about my hero, Sandy Koufax, while he watches a rerun of *Gunsmoke*. When I rest my case: Koufax is the greatest lefthander of all time; he just grunts and turns his full attention back to the television. But tonight I step right in his line of sight.

"I hate you!" I scream it at him. "You're a lousy father; I wish Joe was my dad, not you! He taught Ben how to shoot pool, how to work on cars and shit like that. You ain't ever showed me shit!"

Passively he sits and listens, he does not argue back. Then, with a creak of his knees and a bit of a sore limp that takes all the wind out of my tirade, he gets up. "aye-yiyi," he moans as his tired joints begin to move him, jerkily, almost against his will, and he slowly makes his way down the hall to bed.

It is only 8:30 as he crawls in. The bedroom is at the end of the short hall, a half-dozen steps from the living room. He always leaves the door open. I can see him in the slice of hall light, lying on his side, one arm propped under his head, the other, the one with the welts, on top of the covers, fingers tucked up under his chin like a cartoon drawing of someone sleeping.

Observing this Mom does not yell or hit me, her usual reaction if I am within reach when I am annoying. Instead she does something else, something that actually scares me: she softly and calmly tells me: "You hurt your father's feelings real bad this time, and you ought to go in and apologize to him, right now."

I cannot remember ever before hearing Mom whisper, her voice only knows how to boom. I can hear her from the other end of the block when she calls me home for dinner. She wants to keep Dad, and Gramma and Grandpa, who are in their bedroom, from hearing what she has to say.

My family, the Russo's, does not apologize. We blow up and storm off. Then, when we cool down, we go right back to our normal relations, such as they are. An apology recognizes that you might have hurt someone, made them uncomfortable. But in our family no one gives a shit. You can say anything at all and it is supposed to just roll off the other person's back. So I take it seriously when Mom speaks so softly *and* asks me to do something so out of the ordinary.

Slowly I make my way to my parents' room. I pass the bathroom, pass the big hall closet I liked to hide in when I was smaller, pass my own room on the right, and my grandparents' on the left. My mind is blank – what do I say? For a while I stand at the foot of Dad's bed, watching, hoping he has gone to sleep so I can just go. But as I am about to turn around his eyes blink in the semi-darkness and I know that he knows I am there. So I walk around to face him and tentatively say his name. He grunts in return, signaling that he has heard me, nothing more.

I tell him, "I'm sorry, I didn't mean it. You're a great dad." I do not sound convincing. But he is my father and that is how you apologize, right?

"You know, I ain't da best fahder in da world," he says in a low voice. Everyone is whispering tonight. "But I ain't never hit youse." He pauses, like that settles it. "Ben's dad, he smacks dem kids around but good all da time, so does Al. Dey all do, but not me. I ain't never hurt youse," he repeats.

He hasn't moved a muscle, even to take the hand from under his chin. Lying there immobile he looks as vulnerable as a sleeping child, but he is a grown man, with a day's stubble on his face. He is my father but what I feel in that instant is the twelve year old equivalent of contempt: he is pathetic.

I usually try for pride in his quiet toughness, strong and silent, like in the movies, but it just won't come tonight. It is always a stretch to admire him; there is nothing to admire beyond the stark fact of his existence. Other than work he does nothing, he says nothing, he knows nothing and so, he is nothing. He is five-foot-nine and weighs one hundred sixty pounds. He has slightly thinning, wavy black hair and brown eyes. Even in his fifties, he has added not an ounce of fat. From his pictures I can tell that as a young man he was quite handsome. He still is.

But his mind, his likes and dislikes, his hobbies – I cannot describe any of them because I have never seen a sign of any of them. Still, for my own needs I try to concoct a past for him, one I could admire as a son. When I was younger these stories involved him getting those terrible red welts on his arm in some daring scrape worthy of a comic book superhero. He saved his family from a burning building when he was about my age. He battled Hitler to a standstill just like Superman. He single-handedly fought off a group of muggers, saving his week's pay – our rent money. The stories were silly, but my need for them was real.

Now here I am at his bedside and he cannot even face me, his own son, even though I am really just a kid wanting him to be my small hero. He has run to his bed like a frightened child, and now that I, his child, have worked up the nerve to apologize, he cannot even look at me.

Still I feel that maybe I have an opening, since we are talking, in a way, so I use it. "You coulda hit me when I said that shit to you. I wouldn't'a minded it. It's what you're s'posed to do."

"Oh, sure, hit youse." Without otherwise moving he shakes his head in disgust. He scoffs: "You'd like it if I hit youse."

—⚫—

My father could never bear the thought of striking me, and not because he had read or even heard of Dr. Spock. It was only that he could not get all that worked up, certainly not over me, and I doubt over anything. But he was still the adult, the parent, and he was supposed to care.

He was a good, steady provider, as he told us nearly every week when he brought his pay home to Mom. He was proud of that, and rightly so, but otherwise he was a grown man acting like a maiden aunt, lost in her own world. I could not get anything from him, especially the one thing only he could have given me at that point in my life – someone to show me the way in the years ahead. Because, at twelve, I was about to grow up.

My entire childhood he never once hit me. This was certainly unusual for fathers in our neighborhood. Pico Rivera, east of East L.A., was mostly working but poor, overwhelmingly *Chicano*, and crowded, so men used their fists without much thought, both within their own homes and on the streets. Mom more than made up for Dad's pacifism; she hit me, threw her shoe at me if I tried to run, and screamed at me on a regular basis. But I was certain Dad's gentleness came less from love or forbearance than from a lack of interest. You have to care what your son does in order to be angry enough to hit him, it seemed to me. A steady provider is all he could ever be, no matter what I said or did to try to change him.

I went out on a limb that night, telling him that he should hit me when I deserved it, to show he cared. This was an idea that I had been developing for some time. It went like this: How is Dad different from the other dads in the neighborhood? Two ways: first, he never shows me how to do anything or does anything normal with me; things like playing catch, fishing, working on cars. . .and second, he never hits me. So, in my child's mind I linked the two. Since I could not force him to play catch maybe if I could move him to hit me, then the other would come. I worked it out slowly, lying in bed, over many nights. I considered the connection between the two elements and refined it as best I could; it was all I had.

—⚓—

The whole effort to reach him has been a waste of time. I am back to where I was when I started screaming at him minutes ago. Except I feel even more savage, more disgusted, and I do not care if he is lying in bed and if everyone is whispering.

I shout: "You don't give enough of a shit to even hit me, do you?" He just sighs softly and remains quiet. I stand taller, towering over him as he lays there, helpless. I screech, tears in my voice. "Or even to talk to me, eh man?" Now I am not talking to him like a father at all, but like one of the kids outside on the street; I am screaming mad.

I do not want to talk to my father this way, but here I am. To make it worse, I cannot stop the tears in my voice from migrating to my eyes. Shaking with anger, I want to pull him from that bed and force him to come alive. It makes no difference to me if he stands up and hugs me or pulls a machete from under the mattress and hacks off my arm. I need him to do something, to act. Because I am standing so close I start to grab him, to drag him out of bed if necessary. But as I lay my hand on his arm, it lands on top of those welts, which gives me a physical surprise, a kind of jolt. He does not react, I am not sure he feels it at all. Touching him is like touching a corpse, a living, breathing, warm-to-the-touch corpse that is supposed to be my father. But his arm is hard, like granite, I can feel the muscle and see the vein that pops just below the skin. It is the arm of a man who has worked hard his whole life, and who once had a terrible accident that scarred him.

I stop. Touching him is painful. The warmth of his body promises something, but it is biological warmth, nothing more, a consequence of life; and it is the only connection we have: we are both alive. The touch ties me to him in a way I can feel but not understand.

I am still tearing up, but now I say again that I did not mean what I just said. I say it and take it back, then say worse still and then take that back as well. I am fighting with myself; he does not fight.

I have not cried because of a sudden recognition that I do in fact love this man the way he is, or of how good I have it, think of all the kids whose fathers are drunken bastards, or those who do not have fathers at all. No, I would gladly take an occasional belt-beating along with all the ways other dads raise their sons.

I find that I am still touching him. Almost involuntarily, I start to rub his arm and soon he moves, putting his other hand over mine. I can see his eyes glistening in the darkness and I hope that, after everything I have said, maybe he feels something. Maybe this will change him, clear the air, show him I need him.

We sit together, my hand on his muscled, scarred arm, his other calloused hand, rough, but warm to the touch, covering mine. Strange, but for once I don't want to move, to get away from him. I feel closer to him then, with my hand on his arm, than ever before. Still I know that when I release him I will have to start growing up – and I will still be on my own.

That night changed nothing. His sad eyes had nothing to do with me; they had been looking somewhere, searching for someone, but not for me. Growing up I had no idea who he was or what his life had been. He never talked about what it was like when he was young. Mom was no help. She talked freely about her own life as a young girl, and about her early life with Dad, after the war, before me. But her stories were always more about herself than Dad. For her, he only existed as her husband. It always seemed to me that the key to him had something to do with those welts. How tough he had to be. If I could unravel their mystery, I thought, I could figure him out. That, at least, would be something. So I started on a story, not the cartoonish ones I invented to explain those welts when I was little. I needed a real history that explained him to me, and I found one.

II

Got any letters goin' home?

There was no denying it: she was now a wreck, a useless lump of scrap. What a waste, John Russo thought, after all they had been through together. He recalled the frenzy of the hurried loading of five hundred trucks onto eighteen different transports in Norfolk: trucks, self-propelled artillery pieces, jeeps and tanks went onto ships helter-skelter while their fuel, ammo, spare parts, and crews were dispersed to others. Everything was crammed together with no thought to what went with what, or to what would be needed, where, when, and by whom.

His transport, the *SS Earl*, had carried two million .50 caliber rounds but no machine guns to fire them; hundreds of cases of Coca Cola; tons of white flour – although no one actually saw a loaf of bread, it was argued, throughout the entire North Africa campaign; ten thousand M1 rifles, but none of their .30 caliber ammo; and a thousand pairs of ladies' stockings, brought along as trade goods, ordered by some staff officer who clearly knew nothing about how local women dressed. Since the *Earl* carried no trucks the Navy brought Russo on it, along with what seemed to be most of the division's other drivers and mechanics.

Once loaded, the task force, plus escorts watching for U-Boats, made a rushed, zigzagging crossing to the Algerian seaport of Oran, which had recently fallen. He and the other drivers then spent a full week searching for their mounts among the crowded docks where enough matériel to build a small city, and enough firepower to destroy several, were being unloaded with no more care or organization than that of a greedy four-year-old tearing into an embarrassing hoard of Christmas presents.

Navy dock masters tried in vain to bring a semblance of order to the unloading process, mostly by waving their clipboards and yelling. MPs wearing white Sam Browne belts and matching spats chased away local thieves, eager to get their hands on the division's treasure, the likes of which they had never before imagined. Navy Shore Patrols, deftly swinging billy clubs from lanyards looped around wrists, dragooned shirking stevedores, hiding in shadows, into helping with the unloading. Sailors and soldiers by the thousand, despite the lack of any official leave, roamed the town of ancient mud-brown houses and imposing, white-washed colonial edifices, stretching their legs while looking for women and drink after the long passage. French Colonial officials struggled still to decide whose side they were on – Vichy and the Germans, or Uncle Sam and the British, both sides detested equally. Local Algerians tried to salvage their ruined homes after the bombardment and invasion. Bedouins wandered down to the port with their camels, seeking goods, traders, or shelter.

All these and more overran the port of Oran like ants after a careless boot kicks down their hill, with the added excitement of occasional *Luftwaffe* strafing runs on the fat target posed by the groaning port. Before each attack the shipboard alarms sounded and men would drop what they were doing. Anti-aircraft crews ran for their guns but most others simply flattened themselves where they stood, on the deck of a ship or somewhere along the loading docks. The alarms only sounded after the planes came into sight, so there was not much of a chance to run anyway. The sky would fill with the exploding *ack-ack* of anti-aircraft fire, a bomb or two would drop near the ships, British Spitfires would come to chase away the German raiders, and after a few minutes everyone would return to work like nothing had happened.

Finally, almost in spite of itself, the division was ready to move east, toward Tunisia and the war. Regardless of what might lay ahead by that point everyone was glad to see Oran in the rearview mirror.

Sometimes, when Russo turned in at night, he dreamed he was still behind the wheel. It was a pleasant dream because he loved to drive. What had kept him going during the past weeks, when he was often scared half to death, was sitting high up in that cab, cruising along some desolate stretch of road, day after day, just driving. He sometimes dreamed about his best friend back home in New York City. The Bull had an almost-new '38 Ford. In the old days they liked nothing better than to drive around the neighborhood together on a warm evening, windows rolled down and shirtsleeves rolled up, smoking and laughing. They went out hoping to impress the guys and to attract the girls, but mostly they went for the sheer pleasure of driving. Now that the Army had taught him how to be the one in the driver's seat, when he got home he was going to make The Bull let him take a turn behind the wheel himself. He would show the folks how well a man could handle a '38 Ford on a city street after he had driven an overloaded, deuce-and-a-half across most of North Africa on roads that were little more than camel tracks.

Russo was driving and the division was finally moving again under its own power. As they crossed the sands and scrub of Algeria there were days of convoy, with patterns of movement reminiscent of maneuvers back home, although the dessert, the scrub hills, and especially the narrow dirt tracks were nothing like the green, forested terrain and well-paved roads of Upstate New York, where the Army had taught him to drive. Then, often unexpectedly, there were days of fighting. And now, he was in the middle of the lousy back-and-forth fight for Tunisia, where instead of the inconsistently resistant Vichy French and the consistently unresisting Italians, they faced the real thing: German *Panzer* divisions; Von Kesselring, Rommel, Von Arnim, and the Afrika Corps, with three years' experience of desert war. The American II Corps, tasked with defeating this experienced enemy, had been hastily mobilized and minimally trained. With the exception of a few senior noncoms who had fought in the Great War, when the Americans arrived in North Africa they were totally innocent of combat; an innocence that had been lost somewhere along the great sandy highway traversing Tunisia.

Through it all she drove on, never once breaking down; never disappointing him. His once-beautiful, once-new love carried gracefully the scars of her many miles and many fights. Her paint was half gone, her body pitted by the incessant sand churned up from the unpaved roads. Her canvas troop cover was in tatters, her leather rifle sheath, a cavalry-era artifact where the driver kept his weapon strapped outside his door, now lay inert across the seat, rotted from its mounting bracket. Her undercarriage had been pierced by a single bullet hole that did no harm but was already collecting rust. Her engine wheezed, having ingested too much sand and dust, and her clutch smoked and ground every time he shifted gears. He kept telling himself she really could use an oil change, if not a total tear-down.

But none of that mattered. To him she was still a beauty. He only wanted to keep driving. He loved the feeling of movement, the simple joy of pressing his foot down and seeing her move in response. To him the object of the war was to keep moving, and stopping to kill the enemy just got in the way of that purpose. He hoped they would drive all the way to Egypt.

But that was before the sixteen Stukas came screaming down on them as they neared their latest destination, the foot of the Djebel, "the Dj" as the men had come to call the steep and craggy North African hills that alternated with scrub plains in this part of north-central Tunisia. This one appeared on the maps as Djebel Lessouda. The German planes had approached at nearly ground level, so no one saw or heard anything until it was too late; until they popped up over the closest Dj and made the first of three runs, two for strafing and a final one for each plane to drop a single two hundred fifty pound bomb on their immobilized targets. Dozens of high velocity machine gun rounds struck her on the first pass. He had still been in the cab; through the floorboards and the steering wheel he felt the shuddering impacts as they struck the engine compartment just a few feet in front of him. Now she sat useless, half blocking the road, the same road a relief column would need to use to get to them, if one came.

He'd been lucky to get out of the wreck alive. Lucky the troops' ammo load in the rear or her fuel tank had not blown. Most of the infantry he carried had gotten away from her at the first sign of trouble, all except for slow, scared Jimmy Pete, whose ruined body he found dripping over her tailgate, a pool of blood collecting in the sand behind the exhaust pipe. Once the Stukas were gone a couple of the men retrieved Jimmy Pete's body and buried it right beside Russo's truck.

"Hey Jimmy Pete!" Sarge had yelled at breakfast only a day before, as the soldier, carrying his mess tin to a makeshift table, managed to drop his spoon into the dust and scald his hand with coffee slopped from his canteen cup at the same time. "We don't need no entertainment when we got you to watch."

Russo got to his feet, picked up his helmet, pack, and rifle, and joined the long line of frightened men headed toward the summit of the Dj on foot. He took a last brief look at her: two flat tires, passenger side shot all to hell. But it was her face he saw last, and that provided the image that would stay with him. The four evenly spaced holes through her engine block – radiator water, hydraulic fluid and black engine oil staining the desert beneath her – that's what killed her.

—ᴍ—

Djebel Lessouda is a lousy place to die, he thought, now digging his hole deeper in the shifting scree of shale below the brow of the Dj. He was thinking of himself, and of his beloved truck, not of Jimmy Pete, whose memory he had already filed away in that dark room all soldiers must create and then fill with the memories of their dead if they are to keep going. For Russo, that room was already getting crowded.

There had been too many guys like that, OK guys who were only doing what they were told and hoping for the best, maybe a hot meal or a full night's sleep – simple, immediate, physical pleasures that reminded a guy he was still alive and, equally important, that life was still worth living. They lived together for days and weeks and months on end, no relief from one another, until they ceased to be separate men and became, not exactly a family, something more like a machine: a loud, grumbling, itinerant killing machine. And then suddenly someone was gone: a bullet, a shell, a flash of fire, and a part of the machine was missing, a hole opened where someone had taken up space.

Sometimes they were killed outright and left where they lay for the graves registration people to deal with, never to be seen again. But there were other times that were much worse. Times when guys were still alive for a while, screaming for their mothers, or their god, or cursing the Army, the enemy, or God himself, as medics worked in vain to stop the bleeding before finally giving in, administering a dose of morphine, and leaving the man to sleep and to die.

It might have been more manageable if it happened just once and then stopped, like seeing a bad car wreck back home, but it didn't. One, three, eight, or thirty men were taken in a single day. So many were lost that Russo could not think about it or he might start to doubt whether he himself would survive; and he might begin to question the wisdom and skill of his officers.

The killing machine had spare parts, apparently lots of them, and a new replacement was usually only a few days away. Which somehow made it all seem unimportant – who lived and who died – so long as the machine continued its movement, continued its own killing, its destruction of enemy men and armor, occasionally chewing up the miserable Arabs and their orchards and fields and towns encountered along the way, or the thieves, usually half-starved natives caught red-handed stripping the dead and dying from both infidel sides before the stretcher parties could get to them.

—∿—

From the position on the sharp heights of the Dj that half of the battalion now occupied he could see the wreck at the edge of the plain below. She was keeping company with several other trucks, plus a jeep and a Stuart M3 tank, near the base of the Dj. The Stuart's hulk was still smoking even now. Its turret, blown fifty feet away by the force of an internal explosion, lay upside down in the sand. The plain looked like a ready-made graveyard for armor and vehicles. He scanned the desert toward Faid Pass, a deep cut between Dj Lessouda and its neighbor, Dj Ksaira, offering entrance to the dry, flat expanse that carried away toward the horizon.

The attack would come from the pass, Sarge had told them: "Through the pass and right up our assholes."

The battalion had been split between the two hilltops, Dj Lessouda and Dj Ksaira, visible a couple miles away. It might as well have been a thousand miles, for all the support the two groups of roughly nine hundred men could lend to each other now. Every dogface knew light infantry, arrayed like this, was a weak force if this was where the *Wehrmacht's Panzers* decided to make their main assault. Corps Intelligence said the Germans would not attack here but were moving farther south. That judgment justified only a light force occupying the hills astride the pass. And that confident prediction pretty much sealed their fate, according to the pessimists in the battalion, which at this point included almost everyone.

Colonel Wayne, the CO, had argued strongly against splitting his troops between two distant and isolated hills, with no possibility of mutual support and no line of retreat if things went badly, as they had recently developed a habit of doing. He had argued for artillery, so he could defend his positions against armored attack. He had argued against placing the battalion's supporting tank company in the plain below. But there his armor sat, right in the downhill path of any *Panzer* offensive, which, if it came at dawn, would have the sun at its back while the Americans squinted into the morning light at targets across a desert full of glare. Worse yet, his tanks would have to engage those targets head on, where their armor was more than four inches thick, when the only chance an M3 had against a German Tiger tank was to take it enfilade, and even then, it had better shoot first. Wayne had argued that if Field Marshall Rommel himself had dictated a defensive array for the American battalion he sought to destroy he could not have improved upon this plan hatched by the division's own staff officers.

But in the end Colonel Wayne had his orders, and he did what good soldiers have always done – he followed those orders, he tried to make the best of them, and he cursed those who gave them, from the safety of the rear echelons, to the men out in front who would live or die when the issue was settled. This early in the war the supreme commander's staff, three hundred miles from the front, and even the Corps and Division commanders' staffs, still fifty miles away, had not yet made enough mistakes, had not yet learned their trade. Their education would be paid for with young men's lives.

In the cold pre-dawn quiet he heard a crunching from behind on the shale. Then a body slumped down beside him in the hole.

"Where'd you go to take dat crap, Goldie, Division HQ?" Russo asked, a goofy smile on his sooty face.

Goldstein ignored the jibe. "Hey Johnny, you got any letters goin' home? They're collectin'."

Adam Goldstein was, like Russo, a driver from Baker Company. As the company no longer had trucks to drive they were now just a couple of infantrymen sharing a fighting hole. Goldie sat with his back against the hastily-dug parapet wall, his knees propped up in front of him, M1 cradled in his lap. Several days' growth of beard and an oversize helmet pulled low on Goldstein's brow obscured Russo's view of his buddy. It didn't matter. He knew Goldie's features, silhouette, and smell as well as his own. The thin, hawk-like face could not have differed more from Russo's smooth oval flanked by high cheekbones. Goldie's watery blue eyes and thin brown hair that, even at twenty-two, was already receding, contrasted with Russo's olive skin, dark eyes, and abundant black curls. The smell was something they shared: a combination of diesel fuel, gun oil, urine, and sweat.

"How da fuck are dey gonna make a mail run from here?" Russo bitched. "You'd tink if dey could get mail inan outta here maybe dey could get us some hot chow?"

They were down to once-a-day rations, chocolate bars, and a few cartons of cigarettes, having lost much of their supplies in the Stuka attack. He loved to eat, and he loved to talk about how much he loved to eat, which meant that he complained about their unpredictable flow of rations to anyone who would listen. And that was before the current starvation diet was implemented. Next to driving, regular meals was the thing he liked best about the Army, and it didn't seem fair that just when he had been getting plenty of the one, he had so little of the other, and now he had neither. Unlike the other soldiers he never complained about chow. It didn't matter to him what was on the menu, so long as there was enough to eat he was happy.

Before the war John Russo had been a scrawny nineteen-year-old of one hundred twenty-five pounds, raised in New York City on a Depression-era Italian-American diet that consisted mostly of pasta and bread, and not much of either. Modern nutritionists would call it protein-deficient. Mrs. Russo called it dinner for 11. He enlisted on December 8, 1941, motivated equally by anger at the Japs and hunger in his belly. Before shipping out for North Africa he had weighed in at one-fifty; through regular meals and physical exercise the army had built his 5' 8' frame into a wall of muscle that filled out a uniform in a way women found difficult to ignore. That night at Djebel Lessouda he was just short of his twenty-first birthday.

"Hey, Johnny," Goldstein said, looking at his watch under the moonlight. "It's 0200, a new day, and you know what today is?" Russo stared blankly back at Goldie. "It's February 14, Romeo, fuckin' Valentine's Day. Don't you got no Valentine's card to send home to that girl of yours?"

"Goldie, we passed da last goddamned stationers about six tousand miles back. No, I got no fuckin' card. Besides, she ain't 'my girl,'" He protested. "I only went with her for two lousy weeks before we shipped out, we took in a couple of matinees, went for a walk by da Hudson, sat on a bench in da Park and fed da goddamned pigeons, and dat was it. I was too broke even to buy her a lousy dinner, and she knew it." By the Army's grand design, even before shipping out most of his pay went home to his parents in the Bowery. He would have liked to drive her around town in style but he had no civilian license, no car, and no gas rations anyway.

He recalled her auburn hair, a silky dress, and that sweet girl smell, like soap. Girls were still largely a mystery to him, the middle of nine sons. He had never given much serious thought to any particular girl – although he had spent most of his free time stateside thinking about girls in general – until this one.

"I shoulda wrote to her," he finally mumbled, "she was real nice; a real looker too."

Goldstein was shocked. "You mean to tell me you ain't never wrote to her, not even once!" He was the kind of guy who was easily shocked, especially when it helped his cause. And tonight, in honor of Valentine's Day, his cause was his friend's love life. "But she wrote you, plenty, I seen you readin' the letters."

"Yeah, she wrote a lot at first, den less, like she lost interest. But she still goes ta the Bowery to see my folks and writes letters ta me for dem. Dey talk in dialec' an she writes down what dey say. I can tell it's her handwritin'. Anyhow, Mama and Papa, dey can't write for deyselves – eader in English or Eye-talian."

"You write to your folks, but not to your girl?" Goldie asked, his eyebrows disappearing up under his helmet. "What are ya, nuts?"

"Nah, I don' write ta nobody, my folks, my brudders, her, nobody. Dey just write ta me, when she helps 'em."

"Well here's a goddamn piece of GI paper," Goldstein said, his voice determined, forcing a smudged and rumpled sheet of US Army note paper into Russo's hands. "Write to her now for chrissake, before it's too late." He paused, "And then write to your ma, I got another sheet here somewhere. She must think yer dead. And I'm tellin you man that's what I would be if I didn't write to my ol' lady real regular. Mrs. Goldstein would come all the way over here, walk right through that minefield down there, pull me out of this fuckin hole by my ears, and slap me silly with that big ol' purse a' hers."

Russo held the paper dumbly in his hand, like he had never seen such a thing before. To his ears it sounded like Goldstein would welcome his ma coming all the way to Tunisia in order to smack him, right here in the middle of a battlefield, like a little boy who'd wandered away. Come to think of it, he wouldn't mind that too much himself right now. He missed his mama's voice, her threats, even her swats with a wooden cook's spoon. He missed sitting at the kitchen table shelling peas for her, listening to her singing one of those old Italian songs. She must be terribly lonely right now, with seven of her nine sons in uniform, spread all over the world. Briefly he wondered if his brothers were ok, then he thought about the girl.

"You don' tink she found anuder guy by now, eh Goldie?"

"Lemme see," Goldstein considered, looking thoughtfully up into the starry night sky, recording points on his fingers as he made them. "You only knew her for two weeks, you took her on a couple of cheapskate dates right before shipping out, you never called her after, and that was what, eleven months ago? And ever since you left the states you ain't never even wrote to her?" He paused, a contemplative look on his face, as if he were totaling the score.

"Nah, you're OK. Who the hell's she gonna go out with? Every swingin' dick between eighteen and fifty is over here, or out in the Pacific fightin' Japs." He paused again, looking up at the stars. "Besides, she loves you."

Russo perked up and turned to face his friend, "What makes you say dat, Goldie, you ain't shittin' me, is you?" He rubbed his coarse stubble with a wide, filthy hand, the scratching sound loud enough for Goldie to turn and look.

"Well, it's real simple, Johnny boy. Here's how I see it: you love *her*, you're a million miles away, and you don' know shit about anything that's happenin' outside of this little piece of heaven right here in front of us. So, she loves you," he concluded, a philosopher proving a difficult point of logic.

"Yeah? Dat make sense Goldie, does it?"

"Just believe me, pal, it's true. Now let me find my fuckin' pencil and you can write her a fuckin' love letter. OK?"

"I can't," he said flatly. When that didn't seem to deter Goldstein, who continued to stare at him, he decided more explanation was going to be necessary.

"First off, I dunno her address, only her parents' landlady's phone number, and . . ." he paused, at a loss for what to say, how to express himself. "I ain' much good at writin'. I dunno how to use da words like you." He wasn't embarrassed, just stating a fact: writing was one of those only occasionally useful skills he had never acquired, like sewing a button on a shirt or boiling an egg.

"Oy!" lamented Goldstein, "It's a wonder you Dagos ever get married at all. What's all this crap about Italian Casanovas? How do you expect to stay in this girl's heart if you don't never write her, tell her what a big hero you are?"

That fine point was lost on Russo. "Sometimes I tink about it, but den I always figures dere's no reason to lead her on," he said evenly. "I wasn't never too sure I was comin' home again anyhow." He looked around at the desolate plain below and at that moment such a statement seemed not at all melodramatic; in fact it appeared a pretty safe bet.

"Whadda you tink?"

"Christ almighty!" cursed Goldstein. "Here, give me that paper. I'll do the writin', we'll mail it to your ol' lady and she can pass it on." He ripped the sheet from a willing hand. "Ok, now turn around." He pulled a stubby pencil out of his blouse pocket, licked the tip and started to write, using his friend's back for a desk. "Dear – what's her name again?"

"Gina," he said and suddenly smelled that sweet girl smell again, like she was close by. The sensation was so real that he looked around briefly, half-expecting her to appear, to slide down the scree into the hole and say "hi;" to sit on the ammo box with her legs crossed in that really tight arc only girls could do, thighs right together, one foot wagging, shoe hanging by her toes, heel down. He thought of her perfect face, her perfect hair, her perfect silky smooth dress and legs, her shiny black high-heeled shoes, and then he thought about what would happen to her if she were actually here and did in fact try to slide down next to him like Goldstein had just done. He saw the sharp scree ripping and tearing at her, the bloodied ankles, the dirt and rock chipping at her immaculate hands. He didn't like that image, didn't like to think about her except as he remembered her – perfect, smiling with white teeth, smelling that girly smell. He didn't want her here, didn't want her to see him like he was, filthy, emaciated, and exhausted. Sure, there was danger to be avoided, but mostly he thought about the filth.

He looked down at his own hands, his nails broken and blackened, palms a mass of cuts covered with calluses, oil ground in under the skin. He couldn't even smell himself anymore but he was pretty confident that inside his ragged uniform he reeked as badly as Goldie. He had not had a good wash, or for that matter a change of clothes, for. . .how long had it been? Two weeks?

"Dear Gina," Goldstein wrote, speaking the words aloud as he did so. "OK Johnny, go on."

There was a distant thump, like thunder, but a bit too muffled for that. Their experience, working against their hope, told them what it must be. This was confirmed by another thump, immediately before the first round impacted below them, on the plain in front of Dj Ksaira, well over a mile distant from their fox hole. They craned their necks to see over the mound of scree and dirt their shovels had thrown up in front of their hole, looking for a flash in the dark.

"Registerin' fire?" he whispered to Goldie in the sudden quiet after the first two rounds landed short of Dj Ksaira. Another thump followed, this one landing right on Dj Ksaira as if in answer to his question. After a moment's silence the night awoke with the din of artillery shells, 88's and 75's, fired from safe positions behind the pass and aimed at the Dj across the valley.

"Shit. Happy Valentine's Day, Gina," Goldstein said, tucking the pencil and paper back in his blouse, and crouching lower in their hole. "Now it starts, but good."

III

Strays.

M om tried hard to raise me right, and to her mind that meant protecting me from the roughness of life, controlling me, even telling me what I should think before I had a chance to figure it out for myself. She told me which of my friends I should spend more time with and which to avoid. She told me how I wanted to spend an afternoon – helping her bake cookies, not risking life and limb riding bicycles with Ernie. She even told me what I remembered from past events, and when my memory differed from hers she worked to convince me that mine was faulty.

It was for this reason above all others – her uncanny ability to climb inside my head and implant her own thoughts there – that throughout my childhood I stayed as far away from her as possible. I needed the distance in order to think for myself. As a teenager I wondered if maybe that was what had happened to Dad – he had lived with her for so long, relying on her version of reality, that he actually forgot how to think for himself.

Mom's efforts had focus: keeping me safe from a world she saw full of danger. She feared everything from summer barefootedness – "You could step on a bee and get stung." To playing in the nearby riverbed – "It said on the news those *cholos* put glue in some kid's eyes down there." To the heavy traffic of trucks, commuters, and lowriders along the route I walk to school – "They'll drive up on the sidewalks to hit you."

What she feared most of all though was the other neighborhood kids. She knew we would grow up, all too soon, and she feared letting me grow up to be who I would be, with my friends, not her, pointing the way.

Despite her ongoing warnings about "bad kids," Mom naturally loved all young people in the same smothering and controlling way she loved me. That meant she took them all in and fed them. The half-wits, the *cholos*, the drop-outs, and all the rest; if they were hungry they were welcome at our house. More than once I came home to find her feeding kids I did not even really know, and at least once it was a guy I was actually afraid of.

—m—

I walk in while she is talking to Gustavo Fiero, one of the most notorious kids in town. He sits at the dinette, the handle of a Bowie knife sticking out of a sheath stuffed into the back pocket of his starched khakis, eating a big square of thick Sicilian pizza hot from the oven. The house smells of anchovies and oregano, garlic and tomatoes, mixed with the glorious scent of fresh risen yeast.

Mom is rolling out more pizza dough. "So, to make the dough like this is real easy Gustavo – do they call you Gus? Get your mama to try it, its sooo damn easy! You just got to make sure you don't kill the goddamn yeast when you pour in the water – warm water, never too hot."

I try to ignore them as I walk by but he nods and so, of course, I return the greeting. There are two nods in our world. Both are delivered with otherwise blank expressions. The message is all in the nod itself. One nod involves a long, relatively slow upward movement of the head that flows immediately into a short downward stroke that – and this is important – only goes about half way back down. This is the nod of recognition. It is a good greeting. If the nodder wants to make it extra friendly he adds a bobbing motion at the end. The other nod involves a quick, flicking upward motion of the head – the movement originates in the chin – and little if any downward return. This is the nodding equivalent of "fuck you." It sounds complicated but believe me every nine year old in our neighborhood understands the difference. If he doesn't, he won't make it to ten.

Gustavo, whom I do not really know except by a fearsome reputation for *chingazos*, a real ass-kicker, for carving people with that huge knife of his, gives me the basic friendly nod, which I return, bobbing maybe a little too much, which is like kissing ass. While I make like a bobble head I also cringe, because Mom works in a comment about that #13 tattoo on his neck. It stands for the letter "M," the thirteenth letter in the alphabet, and "M" stands for *Los Mexicanos*, a prison gang.

"You know, Gus, that tattoo is gonna make it hard for you to get a job, bosses don't like *cholos*, you know what I mean?"

I cannot believe she is talking like this to a Mexican gangster, a guy with about as much chance of getting a real job as I do of pitching for the Dodgers. But the kid listens politely, with his shiny black hair slicked back, his crisp white t-shirt sprinkled with tiny pizza crumbs. He listens and nods, and then asks for a second piece, "*Por favor, señora.*"

Plenty of kids around town need a better home, a better mother. "Strays" Mom calls them, and she always has a place for them. It makes up for her greatest disappointment in life – me; or rather, only having me, just one kid of her own. At the same time she distrusts every adult who is not related to us by blood and constantly feuds with those who are. This includes her parents, who live in the back bedroom of our little stucco rental, and all of Dad's family, which she never much cared for and cut off nearly all communication with when we left them back in New York.

IV

Ambition.

O n a hot summer's day near the end of the school year I come home for
lunch. I bring Ernie, who lives across the street and is a year older, but
is still my closest friend. We head directly for the shade outside. The house is
stifling. Over the years Grandpa has turned our rental's dusty, garbage-strewn
backyard into the little Sicilian garden he never knew in New York or, for that
matter, in Sicily, where he had grown up an orphan. The L.A. climate is much
like Sicily's so he grows what he would have grown there: a big, leafy fig tree,
two orange trees, and vegetables and herbs that change with the seasons. This
early summer day he is starting corn.

Where in L.A. does he find grapes? He doesn't drive or speak much English,
but somehow he locates fat red grapes in quantity, and from these he makes
wine in the tiny garage. "Dago Red," Mom calls it, fermenting in a steel barrel
sitting next to the rusty push lawnmower, but we all drink it.

Grandpa is tending to his tomatoes, which in June are already threatening
to topple over so he ties them up with old shoe laces. It is lunch time and the
table is set outside under the trees for coolness. He decants a measure of his
wine into an old Aunt Jemima pancake syrup bottle as he does for lunch each
day. My cousins and I must be the only kids who return to our elementary
school with wine on their breath – we live only a couple blocks away and coming home for lunch is a treat. At mealtimes he gives us each a little bit of wine
mixed with water, his immediate concern being that the bottle, rationed by
Gramma, last him through lunch.

I bring Ernie home because he forgot to make himself a bag lunch and it is a good excuse for us to hang out together. By the time I was in fourth grade and he was in fifth he had become my best friend in the world. We have known each other since we were little and my grandparents welcome him warmly. Quickly Gramma runs to set another place at the table. My cousins – Linia, Lani, and Louisa are already sitting at the table chattering away, but at the appearance of Ernie, a boy, and not strictly speaking family, they quickly shut up and stare earnestly at their empty plates.

"Linidu, pora da boys *un po' di vino*, eh?" Gramma asks the oldest, Linia, who is my age.

Grandpa adds a little water, since we are still kids, and Ernie and I sip our wine, exchanging glances. He is trying to look sophisticated in front of the girls, like he drinks wine with lunch every day. Then Gramma reappears with an enormous platter of *spaghetti*, which lands with a caloric thud in the center of the table.

"Gramma, who you spectin for lunch, an army," I offer, the usual joke. We all help ourselves to big, sloppy tomato sauced servings of *spaghetti*, as Grandpa passes around a bowl filled with *salsiccia*, meatballs, and pork neck bones.

Ernie eats two bowls of pasta, several sausages, and a half dozen meatballs, which makes Gramma's day. She pinches his cheek and mutters something encouraging in dialect; then she goes back in the house with a load of dirty dishes.

"Linidu, *veni ca*," she calls again to my cousin. Ernie understands. It works the same way across the street at his house. *Chicanos* and Italians both train the oldest girl best, assuming that she will be getting married pretty quickly and needs a head start developing housekeeping skills.

Gramma and Linia reappear with a plate of hard cheeses as Grandpa walks up holding a bulging cloth napkin by the corners, announces *"Ficchi, mangia,"* and dumps onto the table a pile of figs he has just picked, still warm from the sun. We dive in. To eat figs fresh off the tree is as close to heaven as you can get while sitting at a faded red wooden picnic table in the backyard of a little stucco rental just east of East L.A.

Finally, Gramma brings out a pot of coffee. It's not *espresso* or *cappuccino*, which she has never heard of, but Hills Brothers made in the percolator. She pours a cup all around. We are going to need it. Grandpa could finish off the last of his wine and take a nap in the afternoon heat but the rest of us have to return for two more unbearable hours of school and, in our airless classrooms, after this meal just staying awake is going to be a feat.

—⚂—

For dinner each night throughout my childhood Grandpa brought out a half gallon of his Dago Red for the table. We all drank, but again, it was mostly Grandpa. He stood only about five feet tall but that man could put away more wine than anyone else in the family. He was drunk after most meals. In fact he was drunk *before* most meals, the kind of drunk who suddenly remembers with more enthusiasm than skill favorite snatches of old Italian folk songs, bits of arias from operas he does not really know, and dance steps from the *Tarantella* long forgotten. He greeted visitors with a hug and a glass of wine, speaking slowly in that Sicilian dialect that is largely incomprehensible to other Italians let alone to our *Chicano* neighbors in L.A. To them Grandpa was just another kindly, drunken old *abuelo* and they liked him fine.

Grandpa had the clearest blue eyes, almost translucent. I loved to look at them as he sang or told his old stories. When he was animated, in the midst of a tale I had heard many times before, the eyes sparkled, growing so bright you thought they must be lit from within. The lightness of his eyes was especially dramatic since he was otherwise quite dark, almost African, the genetic product of an island that has been invaded repeatedly, and from all four compass points, since long before Christ walked the earth.

I grew up with Grandpa's stories, the unofficial Italian version of the First World War, and with no mention whatsoever of the Second World War from my parents. Grandpa was a cook in the Italian Army in The Great War, so I grew up believing that Italy played a pivotal role in the defeat of Germany. In fact, it sounded like Italy was singly responsible for that victory. Historians may differ, but as Grandpa would say, flicking his finger from his eye, *"Iu la vistu"* I saw it. Once you felt his martial pride you wanted to believe he served in the conquering Roman Legions of old rather than the forever-in-retreat modern Italian army.

Grandpa never attended a single day of school in his life. That was not unusual in Sicily, where children were lucky to get two or three years, enough to read a bit and perhaps to write their name. Grandpa never learned either. He was an orphan from as early an age as he could remember and the only parent he ever knew was the mine. When he was a boy, Sicily had a monopoly on the production of sulphur, that foul-smelling, bright-burning substance long associated with the underworld. The ancient Greeks thought smoky Mt. Etna was the entrance to hell. In Grandpa's case, that turned out to be about right.

Sicilian mining made little use of machinery or even animals. Nearly everything was done by human hands and ore was carried out to the donkey carts, for transport to market, on human backs. Because of their size children like Niccoló were lowered into the shafts to load chunks of raw sulphur into buckets. Each bucket, tied to a rope, was lifted out and immediately an empty one was lowered in its place. Day after day, year after year, this was his life, until he grew strong enough for harder work. Then, while a new generation of smaller boys went down the shaft, he was given the task of transporting the mined sulphur to the donkey carts in wooden crates carried on his shoulder. Through all of this he was entirely unpaid and was fed only the absolute minimum to ensure he was able to work. He dressed in rags, wore sandals he made from scraps of leather, seldom bathed, but was dutifully brought to church each week.

One Sunday after mass Grandpa and a couple of other boys began kicking an empty oil tin around the lean-to hovel where they lived beside the mine in a makeshift game of soccer. Give two or three Italian boys some free time and any object becomes a soccer ball. The overseer came upon them and the game ended as quickly as it had begun. The boys stood at attention to await their punishment. The overseer crushed the can flat with his boot then picked it up and slapped each of the boys hard across the face with the flattened end, cutting their jaws and cheeks with its split, jagged edges. The boys waited their turn, with Grandpa at the end of the line. The urge to run, to fight back, or at least to raise his hands in self-protection must have been overwhelming as each successive boy was struck. But Grandpa knew that any resistance, even cowering, would bring a far worse beating, so he stood stock still and took his blow. The resulting scar was still plainly visible in his old age, a thin white line running from cheekbone to nose. When he told me this story it was like it had just happened yesterday, right around the corner, not half a century ago on the other side of the world. Grandpa's anger, from a thousand causes, simmered just below the surface until the day he died at ninety-eight.

This was Grandpa's life until he was old enough – eighteen, in 1914 – to join the army and escape. He was sent north to the border, where he met Italians from other regions as well as strangers from other parts of Sicily. From his comrades he heard wondrous stories of the great land across the sea, America, but it might as well have been the dark side of the moon for all the chance he had of actually going. Throughout the war, in which he cooked at a prisoner of war camp, emigration remained only a daydream.

After the 1918 Armistice Grandpa returned to his village, near Caltanissetta, but not to the mine. He took odd jobs on farms and in the few shops in town, and soon married a simple girl from a destitute family – my grandmother, Antonina. They took over an abandoned, falling down, one-room stone hovel. It was part cave, part shack, on the outskirts of the village proper, and no one seemed to have claimed it. They grew vegetables in the patch of dirt in front of it, bought chickens as finances allowed, and started a family. Mom was their second child, their first daughter, born two years after my uncle Alonzo.

After they came to America Mom, who quickly picked up the new tongue, painstakingly taught Grandpa enough of his new country's language for him to pass his citizenship test, conferring that prize upon the whole family. Somehow he got through the examination, which was administered orally for the illiterate. Then he promptly forgot nearly every word of English he had learned, and every American history lesson, except one. He always believed that George Washington, whom he called *Joe Washing Machine*, was a great man, a fine farmer, a brilliant *generalissimo*, and that he was, eternally, the president of the United States. Roosevelt and all the lesser men who followed were only pretenders in Grandpa's mind.

"*Joe Washing Machine, he a guda presidente*," was Grandpa's expectable contribution to any discussion of politics.

Dad worked hard in the paint factory but wouldn't turn a hand to anything around the house. Mom would occasionally remind him of how much he used to love cars and driving when she first met him, but he never rose to the bait, seeing car repair, even a fill-up at the corner station, as just another chore he would as soon avoid. I wonder when it was that he supposedly loved driving since he paid so little attention to our car. In fact, so far as I can tell, and I made quite a study of it, he had no interests whatsoever, no passions, no hobbies, no vices.

Sometimes Dad doodled, when he found a pencil and paper before him. It was always the same image: two small circles connected by a straight line, I thought of it as a two-dimensional barbell. It was neat and orderly but gave nothing away.

I sometimes studied his discarded doodles, making my own copies, hoping that by duplicating the movements of his hand I would follow the process of his mind, feeling what he felt when he made them. Much as I urged the little drawings to tell me something of my father, they did not.

I was not much of an artist myself. Mom was once summoned to meet with my Kindergarten teacher, Miss Kramer, who told her that I might have visual problems or a brain defect since, unlike normal children of my age who are eager for any kind of art activity, I only drew when urged on by her, and then would only use the black crayon. She also thought maybe I was color-blind.

Most of the other men in the neighborhood tinkered with their cars, many had an old clunker, a '54 Chevy or even a '49 Ford, parked semi-permanently on the front lawn, their engines dismembered on the garage floor awaiting some part or perhaps some inspiration. Their kids were the lucky ones. They learned all about the magic of driving machines from an early age. Many of these same men also hunted and fished on their vacations, and gambled and drank themselves into a stupor each weekend. Not my dad. He worked hard and then flopped down with a single beer to watch television. That was all.

When Mom scolded him to get off the couch and do something, anything – mow the lawn, play ball with his son, take out the garbage, answer the phone while she has her hands full of laundry– he invariably whined something like, "*Managgia*! Jeez honey. I work. I bring youse all my pay, not like some a dem guys dat drinks it all up and bring home *cazzu*. What more do youse want, huh Gina?" His massive hands were upturned in supplication, his eyes pleading the simple righteousness of his case.

—w—

It was true. Dad brought his paycheck home each Friday night. Given the other men in the neighborhood – many of whom drank a good portion of their pay, beat their wives and children, and drifted from job to job – it was hard to argue with him, but she did. Mom wanted to control Dad, too; to make him into the man she thought he was going to become when she married him right after the war. She wanted more from him than a paycheck. She wanted him to have Ambition. It had something to do with making more money, buying a house of our own, and getting a new car. It involved getting out of the neighborhood, moving to someplace nice, someplace safe for me to grow up in, someplace White. I never wanted this. I wanted to stay right where I was, with my friends. Anyway, it was not a serious option, since we didn't have the money to do any of those things, least of all to move. We rented the same little stucco house for fifteen years.

The dream of a happier life in a nice suburb was only a fiction of Mom's making. If we had ever been able to afford it, the prosperous Anglos, our new neighbors, would only have shunned us. We were not Anglo, not middle class, not polite or educated or cultured by any modest standard they might apply. We were Sicilian immigrant laborers, short-statured, squat-bodied, olive-skinned, uneducated, poorly spoken, unread, crude, un-ambitious, lacking in curiosity about the world. We were in America, but we were not yet American.

Grandpa and Gramma, Mom and Dad, feared the teacher as they feared the police and the priest. Mom wore her Sunday best to parent-teacher conferences, smiling nervously, like they might expel me if she did not measure up. She usually brought along a plate of food, often it was *cannoli*, as an offering to the all-powerful teacher. I tried to tell her this was not the old country, or even the Lower East Side. I told her she did not need to bow and scrape before Mrs. Allen, with her string of white pearls the size of marbles, her bright orange cheeks, her rhinestone rimmed glasses, and her five months pregnant belly. Mrs. Allen was as White as White comes and the only reason I can think of for her to be a teacher in my school is that someone White had to do it, we had no *Chicano* teachers. This was still 1966.

It made no difference to Mom what I said, she was nervous whenever forced to visit school. Maybe it was because she never finished high school herself or maybe she was remembering that early Kindergarten conference where she was told something was wrong with me. Maybe she was afraid she would hear more bad news on these visits. Come to think of it, she often did. In any case, the *cannoli* were offered, and they were accepted by Mrs. Allen almost as a curiosity. To be fair, this was a long time ago, before Italian culinary imperialism conquered America, before every restaurant in the country was obliged to serve *pasta primavera* and *tiramisu*, before *pizza* replaced the hot dog as the national dish. This was still the age of canned vegetables, TV dinners, and Chef Boyardee, so homemade Italian food brought as an offering to an elementary school classroom was about as foreign – and therefore as strange and untrustworthy – as things got.

—⁂—

Ambition was a word Mom sometimes threw around as an insult – "You got no ambition." No one in our family seemed to believe they could change our circumstances; and they all tacitly believed that trying to do so would only cause us grief, as if such hubris would bring a curse upon us if we tried too hard to jump up in society. A college education was never dreamed of, even for my generation; it was too big of a leap. It would mean leaving home for a strange and unknown world, years of living with strangers, unimaginable and unfathomable dangers of difference. Followed by what? No Sicilian boy was going to become a doctor, a lawyer, or a professor, was he? And who was going to pay for all that useless college anyway?

Dad's lack of Ambition made a nice excuse for our poverty, but it was only an excuse. Mom, Dad and I, and my uncle and aunt and cousins who made it to L.A., were too frightened to risk the things that would need to be risked for Ambition. For us kids, graduating from high school and learning a trade would be the next step forward after Grandpa's sulphur mining and Dad's unskilled labor. That would be more than enough progress for one generation, more than enough to satisfy the family, to make them, in fact, proud.

—⁂—

As a girl, Mom often did her homework late at night in the small toilet room which was shared with three other families, down the dingy hall from her family's Lower East Side apartment. She snuck off because her parents did not approve of wasting electricity on book work. They were also afraid of what she might learn. They were afraid that their children would move away to pursue some dream of their own and leave them stranded in their old age in this strange land. At sixteen she left school for work, and cared for her parents until they died, in our home, fifty years later.

I have no idea how Dad's family came to the United States. When they emigrated from the old country they left all their stories behind. As illiterate immigrants they quickly lost contact with relatives, since neither side could read nor write a letter. I often wondered what all my uncles, his brothers, were like, and what they could tell me about him. But we moved to L.A. with Mom's parents when I was only five, while the rest of the Russo boys remained in New York. Dad was never much good at keeping in touch. Mom said he liked to visit with his family when he lived near them but with the move to California he simply dropped them, except for a monthly long distance call Mom insisted he make to his mother. As a result I never knew any of his brothers and only met one or two of my numerous cousins, whom I knew mostly from Christmas cards and, later, wedding announcements.

Like Mom, Dad was born in Sicily and came to the U.S. as a child. Like her he was reared in lower Manhattan and left high school in his second year. Book learning never interested him. He preferred hanging around the corner with his friends, cadging cigarettes, telling jokes, and apparently, dreaming of cars. At St Mary's parish school in the Bowery he was one of a large group of disinterested, exasperating, non-paying students who were neither motivated by their lessons nor intimidated by their dour teachers. One day Sister approached quietly in her crepe soles and decided to inspire him with the edge of a ruler across the back of his neck. He responded to the surprise of the blow as much as to the pain of it by punching her hard enough to sit her right down on the floor, stunned. He walked out of the classroom, sixteen years old, never to return. That image of Dad as a man of action, with the nerve to punch a nun, of all things, never really fit with the man I knew growing up. But I heard the story enough times from Mom, never from his lips, to believe it. I wanted to believe it. Hey, Dad punched-out a nun. It was something.

Dad's father, my other Grandpa, died before I was born. He was an illiterate laborer both in Sicily and in New York. He was not a drinker like Mom's father and made very little mark on the world before passing from it. His most notable contribution to the family was his unerring aim: nine for nine. He got Gramma Russo pregnant nine times and she bore him nine boys.

Encouraged by his mother to get away from New York before his father came home and learned he had struck a nun, Dad enrolled in Roosevelt's Civilian Conservation Corps the very day he left school. After a couple of years of logging and firefighting in faraway Louisiana, which might have been Outer Mongolia by the family's reckoning, he returned to his parents' tenement home in the Bowery, a tearful reunion, all things forgiven, and briefly took what work he could find. This was 1941 and in a few months he would be in uniform like everyone else of his generation. I never heard a word of this from Dad, of course, but pieced it together from second hand stories Mom had heard from her in-laws.

—m—

Because of the family's lack of Ambition we lived on scraps in the midst of plenty, during the booming years of the 1950's and 60's. We survived in America just as Grandpa and Gramma had survived in Sicily. Mom's and Dad's families both emigrated to America to escape unplumbed stone hovels and work for demoniacal overseers. Instead they raised their children during the Depression in Lower Manhattan. The crowded tenements they inhabited were actually a big improvement over what they had previously known. God bless America.

V

Appendix ain't catchy.

E rnie has so many brothers and sisters it is hard to keep track of them all. The little house across the street from ours is always full of crying toddlers, loud teens, and the smell of beans on the stove. Ernie shares a small room with two brothers but he is the oldest so he gets the choicest bed – the lower bunk near the window. This is where we sit trying to figure out how to assemble a plastic model of a World War II B-29 Superfortress, the biggest bomber from the biggest war ever. Our gray model doesn't look as good as the full-color version on the box cover, with the tail gunner drilling the swarming German fighters while bombs drop on an exploding oil refinery, the pilots flashing devilishly handsome smiles from the cockpit. Our version looks a little tired, and the smudges of our gluey finger prints on the fuselage do not help.

After the umpteenth attempt to affix the wheels so they will fold up when we want them to, Ernie stops and lowers the model to his lap, lying back against the pillow. He is exhausted, so am I. We are wearing our old and tattered pajamas even though it is three in the afternoon on a school day, because we are recovering from nearly simultaneous appendectomies.

I balled up with a stomachache on Easter Sunday. Mom put it down to that foot-high chocolate rabbit she bought me. Whatever happens in my life, she takes responsibility for it. She cannot conceive of any other power than her own, even nature's. Eventually the fever and vomiting overcame her thrift and she decided to take me to the hospital. They operated immediately.

"A few hours later," the doctor told her, "and it might have burst." When I hear this, I conjure an image of an explosion inside my gut like that bombed oil refinery on the B-29 box cover.

The day after my surgery Ernie, my best friend, accompanied my parents to the hospital. Mom figured it would cheer me up. We didn't talk much as we were both uncomfortable in the strange surroundings. Besides, we never talked to each other around adults. He left and soon after arriving home doubled over with the pain. A week later we are convalescing, comparing our scars, and assembling the model airplanes that Ernie's father, Al, has brought us. We have plenty of models to build, an embarrassment of riches really, except for the fact that they are all the same plane. Al has somehow – we can guess how – gotten his hands on an entire case of B-29s, which he presents to us with such pride and solemnity that we know better than to ask about their origin, even jokingly.

"So," Ernie asks, "Do you think I caught it from you, man?"

"No," I reply with absolute certainty, more certain then than I am today. "My Ma says appendix ain't catchy."

After a reflective twelve-year-old's silence, Ernie says, "That's pretty weird, eh? Both of us getting it at Easter." He shrugs, I shrug, and we go back to the B-29; it is our third model and we are actually getting better at it.

"You know, *carnal*," he says a few moments later, "When Jesus was hangin' up on the cross, them *cholos* stabbed him through the side." We both look up at the crucifix that adorns Ernie's wall.

"Yours looks like a different guy from mine. I thought he had brown hair and blue eyes," I say, recalling the crucifixion painting from my own bedroom. "But yours looks *Chicano*. He's Brown, man!"

Unconsciously we both locate our scars through our pajamas. The steel staples are still in place. Sure enough blood is dripping from Jesus' side at just about the same place we have our scars. The sad face looks down on us and we both feel the pain *El Señor* underwent for us.

"He got His on Good Friday; we got ours a couple of days later. It's like, what is it? The stigmata or something," Ernie says. We leave it at that.

—⁓—

In our neighborhood in the early 60's everyone left their doors unlocked and you could drop your bike overnight on the front lawn without a kryptonite chain securing it to a lamp post and expect it to be there in the morning. It was a close little *barrio*, where people still looked out for one another, where it would be a few more years still before drugs, and the money they brought, would lead the gangs to abandon their fists and knives for guns, to go from protecting turf to terrorizing neighborhoods. This was our home, and nearly everyone was a thief. I didn't think anything of it at the time, it just seemed normal.

Al steals a case of model planes off his truck to help with our convalescence.

Alejandro, Mario's father, has a garage full of candy that he skims from his delivery route and sells to the neighborhood kids at cut rates. His little garage is even referred to by both kids and adults as "*La Confitería.*" When we have some loose change someone will say, "Let's see if we can get Jandro to open up The Candy Store." Then we troop around the corner, knock on the door, and beg him to open up, even if it is for a total sale of less than one dollar. It doesn't matter to Alejandro, he has very low overhead.

Every summer Mom tells us to sneak out to the nursery run by a Japanese family on part of the back lot behind our side of the block and pick the berries off the vines for her strawberry shortcake. She doesn't have to ask twice. When she wants a shelf built in the garage we know the nursery owner has some construction underway so Ernie and I put on dark sweatshirts and beanies, sneaking out on a nighttime commando raid. We return in half an hour with a ten foot long two-by-twelve.

Mom never buys me a pair of shoes. She knows my size and just takes them out of the box when she is alone near closing time at the shoe store where she works. They aren't shoes I would choose, they are hard with shiny leather when what I want is Converse All-Stars. But they are shoes, and free. When I ask her why she never finds me any sneakers she says they aren't good for my feet.

When we are hungry after school and we don't have enough money, we pool our resources and do a double-buy, sometimes a triple- or even a quadru-ple-buy. Kid number one goes into the Market Basket; it works better in a big, impersonal place with lots of different checkers. He buys a bottle of soda, a frosted fruit pie, and whatever candy bar we have all agreed upon. He pays for it and politely asks the checker to put his purchases in a bag, avoiding eye contact.

He makes sure to get a receipt. Then he comes outside where we are waiting. Kid number two takes the empty bag and the receipt, goes back into the store, and refills the bag with the exact same contents kid number one just bought. If someone from the store stops him he shows his receipt and they have to let him go. Kids come in and out and no one remembers if this is the one who was in the store five minutes ago. We keep this going until each of us has his own stuff or until someone gets questioned. When this happens we know that for a while they will be more alert, so we divide what we have and call it a day. It always works.

No one saw any of this stealing as bad. If we told our parents about the double-buy their reactions ranged from a lack of interest to a hint of familial pride at our ingenuity. Some people had more money than they needed. They were the bosses, the big shots, and who would it hurt if a few model airplanes, a little candy, some new shoes, some nice juicy strawberries, or a bottle of soda were taken by people who had so little?

—∞—

Al comes into the bedroom while we are working on the model planes. We can smell the tequila as soon as he crosses the doorway. He is one of those men whose naturally quiet, even meek, personality shifts in an angry, violent, unpredictable direction whenever he drinks.

"*¿Dónde está tu chingada puta de madre?*" He slurs.

I notice that for once it is quiet in the house. I also know from experience that when he is drunk and calls his wife a whore, Al is starting on the path that is likely to end with him giving Marta a beating and then passing out in a chair.

"*¿Dónde está, Mijo, eh?*" He asks again.

Marta is in the yard, hanging laundry. From where we sit I can see her through the window. Ernie can't rat-out his mom, especially when he knows what is coming.

We are in a tough spot. I can't tell if Al is going to walk over and smack Ernie, or me, or turn and leave. He just stands for a minute, babbling something neither of us can make out. Then, suddenly he lunges over to the bed where we sit, his head barely missing the upper bunk frame, and lays down. It is crowded with the three of us on that single bunk mattress, we are practically on top of each other, and Ernie and I have these damn staples in our sides, but we don't dare move, don't want to give offense. Al is dangerously sensitive to slights against his honor when he is drunk.

Al picks up the latest model we have been working on, looking it over like someone who knows what a model airplane is supposed to look like. He points to the clear-plastic tail of the plane and says, in his heavy and broken English, "I rode back here, *aquí*, hangin' *debajo del chingado* plane *como un pendejo*, catching all the treepul-eh flak they threw up at us."

He shakes his head. "*Treinta y cuatro* fuckin' *misiones sobre Alemania*." Then he lays his head down on the pillow, the plane on his chest, and immediately begins to snore.

Ernie's eyes get wet, either from relief or embarrassment, but you don't cry if you can help it, and never in front of a friend. So he slinks his way out from under his father, which is not easy. Eventually he gets up from the bed and walks out of the room, and I just crawl out after him and pretend I don't notice.

When we are outside I ask: "Your dad flew as a tail gunner on one of them bombers in the war? Thirty-four missions bombing Germany?" Ernie nods. Al is about the same age as Dad, who has never mentioned the war at all, and I start to wonder if he too has flown in a B-29. I take the model home and put it out where he can't miss it. He does.

VI

Think of the children.

G randpa – *Nonno* in Sicilian – never seriously considered immigrating to America, although he had heard from some of the many men who had gone and returned that indeed the streets of New York were paved with gold. He may well have wondered why, with so much gold lying around for the taking, they returned to Sicily as destitute as they had left it. Occasionally he heard another version of America: "Niccoló, the streets are not paved with gold and often they are not even paved, but we are hired to pave them!"

With a growing family to support after the Great War, he had little time or inclination to think beyond today's work and tonight's meal. Besides, he could never have saved the money for the trip. Then one day a single event changed everything, for him and for the whole family.

It is late summer and in the evening Gramma returns a little stiffer than usual from threshing wheat for Don Carlo. She raises the children, feeds the family from the scraps they can afford, and once Gina is old enough to watch the little ones, she works. In winter it is a job scrubbing buckets in the back room at the sheep milk farm. In spring it is planting, whatever fields need her labor. At harvest time, when everyone is fully employed, it is threshing, separating the edible wheat from the mass of stalks. The work is done without mechanization by peasants like her, as it has been done for millennia.

Grandpa has just returned from his own harvest work at the grain silo, covered in a fine wheat-dust. He notices her slowness this evening as she cooks and tends to the children. The oldest girl, Gina, is eight. After a day of chasing the two smaller ones around, while her ten year old brother, Alonzo, is off with his friends, she helps Gramma make dinner. Grandpa asks his wife what is wrong, you don't look right, but she begs off. He keeps after her as she cooks the evening supper, suspecting that she is hiding something worth knowing. He will not tolerate her avoidance for much longer.

When the children are all fed and Gina is telling the little ones stories, he will wait no longer. She mutters something about her back hurting so he forces her to unbutton her dress and show it to him. She does not want to but under threat of his raised hand she reveals several great bruises across her shoulders. Some are red and nasty, freshly made, while others are older, various shades of purple tinged with a sickly yellow. It makes his blood boil. His face becomes rigid and his voice quiet and insistent. His warm, liquid blue eyes are now as hard and cold as ice. She resists telling, but he is well beyond the limits of what little patience he ever possessed. Finally, a quick slap across the face, and she relents. When she does tell her story, with much wailing and tears, Grandpa has what he wants – the name of the overseer who has done this, laying a hand on his wife, the mother of his children. *Disgraciada*. He is shaking with anger and disgust.

As Gramma pleads with him, "Think of the children," Grandpa isn't listening. He is beyond all restraint, searching frantically for something he must have misplaced. Eventually he finds his old army-issue bayonet, with its twenty-nine centimeters of blade, lost in a pile of debris, loose bricks, and cat shit at the narrow back of the hovel where it was once a cave. He brings it out, tests its strength, and calmly rubs its double-edged rusty blade all over with a clove of fresh garlic, believed to promote infection in a wound. Needlessly telling his wife to stay with her children, he puts on his coat, slips the blade up his left sleeve, wooden handle last, and walks toward the overseer's house on the edge of town.

She knows what he plans but she is powerless to stop him. She is always powerless when he is angry. He is stubborn, and when he is angry he is dangerous. One moment he is playing happily with the children, a kind and loving father. The next, one of them does something he takes as disrespectful and the game is over. He swats the child with a quick back of the hand and the little one runs to her in tears. But she has never before seen him like this, and she has no doubt of his intention.

As he walks through the village the evening is recovering from the late summer day's oppressive heat. The smell of the turned earth, intensely warmed, is refreshing. People and animals come out to enjoy the relief at day's end. Villagers nod or exchange greetings with Niccoló but, very unlike him, he does not stop to talk or even slow his gait. He passes the café, a dusty stone place little bigger than a chicken coop with a few crude tables and chairs spread around the dirt under the cover of a tile roof. When Marco, an old friend and fellow laborer from his mine years, calls from his seat, invites him to join in a glass of wine, he only waves distractedly and keeps going. This is so uncharacteristic of Niccoló that Marco briefly considers going after his friend to see what has him so troubled as to turn down a cool glass of wine at the end of a blistering day. But remembering his own thirst he puts it out of mind and returns to his table.

The overseer's house is a modest place, to be sure, but it is better than any place Grandpa has ever lived. It is a real house, not a hovel carved out of the side of a hill. It has a real door and windows, made of wood and glass, and a roof of clay tiles, not discarded sheets of tin. As he approaches he can hear the working of a water pump inside the big main room. He thinks about his Antonina, with four small children, scurrying up the hill with bucket in hand to the communal water pump forty meters away. Without a word he walks unnoticed through the open gate and past the three little girls playing in the gravel that fronts the house.

At the open front door he calls out, *"Giuseppe Lampare, é statu qui?"* to see if his enemy is at home.

"Cu c'e?" an impatient voice demands of the visitor from the darkness of the house. The man himself appears in a moment at his doorway. He is short, although still half a head taller than Grandpa. His demeanor is dark, and menacing, with thick black eyebrows, a well-waxed mustache and dull gray suspenders holding up a pair of worn black work pants. He has a small white towel in his hands, having just washed up, probably after dinner.

Grandpa introduces himself. *"So Niccoló Traina, il sposo di Antonina Traina,"* he says, waiting for the man's eyes to flash in recognition: I am the man you have wronged. It is important that he know why he is going to die and at whose hand. When the eyes betray Lampare's recognition of exactly who is standing on his doorstep, and only then, Grandpa's right hand pulls the bayonet by the handle from his left sleeve.

"Chisstu ca e per idda." This is for her, he wants his victim to know. He says it with such malevolence that Giuseppe Lampare is momentarily taken aback and doesn't immediately see the nearly foot-long blade Grandpa slowly begins to slide into his chest, its thinness moving effortlessly between the ribs all the way to the hilt. Lampare gasps and a gush of blood issues from his mouth, splattering the white towel in his hands. A lung has been punctured, perhaps also the heart. He doesn't cry out. In fact he makes surprisingly little noise, only a soft cough and the burbling sound of blood on his lips.

Grandpa stands inches away inhaling the dull metallic smell of Lampare's blood, still holding the bayonet's worn wooden handle, pressing the steel hilt flush against the man's heaving chest. With his other hand he grabs Lampare by the jaw and forces the taller man's head down to look into his own bright blue eyes.

"Vastasi!" Fuck you, he whispers fiercely, then slowly eases the long blade out, pressing downward on the handle, ensuring maximum internal damage as the tip tears new flesh along the entire journey outward. Lampare shudders but remains quiet. His hands are yet clutching the towel before him.

Still holding Lampare's chin in one hand, the dripping blade in the other, Grandpa pushes the overseer back into his doorway where he leans weakly against the frame, his hands loosely clutching the towel over the spouting wound. It is suddenly quiet except for the children's laughter and the crunch of their small feet on the gravel.

Grandpa turns as if to flee, then something stops him. His anger is not paid. Still holding the bayonet, he turns back to Lampare, who stares blankly ahead as crimson oozes from his mouth and chest, spreads across his shirt, and drips onto the doorstep in front of him. Grandpa raises the blade high over his head in both hands. With a quiet exclamation he plunges it wildly into Lampare's chest halfway between sternum and throat, pinning Lampare to the wooden door frame. The hilt stands on his chest like a large, mal-formed button on his shirt, the handle oddly slanted as blood oozes out along the bayonet's blood gutter with each labored breath. His body slowly sags but for a moment the bayonet holds him up, wedged in the firm wood.

Now satisfied, as signaled by a loud snort of disgust in Lampare's direction, Grandpa turns and strides past the little girls still playing intently in the gravel, unaware that their world has just changed forever.

A moment later Signora Lampare screams as she finds her husband in the open doorway, a growing pool of blood on her floor. "Assassino!" she cries again and again after Grandpa, the murderer. This is where the chase should begin, but doesn't.

—ᴍ—

Grandpa gathered up his wife and four children, hurriedly packed his meager possessions, found non-existent money, boarded the train for the capital, and booked passage out of Palermo on the next ship to New York, all without the police finding him. With all the telling and retelling of this story over the years no one ever directly answered my questions about how this miraculous flight was accomplished. Either Grandpa had friends among the local *oumini d'onore*, or Lampare had enemies among these "men of honor," the *Mafiosi* who ran his village. I am certain that someone interceded because police and immigration officials were clearly looking the other way. And someone provided the money, no doubt expecting a service in the new world.

This flight saved the family from ruin and Grandpa himself from the gallows, for Lampare did indeed die on that summer evening, not days later from the dubious garlic-induced infection, but quickly from massive internal bleeding. He was probably not still pinned to that door frame when he expired but that is where he dies in my mind. I feel no compassion for him – he was a bully who didn't realize that this woman's husband was Niccoló Traina, my maternal grandfather.

Grandpa may have been a murderer but in New York he found a strong Sicilian community where few questions were asked and a new life was easily begun. It appears he did repay his debt to whoever helped him to escape. Mom says some nights during their early years in New York he was gone late, returning home with a chicken, a bottle of wine, and gashed knuckles or flecks of blood on his sleeve. He was not a *Mafioso*, at least not formally, he just provided reliable help from time to time.

New York held all the troubles of the old country as well as a few new ones, including children who quickly learned English while he and Gramma lagged hopelessly behind, loosening the absolute control they had exercised back in Caltanissetta. Supplementing his occasional nocturnal jobs Grandpa found sporadic labor, and a combination of Relief and the intervention of the church kept starvation away. Time passed and a tenement on Bowery Street became home.

I cannot help thinking that were my maternal grandfather not a murderer he would never have come to America, his eldest daughter would never have met and married my father, and I would simply never have been. It is strange but undeniable that I owe my life to Giuseppe Lampare's death.

—⁂—

After the family arrives in New York the immigration authorities eventually ferry them from Ellis Island to Manhattan, depositing them in America without so much as a city map. As they stand confused on the Battery, the children clutching their mother's skirt, they hear a man singing a popular Sicilian folk song. He is wearing a decent suit, slicked down hair, and a wide, friendly grin. The familiar sound of his voice amid the Babel of Lower Manhattan is like a gulp of air to the drowning; they are drawn to the soft syllables of their home with relief and gratitude. They ask him directions and he seems to know everything – where they can find food, housing, and work; even where they can exchange their few useless Lira for real American dollars. Desperation and disorientation render Grandpa an easy mark and the exchange rate he receives is no better than theft. He had little to begin with and now he has next to nothing. They find a two-room windowless tenement that for all its filth and decay is superior to anything they have known before in Sicily. Coming after weeks of shipboard life in steerage and the dormitories at Ellis Island, it is a form of deliverance for the family of six.

Gina is a thin, small, fragile girl, sickly even. The entire boat journey from Palermo she is nauseous. Soon after they land in Manhattan and find the tenement on Bowery a social worker from the nearby Settlement House visits and arranges for her and her eldest brother to attend school. Gina loves school. There is no real work do to, no cooking, laundry or cleaning, and no babies to help her mother with during those precious hours in the classroom. There are only books to read in English, which she picks up quickly. Every school day starts with breakfast, and then includes lunch, with an extra serving of milk for the frail girl, who puts on weight and gains in strength. She finds that she can help the family obtain clothing, food, even winter shoes, through the use of English, her new home's harsh, ugly, but effective tongue.

Her parents need their oldest daughter's growing familiarity with their new country, but they resent the power it gives her. Grandpa feels he is losing control of the family. It is not only that his children are learning English; it is also that they are learning to be American.

One day Gina comes home after mastering long division. She is proud of this accomplishment and eager to show her parents and siblings how it is done. For a moment her father watches, half-mystified, as she tries to explain, using a scrap of paper left over from the market. Then, without warning he rips the pencil from her hand, stuffs it in his pocket and, as she looks up with questioning eyes, he slaps her hard across the face. He fears what he does not know and hates what he fears. She will not show him her excitement again, either about school or about any other part of her life.

VII

Where we could afford the rent.

The family migration from Sicily, where my parents were born, to New York, where I was born, to L.A., where I grew up, was unplanned and almost random. Each step made us smaller, took us farther and farther away from ourselves as we shed those parts of the family – brothers, sisters, aunts, uncles, cousins – who were left behind. Each new place furthered our alienation, deracination, and assimilation. We fled from Sicily to America to escape either the law, which was uncertain, or the revenge of Giuseppe Lampare's relatives, which would have been quite certain under the Sicilian code of endless retribution. Next, using our life savings and driving a boxy black 1958 Ford, we fled the cold, and a lack of work, from New York to L.A. We wound up in Pico Rivera, just east of East L.A., because as Mom would say, "That's where we could afford the rent."

Mom, Dad, and I made the move from New York; we were joined by Grandpa and Gramma, Mom's parents; Mom's sister Claudia, husband Jimmy, and their four kids, my cousins. That's it. I was four years old when we arrived in L.A., and these family members were the only Sicilians, or even Italians, I knew growing up.

My parents stayed together their entire lives, but I cannot say with certainty that they even liked each other. Throughout my childhood Mom fought Dad, hurling insults, screaming names, and once in a while, throwing something, like a glass percolator full of hot coffee that barely missed him as it smashed into the kitchen wall. Dad would generally take it all impassively until he reached his limit and blew, yelling at her in an impressive string of profanities; then he left for a walk around the backyard. It was a small house, with a small yard, so he was gone only as long as it took to smoke a cigarette. Eventually, Mom eased up and the night quieted down. With all the abuse she heaped on him, and her disappointment in who he was, somehow I still felt she was protecting him, though from what I could not imagine, and she would never tell, no matter how many times and how many different ways I asked.

From an early age I was proud of Dad's swearing, it was the only thing he ever did with any passion or skill, and he was a master at it. He complained about the weather, the traffic, his bosses, and about life in California. Cursing was his favorite form of conversation. And when he complained, he voiced his feelings in artful strings of expletives or novel turns of phrase. For example, it was a tradition in our family when someone farted, to accompany the act by saying, with disdain: "*Alla faccia di atoburns.*" I took up the tradition, not knowing until I was older that "Otto Burns" was an actual person. He was once my Dad's boss, and a real S.O.B. So, for the rest of all time, anyone in our family who farted must aim it "into the face of Otto Burns." We all did it, but it was Dad who used the phrase with an almost religious observance, and who also put the most body English and facial affect into it.

One night I try to emulate Dad's swearing. I am watching TV well past my official 8PM bed time. Grandpa is snoring in Dad's lounger, Gramma is polishing non-existent crumbs from the kitchen counter, Mom and Dad are quietly sitting on the couch, and I lay sprawled on the floor. As the hour advances I keep a secret eye on the wall clock, expecting to be told to go to bed at any moment. I convince myself they have silently agreed to let me stay up late to finish watching this program, and the tension is killing me, so at the next commercial I chance it. "Hey, this is almost over, so can I stay up another half hour?"

Instantly, I know I have made a mistake. Mom looks at the wall clock, a faux-gold sun dial surrounded by twelve alternating long and short barbed golden spokes, then over at me.

"Oh, shit! It's way past your bedtime. Off you go."

When I get up off the floor I am indignant, if that word can be applied to a boy of ten. Shouldn't my honesty buy me a half-hour's reprieve?

"Damn it, I wish I had never said a motherfuckin' thing." I start toward the hall, quite pleased with my little rebellion against Mom's tyranny. Dad continues to watch the commercial. He may have actually mouthed an absent-minded "goodnight." But Mom is on her feet in an instant, slapping me around the head and telling me off in three languages.

"Where did you learn to talk like that to your mother?" *Slap, slap.* "What are you, some kind of *cholo?*" *Slap, slap.* "*Porcu miseria!*" *Slap, slap,* all the way to bed. I decide it is best not to respond that I learned to swear from her husband. Anyway, her questions were what I would later learn to call "rhetorical."

After I am dispatched she lights into Dad, telling him that my performance this night was all his "fucking fault."

It is oppressive living under Mom's love but growing up I am more like her than I care to admit. Like her, I am determined to call the shots in my own life, I have a big mouth, and it sometimes gets me in trouble. Like her, I don't understand the culture we live in; I don't know the rules and conventions of middle class society. While I have heard plenty about "The American Dream" I am supposed to live out, by the time I reach high school I have also learned that it is an Anglo dream not made for me. Instead, as time goes on I internalize the peculiar and inflexible code of behavior for boys on the street. I remain ignorant of how things work in the bigger world, beyond Pico Rivera – because no one knows enough about it to teach me.

It took a long while for me to learn the rules outside the *barrio*, among people who read newspapers and books, go to movies, travel in order to visit new places, talk about more than the weather, food, and who they are pissed off at. Our world was very small, stretching along Whittier Boulevard to East L.A., from river to river, stagnant water meandering down concrete channels.

Beside the family Bible we had only one book in our household. One day Mom decided to buy a children's encyclopedia that was being sold serially at the Market Basket. She could buy one letter each week as she did the grocery shopping. She had the idea – she must have gotten it from TV ads – that a kid should own an encyclopedia. She started strong, but for some reason she lost interest after bringing home the first volume, the "A." Still I was fascinated by the book. I stared for hours at the picture of Davy Crockett at the Alamo. As a result of her effort I came to know something about everything from Aardvarks to Ajax, at which point my education Abruptly Abated.

We owned no record player. At age fifteen I received a little transistor radio as a present from my confirmation sponsor, Mom's brother-in-law, Uncle Jimmy. I used it mostly for listening to Dodgers or Lakers games. We went to the drive-in movies only once. Uncle Jimmy organized it. We took no newspapers or magazines, visited no book stores or libraries, and went on the same four-to-five day vacation every year.

In the middle of each blistering August we drove to Las Vegas in a car without air-conditioning. We always stayed at the Yucca, the cheapest motel we could find, while Mom and Dad played the slot machines until their money ran out. This motel, I liked to think, put the "yuck" in Yucca. A nicer place with a pool would have made no difference, since I was alone and did not know how to swim.

At thirteen I am big for my age, complete with facial hair. Out of boredom I begin to tag along to the air conditioned casinos, where my parents encourage me to join them in losing a few nickels or, if we were feeling very brave, quarters. As I gain confidence in my ability to pass for an adult in these forbidden surroundings I start playing slots farther away from Mom and Dad.

A very pretty cocktail waitress in a practically non-existent skirt and white, high-heeled plastic boots smiles and asks sweetly if I want a free drink. I ordered a beer. When it comes, so does her manager, a dour hag who never, decades earlier, on her best day, looked half as good as my waitress. She demands my ID. I am escorted out. The waitress looks confused as I leave – had she been flirting with a thirteen year old?

I begin roaming the back streets away from the "Strip" while my parents gamble, and discover that quite a few people leave their windows unlocked while they are at work. Housebreaking has some of the same attraction as slot machines, risks and rewards, but I take nothing. I could not really explain the sudden appearance of a stereo back at the Yucca. Getting in, walking around, watching some TV, and getting out is just a way to pass the time.

—⋙—

Being an only child born in the fifties was just plain odd. People came back from the war and went to work repopulating the earth. My parents tried but after several miscarriages, which Mom blamed on Dad's "weak sperm," they had about given up. Then, when she was thirty-four, when her younger sisters were on their third or fourth child, and when Dad was thirty-nine, she finally got me. That was enough for her, at last she had a baby, but it wasn't enough for me.

Here we were, a large Sicilian family; I could name more than thirty first cousins, four alone from aunt Claudia, one of my mother's three siblings, who moved out to LA before us. It felt like we were hardly doing our part. When we moved from New York to L.A. we shrank to a much smaller clan. We were no longer in the *Provincia* or the Sicilian homeland of lower Manhattan. The family stood out as different in L.A., foreign, and I was odder still, the "spoiled" only child.

For the cheap rent we settled in Pico Rivera, where most people were Mexican, fresh-arrived from *their* old country, or *Chicano*, Californian by birth but of Mexican ancestry, sometimes recently and sometimes one or two generations removed. Our streets were an unrelenting grid of small, hastily built, nearly identical stucco houses. We lived on the last block on the Rivera side of town, which we liked to think was the "nice" side, our side of Whittier Boulevard. Our house backed onto the back lot, an easement under the massive towers of the Edison Company power lines which people used as a makeshift dump. As kids we found the back lot a wonderland of old couches, discarded crates, and assorted precious objects we used to build clubhouses and from which we fought raging make-believe wars. Behind the back lot was the San Gabriel River, fenced to keep us out, not yet buried under concrete, and always accessible through the well-known cut outs in the rusty chain link made by earlier generations.

The dads with good jobs were custodians with the City of L.A. or linemen with the Edison power company or worked the assembly line at the Ford plant. Ben's dad was a tree surgeon with the City, a title which conferred upon him roughly the same status on our block that the profession of brain surgeon might convey somewhere else. But those few with these really good jobs, the ones who owned their own modest homes while the rest of us rented month-to-month, were a minority. Mostly the dads were laborers, just as they had been in the old country for generations, as long as anyone could recall. The moms for their part stayed at home to make tortillas, give birth to and swat at their numerous kids, and endure their husbands' drinking.

It was a poor but mostly working town, and my small family was noticeably among the poorest of all because my father could not land one of those good city or power company jobs or, for that matter, any steady job at all. In order to do that you needed at least some skill or trade and maybe some of that Ambition Mom said he lacked. He could not even land a regular laborer's job. He worked moving furniture, hoping for a permanent position that never came. Instead early each morning he walked to a corner not far from home, next to a perpetually burned out street lamp, where building contractors looking for day laborers drove up, loaded the lucky few who would bring home cash that night, and took them off for the unskilled labor Dad provided.

A new neighbor, a Paddy named John Reagan who was foreman in the shipping department at a paint factory in the City of Industry, got Dad his first and only steady job in California – loading tractor-trailers at the Emerson Paint Company. Dad stayed with Emerson for nearly twenty years doing that same job, refusing seniority-based promotions or an opportunity to become foreman: "Who needs da fuckin' agger'vation?" he complained. His unskilled labor had its dangers. Every few years a man was killed by an avalanche of paint cans falling off the twenty-foot-high overhead racks or lost his footing and plunged that distance from a ladder to the concrete floor. But at least it was a steady job. It was not enough to buy a house or even a new car, but enough in those days to support a frugal family of five.

Dad may have lacked Ambition but he did not lack the will to work. He knew hard work and he welcomed it because it meant money coming home. Maybe it also meant something more to him. The personnel records for Emerson Paint Company, if they still exist, would reveal that Dad never missed a day of work due to illness or injury.

VIII

We're on our own.

"Stay alert, boys, stay the fuck alert," Sarge stage-whispered as he went from hole to hole, cradling his Thompson submachine gun under one big blonde-haired arm. "They'll probably come through the pass right after dawn."

Sarge was a real army pro with fifteen years in before the current mess got started, and he treated the draftees, recent volunteers and other "part-timers" as he called them, both officers and enlisted, equally dismissively. At thirty-five he was the oldest man in the company, and standing a good six-foot three inches tall he was a Minnesotan nobody wanted to cross. That included Lieutenant Connors, a recent college graduate who had become their platoon leader when Lieutenant Mayer was evacuated with a bullet in his hip two weeks earlier. Connors learned quickly that he and everyone else would be a lot better off if he listened to Sarge's advice on how to do things. He was quickly turning into a pretty good officer and, even Sarge had to admit, if he lived another three or four months, maybe he could be trusted to lead men into battle, but not yet, and certainly not in a tight situation like this.

—◊◊◊—

It was like having a box seat at a perverse fireworks display: perverse because the intermittent flashes from heavy artillery were at ground level in the darkness around Dj Ksaira not up in the sky where they belonged. The Germans pounded away all night, both at the distant hill and at the battalion's armor on the plain below, but not, mercifully, upon their position up on craggy, scrub-covered, nearly treeless Dj Lessouda. Not yet anyway. There was no responding fire: the battalion had no heavy artillery of its own and mortars were useless at this distance.

The *Panzers* poured onto the plain at daybreak virtually unopposed, decimating the American tanks arrayed against them looking into the sun. Then they turned their attack toward Dj Ksaira. A counterattack by a full battalion of M3's sent from Division also failed to stop them. Not one of the twenty-six American tanks survived. They had little chance against the more heavily armored Tigers, which could take the M3's under fire from beyond the Americans' effective range.

Russo felt a mixture of fear and anger that the rest of the battalion was being thoroughly beaten up and at the same time a guilty, niggling sense of relief that for now at least his position was spared. He knew, of course, that their turn would come, and that when it did no one would be left to help. They were being saved for dessert.

"Hey Goldie," he said during a lull, his cheek resting on the stock of his rifle, propped against the scree pile in front of their hole. "Looks like you saved yourself a bunch a work on dat motherfuckin' letter of mine. How do ya make our chances of livin' tru da rest of Valentine's Day?"

"All I know is I ain't goin' easy, pal. I ain't gonna just lie down and die, I'm gonna fight like a sonovabitch. I'm gonna stay alive as long as fuckin' possible, if I have to kill a hundred Krauts with my bare hands to do it. I don't plan on dyin'."

"Den let's stick close and keep each udder alive," Russo replied. He believed in Goldie's confidence, even though he did not share it. He figured his odds were better if he stuck close to his buddy.

"That's right, Johnny. Let's keep an eye out for each other and we'll pull through fine." Goldie sounded like he was trying to convince himself as much as anything, but Russo still took comfort in his friend's words.

A few minutes later, "Whatta loada bullshit. . ." Russo started to say, about nothing in particular, when he was cut short by Sarge dropping into their hole, making his rounds again. One moment he was not there and the next he was, slipping over the edge silently, like a big cat. He spat as he looked over the low scree parapet toward the plain. Then he nodded slowly and it drew both Russo's and Goldie's attention to his face.

"You two assholes awright?" They stared back at him, not knowing what he wanted. "This ain't gonna be no cake walk fellas, make sure you got plenty'a ammo, and while you got time dig this here hole deeper, the deeper the better. Dig it so fuckin deep you think they're gonna come after you for desertion. Then get ready to do some serious killin'." His face was filthy, serious, and unwrinkled.

"Where's da relief, Sarge? We was s'posed to get some fuckin' relief," Russo whined, sounding more desperate than he had meant to, and knowing the answer, but not wanting to hear it.

Sarge smiled, a mouth full of those shiny white teeth, but without happiness. "There ain't no fuckin' relief you fuckin' shitbird," he said quietly, almost gently. "Never was."

It was a fact neither Russo nor Goldstein could dispute but one they didn't want to believe either. "When they put the battalion up here like this, so's we just have to sit here and watch the Krauts cut up them fellas on Dj K, they might as well invited the Krauts to attack. First they go over there," he motioned with his thumb over his shoulder, over the fox hole's parapet, toward Dj Kasira, "then they come after us. Watch what is happening to those poor bastards over there – cuz we're next. So dig." Then Sarge grunted, tapped Goldie on the leg for him to make way and scooted out of their hole, on to the next one.

Russo caught Goldie's eye and they both shrugged.

"Hell, you think Sarge knows what's up?" Goldie asked. "You ask me, he's just being his usual cheerful self. He don't know shit, just like Lieutenant Connors don't know shit, none of the officers, even the Colonel don't. We're stuck sitting up here and if the Krauts turn away we're ok, but if they turn on us, then we're fucked. Relief or no relief."

Russo tried to swallow, his only response, but his throat suddenly felt tight and dry and wouldn't cooperate. By silent mutual agreement each man got out his entrenching tool. While digging, they listened as the pounding of Dj Ksaira continued. They had been under bombardment more than once themselves. It was the worst experience of all the lousy combat experiences they had been through. Occasionally they stopped digging and looked across the valley, imagining in spite of themselves what their comrades on that hill were going through.

Instinctively, Russo made the sign of the cross. Goldie saw it. "I thought you hated all that Catholic school crap?"

"I do, sure, but dat's just da church. It's just like da fuckin' army, run by assholes. Don't mean I got no fait in god, just like hatin' da assholes dat runs dis man's army don't mean I don't love my country."

"So you're a believer," Goldie asked, tossing a shovel full of shale over the parapet, where it spread downhill.

"Hell yeah," Russo answered. He still had the simple faith his mother had taught him. That Jesus, the Son of God, had come to earth, taught people to love one another, and died for our sins. If he died believing that, he would go to heaven.

"It's sometin, dat fait, no matter what else happens in dis fucked up mess."

"So you believe," Goldie pressed, "even though we're in the middle of the biggest fuckin' killin' spree in history?"

Russo didn't like to think too deeply about such things. He was happy with what he knew and what he believed, and he didn't really see much difference between the two where God was concerned. He did what he was told and trusted to God, and to his buddies, especially Goldie, who was a Jew.

"So waddya believe Goldie, I mean, you Jews?" He imagined some strange rituals, like that one where they make circumcision into a public event, and then he realized he had absolutely no idea what Jews believed, or for that matter, what made them Jews and not Catholics. They were only a foot apart and despite the distant sounds of the battle raging at Dj Ksaira it was still possible at this close range to carry on a normal conversation inside their peaceful little fighting hole.

Goldstein didn't respond. He stared blankly over the parapet, across the plain, emptying himself of all feeling, then went back to digging. Every few minutes he muttered an incomprehensible phrase in Hebrew, the one Russo knew he repeated whenever he saw someone killed.

"Hey, Goldie, I tought you didn' pray, taught you made fun a' all dat."

"I ain't got no crucifix, Johnny," he responded. "Not something for a Jew to wear. But damned if it don't help to pray when you're in a situation like this. It's all the same God anyway, so what the fuck?"

Russo had never thought of that possibility, that the Jew God was the same as his Catholic God. He remembered once as a child, when someone had asked if he was "a Christian," and he had answered, "Hell no, I'm a Catlic." It made his head swim to think about these things so he fingered the crucifix attached to his dog tags and started praying, lips moving in silence, "Hail Mary, full of grace. . ."

Incoming artillery erased all physical landmarks, leaving a world without reference point or reason. A man could hear nothing – not shouted orders, not the screams of the dying, not even the individual shells exploding. It all merged into a single deafening roar. The concussion, even from a substantial distance, could knock the breath out of a man, again and again, until he passed out from lack of oxygen. The eyes could not see; dust and dirt obscured his hand in front of his face, had he dared to look. Even thought was impossible. The fury of the attack blotted the mind clear of everything but fear. If a blind man develops more keenly his other senses, so does the infantryman under an artillery barrage. Deprived of sight, hearing, and reason, hugging the ground as if trying to get below it, terrorized to the point of fouling his pants, he experiences his remaining senses with increased acuity. The smell of cordite mixed with freshly raised earth crammed the nose, the taste of dust and blood mixed in the mouth. Teeth shook and jostled, the intestines jumped, and the mind screamed for it to end. But the barrage ruled, it would continue for its appointed time.

Mid-day and the slaughter continued on the plain below and the hill across from their position. *Wehrmacht* infantry had joined in the killing, and half of Colonel Wayne's battalion, some nine hundred men, was catching hell. Despite the ungodly din, and concern for the inevitable attack on his own position, Russo had managed to doze off at the loose scree parapet. It was his first rest since they had dug in nearly two days earlier. Sleeping through the cacophony of the battle below, he was awakened by the much closer and distinctive crack of an M1 rifle only a few yards away.

"Oh shit, oh shit," yelled Lupe Perez from a neighboring hole. "I shot him. I fucking nailed him in the chest. I seen it. He musta been a Kraut, wasn't he?"

Hysterical, his terrible mistake dawning, he tried to climb out of his hole and go after the intruder but his squad mate held him back.

Instantly awake, Russo whispered to Goldstein, "Whadda hell! Krauts up here?" This while chambering a round and slipping the safety off his M1. He could hear shouts and crying from the next hole.

Goldstein's response was silence as he peered cautiously over the parapet. Then, he yelled at the neighbors: "What the fuck is going on over there?"

"I think Loo-pee maybe just aced one a our own guys, prob'ly a messenger sent up from the tanks. Guy just popped up out of nowhere behind that swale down there and Loo-pee fired." That was Miller, the Bible-thumping Georgian sharing Perez's hole. Lupe was a *Pachuco*, a zoot suiter from East L.A., and had talked real tough throughout Basic and on the transports over. Day after day on the crossing he picked one fight after another with anyone who even looked at him sideways as they squeezed through the ship's narrow passageways. Ever since they had gone into combat, however, he had been scared shitless, just like everyone else. Now he was screaming like a child and Miller, who was twice Perez's size and wanted to be a Baptist minister when the war was over, was restraining him.

"Stay where you are, cover us, we'll check it out," Goldstein yelled. Then, turning slightly, he whispered, "C'mon Johnny, let's leapfrog it down there and see what Lupe really shot at." Before jumping off, he craned his neck back to yell to the neighboring holes on either side: "And hold your fuckin' fire until you see Hitler's own mug, awright?"

Raising himself, ready to move, Russo muttered, more to himself than to Goldie, "Tank messenger my ass. If he's really a G.I. he's just tryin' to get to high ground."

Goldstein nodded slightly at this observation and they took off low over the parapet, the scree tumbling back into their hole as their feet pushed against it. They moved in turn, each providing over-watch for the other as they quickly circled the area that Perez had fired into, downhill from their positions. They crossed the barbed wire defensive perimeter, hung with old ration cans filled with small rocks as an early warning line, and lowered themselves over a small ledge. The rocks rattled, making them feel even more exposed as they crept through the jangling wire.

"Whadda useless pain in da ass," Russo quietly swore, steadying a can to silence it. "Dese fuckin' rocks. You can hear a tank comin' from miles. Da

Krauts ain't gonna come sneakin' up here less dey walk across two fuckin miles a open plain."

At the base of a small, pathetically twisted shrub they found him: an American with a bullet wound through and through, just as Lupe Perez had said. The slug had apparently missed his heart, since he was still alive, but he was out cold and had lost an awful lot of blood. "Medic!" they yelled in unison as Russo got out the man's compression bandage from his web gear and pressed it to the entrance hole as they had been taught in the first aid course.

—∿∿—

While the medics were trying to stabilize the wounded soldier for transport to the battalion aid station up the hill and Sarge organized a patrol to go downhill a bit and look for any survivors of the tank slaughter, Russo pulled open the pouch the messenger had been carrying across his chest. It was soaked in blood but still intact. Inside was a coded message for Colonel Wayne, the battalion commander.

"This guy didn't come from the tank company," Goldstein said, looking at the wounded soldier's unit designation. "He came all the way from fuckin' Division HQ! Imagine that shitty luck. He snuck through eight, ten miles of Krauts only to get a bullet from an M1 for his trouble. Goddammit, but I hate the Army."

While Goldstein tried to get everyone back to their positions so they could provide cover for Sarge and his patrol Russo ran the message pouch uphill to the command post, a small, deep hole, hastily dug and massively sandbagged. He found the colonel screaming at his two radiotelephone operators, who were cowering like kicked dogs, pleading that the landlines must have been cut by all the artillery fire. Russo figured from the exchange he overheard that they had no comms with anybody not presently on the Dj, and he had the common sense to know this was not a good thing.

Colonel Wayne was tall and wide-shouldered, with a face that could have been found on a piece of driftwood, crags and wrinkles aging him well beyond his thirty-two years. On his uniform and helmet he wore no "crosshairs," the insignia of rank snipers often looked for in choosing targets. This was counter to General Patton's explicit orders that all officers in theatre conspicuously display their insignia, so as to better motivate the troops. Patton actually thought it was good for the troops to see their officers getting killed, that it made them feel less alone.

Along with most of the battalion, Russo liked Colonel Wayne. He liked him even better for giving Patton the finger. Unlike the distant generals, their colonel seemed to want to keep as many of his men alive as possible. That tended to make a commander popular with the troops. Although he was a West Point graduate Wayne growled, swore, dressed and, Russo could now attest, smelled more like a platoon sergeant than a battalion CO. Keeping Wayne alive seemed to have been a good deal all around. If anyone could get them out of the fix Division had put them in, it was probably him.

As soon as Colonel Wayne saw the dispatch pouch he tore it from Russo's hand. While opening the message he looked up at the man bringing it, recognized him as one of his own, double checked by glancing at the shoulder insignia, then barked: "Where's the messenger?"

"One a da pickets shot him, sir. Everbody's real jumpy," was Russo's uncertain reply. Wayne glared at him for a moment, letting that added bit of misery sink in, then noticed that Russo's hands and parts of his uniform were smeared with blood that was fresh enough to bear that peculiar iron smell.

"You shoot him?" Wayne asked evenly, no emotion in his voice.

"No sir," Russo said. Looking down at his blood-soaked hands he added, "I just got dis on me taking his pouch."

Wayne's own hands got a smear of blood as well. He wiped it on his pant leg without a change of expression then turned to the closest radiotelephone man, who had already gotten the code book open. Together they quickly deciphered the message.

Since he had not been dismissed, Russo stood waiting. The CP was stuffy with cigarette smoke, crammed with ration tins and extra radio batteries, laden with maps, radios, and the occupants' personal weapons. He stood beside a sandbagged wall to wait for orders.

Colonel Wayne finished reading the decoded message. Even before he spoke it was clear to Russo that he was not happy with its contents.

"First they put us up here on these fucking hills like a goat tied to a stake," Wayne said to no one in particular. "And now the whole goddamn division is retreating, so we can just shift for ourselves."

A pause, long enough only for the slightest of sighs. Then, "Shit!" he exploded, with enough violence to cause both Russo and the two much-abused radiomen to jump. "Johnson!" he shouted.

A young officer, barely older than Russo, wearing a tattered uniform blouse, also minus insignia of rank, a cigarette dangling unlit from his lips, appeared from behind the wall of sandbags. "Sir?" His voice sounded several decades older than its owner.

"Message from Division, Lieutenant. We're going to fight our way out of here down to these crossroads," he pointed on the wall map to a dot about eight miles distant along the plain between Lessouda and Ksaira, pressing his body past Russo.

"We're on our own, and it's got to be done tonight, before the Krauts finish off Ksaira, regroup, and attack us. Bring the company and platoon leaders in for a briefing at 1700. We jump off at 2200. That gives us half a fucking chance to get away before first light. Spread word to prepare to debouch. We'll take only what we can carry. Spike the mortars and wire any extra ammo or supplies we have to leave behind. I don't want anything blown, it'll give us away. But I also don't want any of our stuff used against us. Got it?" Johnson nodded and scooted out of the CP without a word.

Wayne suddenly remembered Russo standing against the wall and turned to face him. "Is he dead?"

He was confused for a moment, then realized his CO was asking about the wounded messenger. "S'pretty bad, sir, ches' wound, but da medics was workin' on 'im when I left."

"Alright, get back to the line!" Wayne ordered, and immediately turned back to the radiotelephone men. "Any word yet from Morris?" That was the battalion executive officer, in charge of the other half of Wayne's command, situated on Dj Ksaira, enduring the brunt of the attack.

"None sir, still no fucking word from anyone," was the radioman's response.

IX

¡Qué puta noche!

It is a childhood of street baseball and wars fought with wooden guns, played on the back lot all summer long. My front teeth were shattered at age ten by a rifle butt in hand-to-hand combat and proudly remained jagged, a badge of courage. Boys posture and fight, viciously and with little provocation. They join defensive groups run by their older brothers, or they risk becoming targets for other groups of boys. Some of these groups are real gangs but most are just neighborhood boys from a block or two around who grow up together. It is also a childhood of friends who are present every day, year after year; friends who will do anything for you – share their bag of Doritos, lie to your parents about where you are, lie to the cop/principal/priest about what you both have done, defend you in a tight spot.

I am thirteen and reluctantly, after years of battle between us, Mom now opens the front door on a summer's morning, tells me to be back for dinner, and sends me off. Ben, Ernie, Mario, Dave, Gilberto, these are my companions, but especially Ben and Ernie, *mis carnales*, brothers of my flesh.

Ben is my first friend, my blood brother. We met when we were five years old – later we cut open our thumbs and sealed them, mingling our bloods. We were eight or nine, using an old pocket knife that had gutted rotting frogs on the side of the riverbed, had un-popped soda bottles, and had cleaned under too many filthy fingernails to count. We vowed that whatever happened to us when we grew up, we would share it. If one of us got rich, he would give half to the other. If one had a house or a car, the other would have a place to live or wheels to drive. If one of us went to jail, the other would break him out.

Ben and I fight from time to time, hard punches to the head and stomach, whenever honor calls for it. But these are minor scrapes, never involve kicking, and we are never angry for long. Besides, it is good to learn to fight by trading punches with a friend before you need to do it with people who really want to hurt you.

Our moms walked us to Kindergarten, but thereafter we walk to school together almost every day. Throughout the elementary years Ben came to my house in the morning. Then, in junior high, the pattern reversed as his house is on the way to our new school. Eventually, Ben gets a used Grand Prix, picks me up and we drive to high school, two miles away.

Ben is the youngest of three wild boys, so he has a lot to live up to. He is big, tall and wide, with black skin, short kinky hair and massive hands. As we get older he can intimidate grown men with his ferocious scowl. He is *El Mero Chingón*, the baddest motherfucker in town. He is tough, strong, and fearless, with a terrible temper, and not the best judgment. It is an explosive combination. Ben introduces me to everything I need to know: drinking, getting high, cutting school, fighting, and stealing. Not that I am an innocent he corrupts, more that he is my guide to growing up, to being in the neighborhood. He is my age, but with two older brothers who pave the way he is quicker to get into what we call *la vida*. The life, lived on the street.

—∞—

I am sixteen and one night, cruising Whittier Boulevard in Ben's old Grand Prix looking for I don't know what, there is not much action so we decide to drive up to the Whittier hills. We are drinking beer and throwing the empties out the windows at parked cars. A hit brings an appreciative round of *qué bueno*, and a miss a general teasing and calls of "pussy!" It is Ben, Ernie, Mario, Dave, Gilberto and me, the usual guys.

A long way from home, up in the shallow hills where the roads are windy, with nice views of city lights below, we spot a house on the hillside that looks alive – lights on, cars parked all around. Ben stops.

"Looks like a party, man. Let's go get something to drink," Ben suggests, noting that we have run out of beer. His suggestions are impossible to resist. We all just follow along. I don't know what, or even if, we are thinking, but if anyone has reservations, he doesn't want to be the one to voice them and risk being called a pussy.

A pussy is a guy who won't fight, a guy who won't go off for a couple days with his friends without his parents knowing where he is, a guy who won't drink tequila from the shared bottle, a guy who rats out or abandons a friend. On a good day you are called a pussy ten times by your friends, as a sign of affection. But if a guy who is not a friend says it even once, it means *chingazos*, you have to fight. It is a deadly serious business to us, essential to our sense of who we are. We are tested every day and cannot fail that test – not ever.

The door is unlocked so we walk right into the house and sure enough a couple dozen Anglos who look to be in their early thirties are having a nice little party. Fancy food is laid out on a cloth, drinks are on another table set up as the bar, people are chatting in small groups, the women all dressed nicely in the Anglo way – long straight hair and flowery miniskirts. Ben walks over to the bar, looks over at us like this is his house, his party, his booze, and offers us refreshments. *"Órale, vatos. ¿Tomamos una cerveza, eh?"*

He grabs a beer bottle and flings it over to Mario. With his foot-long Mexican afro, thin attempt at a *Pancho Villa* mustache, and mile-wide lapels, Mario looks like he should be in the *Chicano* Jackson Five. He opens the bottle against a door jamb, chipping the wood and paint, and spilling the agitated beer on the nice shag carpet.

Well, what do you know, pretty soon we get noticed: six of us in creased khakis or jeans, white t-shirts under top-buttoned plaid Pendletons, and Ben with a red bandana tied around his big black forehead. A tall, thin Paddy with long, stringy red hair, confronts Ben. "What the fuck are you doin? Get outta my house."

It strikes me as the right thing to say, reasonable even. If it was my house and this guy crashed my party, I would have wanted to grab him by the bandana and fling him out the door. Of course I hope I would have the sense to assess the situation, that is, Ben, and realize *that* was not going to happen unless I first got some help – in fact, a lot of help. The Paddy obviously doesn't have either the sense to avoid Ben or the help to deal with him. He alone is confronting us. The other guys, a good dozen of them, are busy staring into their drinks or "protecting" their girlfriends by keeping them across the room. That is just wrong. These rich guys have it all – nice house, nice cars, probably paid for with nice jobs, but they are all pussies.

This is something that simply would not happen in our neighborhood. Six guys Ben's size could burst into a party in the home of some poor hundred-and-thirty-pound *Chicano* and he would take them on, with a chair, a baseball bat or a gun, but he would take them on, no question. He might die in the process, but he would die fighting. He would not be a pussy.

I am beside the food table, chewing on something that tastes like salt and cardboard. I look over at Ernie, who is also munching on something, and we make a face, like little kids who do not like the taste of spinach. That's the thing about Ernie, he is a year older than the rest of us, and looks pretty tough when his guard is up, but it only takes a moment for it to slip and he seems like what he is, just a big kid.

"These Paddies don't know shit about *refin*, dude," he says to me, sniffing some fish eggs on a cracker. "This shit smells like a *pedo viejo*," an old fart. Ernie is tall and a little chubby. Unlike Ben he always stands in a slumping, non-threatening way like he doesn't know what to do with all that body.

Across the table from us is a pretty blonde woman with her hair in a ridiculous flip no *Chicana* would ever dare try – you could pack a row of hot dogs around her head inside the curl. She is looking at me like I am Jack the Ripper. I smile, try to put her at ease. No one is going to hurt her. We don't mess with girls; that is bullshit. Out of the corner of my eye I notice one of the other women picking up the pink princess phone, probably calling the cops. *Chale!* It's a long way up here so we have time, if we start moving our asses toward the door.

Ben is in no hurry, however. He frowns at the tall Paddy, like his feelings are hurt by the insult. Maybe they are. Maybe he expects to be welcomed with open arms. I know what is coming, though, even if the Paddy cannot see it. After more than a decade of life with Ben, and many adventures like this one, I know exactly what he is going to do. This Paddy must be thirty-five, but he clearly doesn't know shit about how the world, our world, works. I get a weird sense of satisfaction from being in this position – knowing what is about to happen before it does, and knowing that the Paddy does not.

Ben is calm, relaxed, and positively lethal. I finish up the awful bit of food in my mouth as quickly as I can. Ben picks up a beer bottle, holding it out in front of himself.

"This is your *cerveza*, right *ése*?" It sounds funny, to all of us. I am sure no one has ever before called this Paddy *ése*. We all laugh uncomfortably, trying to keep it cool. I know the clock is running before the cops get here.

"*Órale, carnal, vámanos antes que venga la chota*," Mario says to Ben, reading my mind.

I am glad to hear him suggesting we go, but I would never be the one to say it myself. That is part of my unspoken deal with Ben – like him I also have no fear, or at least I don't show any. I'm not supposed to worry about little things like a busload of Anglo cops coming through the door any minute. I am cool.

"Ok, *ése, está bien*," Ben answers Mario. "Just let me give this *gabacho* his beer back." Here it comes. I don't want to watch, but I can't help it. Ben reaches toward the big Paddy with the beer in his outstretched hand. The poor dupe reflexively puts out his own hand to take it, leaning forward across the bar as he does so, and Ben moves very quickly. He grabs the Paddy's outstretched hand and pulls him further forward, off balance. At the same time with the other hand he rams the capped end of the beer bottle hard into the guy's mouth. In the chaos, the blood, and the screaming that follows we all run for the door. Ben purposely knocks over the bar in the process.

We are followed by more screams and shouts – but by none of the guys from the party – all the way out to the car. We drive off, laughing, I am now ashamed to say. We laugh at the shock and pain on the poor Paddy's face, at the mess Ben made knocking over the bar, at the way we really crashed that party. On our way down the hill we pass a cop car going uphill, toward the party, away from Whittier Boulevard and our homes.

"Ben, you are one fuckin' *vato loco*, ain't you, *cabrón*," Mario says.

"Yeah, why'd you do that, you really messed up that fucker's face?" Dave adds. He is the kind of guy who wishes he would have done something like this, and in the retelling, next week, maybe he will *become* the guy who did. I sit quietly, laughing along with everyone else and, if I am man enough to admit it, feeling bad for the dumbfuck Paddy.

"*Cálmate*, Dave," Mario says. "I think his face was pretty fucked up to begin with." More laughter.

"Someday, you guys, we're all going to be working for that dude, that big, pale, redheaded *gabacho*, the one with no fuckin' teeth!" Everyone laughs. "You know that, *ése*? He's going to be *el Patrón*. He has it all over him." Ben is serious, and seriously angry. "So we mess him up now, and he bends us over and fucks us for the rest of our lives. Seems fair to me, man."

Back on Whittier Blvd it is getting late but we are still in a loud and hyper mood after the party-crashing. Traffic is heavy now and we are cruising, stop-and-go in the Grand Prix.

"What happened to them chicks in the Plymouth?" asks Mario. We had passed some girls going the other way half an hour before, tried to turn around to catch up to them, but got trapped in the traffic.

"Maybe they pulled into Bob's, let's check it out." Dave suggests. We are approaching Bob's Big Boy hamburger joint and Dave is probably hungry. It's the kind of place where we like to "throw a walk-out." We order, eat, and then leave without paying.

Suddenly Ben rolls his window down, sticks his head out and yells "Fuckin' pigs!" at a passing cop car. We all stop laughing when we crane around and see the cherry top come on. The cops make a quick U-turn and come up behind us. We pull over at a vacant stretch of the boulevard in front of a used car lot and wait. I can hear the police radio but I don't turn to look. This trouble will come when it's ready.

"You're a fuckin' *pendejo* Gomez," Mario says to Ben. "You *know* what's gonna happen now. *¡Qué puta noche!*"

Before anyone can respond the car doors are pulled open and we are roughly hauled out and lined up along the curb side of the car, all six of us, sprawled over the hood or roof or fender.

"Which one of you's got the mouth?" asks one of the Paddy cops, who is maybe forty, thin and wiry, and, no surprise, extremely angry.

We are silent. That is assumed. We do not rat-out each other, especially when we know the consequence for the guilty party.

"So, maybe it was alla you faggots," again the thin cop. The other one, who is also Anglo, of course, is about six-two and keeps fingering his club eagerly. "You know what PIG stands for, dontcha? *Pride, Integrity* and *Guts*, that's what." So now we are going to get a lecture?

One by one we are roughly patted down. Ben has his small pocket knife in his khakis, the one we used years before to become blood brothers. The first cop makes a big deal about it, calls it a "concealed weapon," then throws it down the sewer drain opening beside the car. Ben starts to protest, pointing toward the drain where his knife has gone, and gets a quick kidney punch before he can utter a word. He takes it, slightly doubling over, and not fighting back, which is both a surprise and a relief. The cop slams him back down on the hood of the car face first.

I must have some sort of death wish, because my mouth jumps in. "Hey, man, there's no need to do that. We're cooperatin'." My next memory is a warm trickle of blood running down my chin. I am also leaning over the hood, next to Ben. He looks over at me and shakes his head as if to say: "fuckin' pigs." Fortunately for us, this time he doesn't say it, we both just think it.

We are all leaning over the car with hands outstretched and behind me I hear the distinctive sound of wood sliding against metal. I have heard it often enough to know it means a night stick is coming out of its holder ring on a cop's belt.

I think to run, before this gets worse, but then remember something Mom said when I got my driver's license: "If a cop pulls you over, be real polite. Call him 'Sir.' Do whatever the hell he asks. Keep your hands in plain view, out of your pockets, and whatever you do, don't try to run. They'll shoot you in the back." So I stay put.

Right then another cop car pulls up and over my shoulder I hear a new Anglo voice. "Thought you guys might use some back-up, heard your call."

I am glad Ben has been so docile, has not made it worse. He is so big and strong that one of the cops might have shot him, in self-defense of course, if he offered resistance. But it is very unlike him to suffer this kind of treatment from anyone and not fight back. Plus he has what people nowadays refer to as "a problem with authority."

The cops back off a bit and confer while we await our fate. Ben whispers to Mario: "At least they ain't opened the trunk."

"Why, *carnal*, what you got in there?" Mario whispers back.

Listening to this I am thinking maybe he has a trunk full of dope or, knowing Ben as I do, maybe a dead body is stuffed in there. Now the cops come back, all four of them. A club whacks Mario across the shoulders. As he goes down onto his knees the cop tells him not to talk while he's "in custody." I start to think we're really going to get our asses kicked now, maybe we better fight back, to have a chance, and I must have moved because a burning pain in the side of my knee tells me where the club has connected. They start pushing us all around, spin us forward, then slam each of the six of us up against the car once more for good measure. They are showing tough, but their words are a relief.

"You punks get in your fucking lowrider and go home to your mama cunts," the first cop says, enjoying the power he has. It takes a huge amount of restraint not to jump on them at that moment, damn the consequences. You don't talk about people's mothers like that. "And next time you are in trouble you can call one of your fucking Spick friends here." Ben still manages to hold his tongue, as do the rest of us. *Cholo, vato*, Mexican, Greaser, these are all terms used as an insult in our world, either seriously or in jest, but "Spick," well that is in a whole different class of insult. It is a word only an outsider, a *gabacho*, would use. Still, we get out quickly, driving the speed limit, and head toward home. Mario brings up looking for the girls in the Plymouth, but no one is interested anymore.

As we drive along, rubbing our sore jaws and knees and backs, each of us is telling how, if they had not backed off like they did, those cops would have had *their* asses kicked. We are making comments about their mothers and generally letting off steam when Ben says: "*Carajo*, I forgot!" He swerves, pulls the car over, jumps out and gets something from the trunk, then hops back in and plops a heavy brown paper bag in my lap. "Open it, *ése*." I do, and inside I find an old Army-issue M1911A1 .45 Caliber semi-automatic and a full magazine lying beside it. No wonder he was so docile with those cops. Too bad he didn't remember this little bit of cargo *before* he yelled out the window at them in the first place. "My old man brought it home from the war," he says.

"¡*Chingado*!" is all I can say. I check the piece to be sure there isn't a magazine in place then jack the slide back a couple of times to empty the chamber, just to be safe. Then I put it all back in the bag and stuff it in the glove compartment.

"Any reason the cops would have a special interest in this particular piece, *carnal*?" Mario asks. Ben doesn't answer. "¡*Hijo de la puta madre*!" Mario continues, but he is just venting.

—⟋⟋⟍—

At some point Ben's father buys a second hand pool table for the covered back patio – after all, he is a tree surgeon, a man of substance – and we spend hours playing. Ben gets to be quite good at it, while I am only fair. After seeing a movie on TV about some big-time hustling, we go to a pool hall on Whittier near Atlantic in East L.A. We are seriously underage but no one really cares as long as you pay up on your bets and you don't make trouble. Ben brags he is going to whip me, but I beat him every game. He keeps betting, and he loses more and more. We play for a dime a point and it adds up. Finally I say I've had enough and leave. He looks around for more challengers and finds one dumbass who is looking to make some easy money from this stupid kid. Ben bets all he has left, $20, on the one game, winner-take-all, and takes the guy's money in a walk. Unfortunately, the mark spots our scam, the mediocre player suddenly clearing the table, and wants his money back or else. Instead, Ben smacks the guy with a cue, grabs the $20 bills off the side of the table, and runs for it. I am waiting outside. We split our winnings, $10 each, which is generous of Ben considering how small a role I played. But then he is always generous. We know we cannot go back to that pool hall again. Like I said, he has a really bad temper, no fear, and very poor judgment. He is also my friend and my role model.

X

Hey, is he really Brown?

B en can also be quite a softie, so much so that the girls call him Gentle Ben, after the TV character, a big, fluffy, tame, brown bear. It fits, and the name sticks. At a party one night, not one we crash but a real high school party – couple hundred kids, no parents in evidence, kegs, tequila, weed, a few small fights but nothing party-stopping – Ben and I meet a group of St. Peter's girls. This is the local Catholic school, where anyone with a shred of Ambition and a few dollars sends their kids so they can avoid having to go to school with us. We think of it as the rich kids' school but I now realize that is stretching things quite a bit. These four girls are very different: blonde, pretty Paddies with names like Colleen and Beth. They smell like clean towels and bath soap, and they wear white lip gloss which somehow makes them look both deathly and irresistible.

"*Qué ruca, ése, ruquitas de aquellas.*" Ben says as we approach them. I have to agree, they are a group of really foxy chicks.

Ben and I are instantly in love, and going against all reason on their parts the girls talk to us. Maybe they are drawn to the novelty we represent in their world same as we are drawn to them. They speak in nice, unaccented English and wear hippie clothes – colorful shirts of a wonderful diaphanous material, hip-hugger jeans with flower patches on the knees or seat, lots of beads, and sandals that show their white feet.

This is a new world for us. We are used to girls with heavy black eye makeup, seriously plucked eyebrows, and long black hair worn in shiny ringlets or swept around their head into a hair sprayed bird's nest. These girls wear their blonde hair long and straight, and don't seem to know about eye makeup. They take our breath away.

I am especially attracted to Beth, who comes up to my armpit, is thin, birdlike, and always laughing. She is so much fun to watch, to be near. Sitting on the back stoop of the house, with the girls standing in front of me chattering away, horsing around, I decide to take decisive action. I try to sweep my arm out casually and grab Beth, pulling her into my lap. It seems like a good plan. Remember, I am sixteen and my romantic repertoire is, well, limited. Having drunk a few beers and with everyone constantly moving around, as I make my move I miss Beth and catch the girl standing beside her, Linda, who not only falls quite easily into my lap but looks over at me and makes no move to get up. I decide if Linda is my bird in the hand, so be it. She is pretty, has light brown hair, not Beth's white blonde, and something I had not noticed before – a mouthful of braces. She smiles at me and I think if I kiss this girl I am going to get badly cut up. With my jagged, broken front teeth she may be thinking the same thing. It turns out alright but it takes some getting used to.

The party breaks up – cops decide we have violated some law or other – underage drinking, curfew, noise, dope. We are sitting on some hay bales in the huge backyard of the party house listening to a band of local guys playing top forty when suddenly a dozen L.A. cops come from all directions. They don't warn us, or even tell us to leave. Night sticks out, they jump on the nearest people and begin beating. The drummer gets cracked on the head and then the cop puts his baton through each of the drum skins. We grab the girls and run for the cars. It's not unheard of for outnumbered cops to start shooting in a situation like this so it is just best to get away.

The biggest surprise of the night is that Ben ends up with Colleen. She is far and away the most beautiful of the girls, tall and elegant, with waist-length blonde hair, light blue eyes, and a gorgeous mouth. Here she is with Gentle Ben, big, black Ben, with a face that could stop a train and hands like two catcher's mitts. As we drive the girls home in the Grand Prix I think: her parents are going to love this.

Over the next few months we double date many times. I am not in love with Linda. After all, she was kind of a mistake. I certainly do not feel toward her the way Ben and Colleen seem to feel, you can see it on their faces. But

Linda is keen on me, is giggly, happy, soft and sweet. She looks at me in a way that feels like this is how a guy is supposed to be looked at by his girlfriend. And I am happy to have a girlfriend at all; it is definitely the best thing going on in my life.

I was dead wrong about one thing. Colleen's parents actually like Ben. He does not seem surprised but I am amazed. They have him over for dinner, they play checkers with him; her dad even takes him outside to look under the hood of his pickup, which in our world is only one step away from giving Ben his daughter's hand in marriage. Meanwhile Linda's parents can't stand me. I am polite, I clean up before going over, but it doesn't help. Maybe I am just not what they had in mind for their daughter. No matter; I am not shopping for in-laws. We decide we'll have to meet in secret so she starts going to the library at night but never makes it past the parking lot.

Many weekends Linda's parents and brothers pack up the camper on the back of their pickup and go off to Big Bear, leaving her at home – she has to work, as a candy striper at Rio Hondo Hospital. Saturday nights on these weekends she invites her friend Colleen for a sleepover and they invite Ben and me to join them. They are of course Catholic girls, but they are not angels, so Linda and I sleep together in her room, naked amid the stuffed animals and pink wallpaper, while Ben and Colleen take the sofa in the family room. To my surprise and amazement I begin to feel a great peace in Linda's arms, Linda whom I do not love. I try to stay awake so I can listen to her regular breathing against my chest and look at her bare white skin up close in the street light coming through the window. I feel protective of her, asleep like that. It feels right.

We can only see each other when her parents aren't around, since I am not welcome. I wonder how much less welcome I would be if her dad knew about our weekend sleepovers.

A few months after we meet the girls Gentle Ben decides he and I need to see the world. We are going to hitchhike to San Francisco and see for ourselves the free love reportedly being handed out up there. Our mothers worry and try to stop us but to no avail. Dad is characteristically silent.

Ben's dad the tree surgeon tells him quite clearly where he stands: "Personally, I don't give a good shit what you do, but if you do anything that makes your mother cry, I'll kick your *pinche* ass."

We need some gear for the trip since we will be sleeping out, but having no money, we improvise. From neighborhood guys recently out of the Army we borrow a couple of Vietnam-issue camouflage jackets for warmth. From the back of Colleen's garage we unearth the parts to several old canvas Boy Scout backpacks once belonging to her brothers and cannibalize them to make two that work – although mine has improvised rope shoulder straps, which are even worse than the unpadded canvas ones Ben gets. We raid our mothers' cabinets for canned foods. The packs weigh a ton even with minimal changes of clothing and some blankets, which will make do since we have no sleeping bags. The morning we set off Mom hands us each a roasted chicken wrapped in tin foil, our first day's food. It is still warm when we eat it that night. Ben's dad gives us a ride to a freeway on-ramp near his first surgery stop of the day.

It is Easter break 1970, and every middle class Anglo kid on earth seems to be out driving, riding, hitchhiking, and camping their way from somewhere to somewhere else on the California coast. Both boys and girls have long straight hair like Linda and Colleen, wear handmade sandals, and use expensive drugs we have never before tried like hashish, LSD, and peyote. Ben and I have dog-sheer buzz cuts that we get behind the gym from our friends, wear our fathers' cast-off work boots, and drink beer or smoke weed when we can get it. We are not hippies, but the real hippies don't care, they take us in and share with us – everything they have.

We make it as far as San Gregorio, a rural beach town south of San Francisco, where we run out of rides and money, so we camp in an artichoke patch, sleeping on the dirt wrapped in our thin blankets. We walk a mile back to a country store, and after counting our pennies try to find enough food to make a meal for two out of less than a dollar. The old couple that runs the store gets increasingly nervous as we shop. They eye us and say to one another, loud enough for us to hear clear across the store: "The Highway Patrol ought to be coming through here any time now, right honey?" And "Oh yes, dear, in fact they're overdue."

It is strange to be in that store, with no larceny in our hearts, only trying to put together a meal, and to be looked upon as thieves or worse. Ben is especially upset by it.

"*Chale*. It's cuz we're Brown, *ése*" he says as we walk back to our campsite with a box of crackers and a small hunk of Monterey Jack. 'Fuckin' *gabachos. Putos.*"

"*Órale*, maybe it's cuz we're wearing these fuckin' army jackets, been sleeping outside for five nights and could use a shower," I suggest. "You smell like a *pedo viejo, cabrón*. Besides, you ain't brown, man." Ben looks over at me quizzically. "You are motherfuckin' black!"

Ben laughs, looking down at his deep black arm as if noticing for the first time just how dark he is. Brown or Black, it stays in our minds. We have been judged a couple of *cholos*, no-goods, and as a result have scared the daylights out of the old Paddy couple. It isn't the only time on that trip that we are treated like thieves or lowlifes. In the end I have to agree with Ben, 'Fuckin' *gabachos.*"

Our L.A. had two types of kids: Brown (*Chicano* or Mexican) and Paddy (Anglo, *Gabacho*, White). If you had blonde, or red, or even brown hair and light skin, you were a Paddy, even if your family lacked a drop of Irish blood. It wasn't until years later that I heard the term *Paddy* used to refer to the Irish, not to Anglos in general. We had one sub-group of Whites who were not called Paddies. These were the Russians, of which there was a surprising number in East L.A., Montebello, and Pico Rivera. They tended to be huge, strong, light-skinned, and heavy drinkers. We did not generally mess with them, and we didn't call them Paddies. We called them. . .Russians.

With my olive skin, dark hair and eyes, my parents who were born in another country, and my grandparents living with the family and speaking no English, I passed the test, I was considered Brown. I remember exactly when it happened. We were choosing sides for a baseball game. I must have been nine or ten. Someone called out "Browns against Paddies," and the sides formed. Ben grabbed me and pulled me along with him. He must have done it from friendship because I was a terrible baseball player. I needed glasses, but no one knew it, so I couldn't field or hit worth a damn.

Someone asked, quite seriously, "Hey, is he really Brown, *ese?*" Ben looked over at me, said that I was, and that was it.

Being Brown held advantages in the *barrio*. When choosing up sports teams on the street we often divided, as we did on that fateful day, into "Browns and Paddies," and since many sports events devolved into brawls, and the Browns outnumbered the Paddies five to one, that put me on the right side.

Leaving L.A. and making that trip north we saw ourselves in a new, different, and not very flattering light. We were not the Brown majority: we were just scruffy, dirty, thieving Mexicans. Not everyone we met treated us badly though, like all those hippies in the Big Sur hills who shared their food, drugs, and love so freely with us.

—∿—

Heading home, unable to get a ride after hours of waiting with outstretched thumbs along the interstate at a low volume on-ramp, we walk down to the freeway and find a place to sleep along the siding. At about five in the morning the ground begins to shake and being from L.A. Ben and I both wake up thinking: "earthquake!" The shaking intensifies and is eventually joined by a roar. The roar grows louder, and finally materializes into a train, which runs past us not ten feet away. In the dark we had not noticed the tracks. It is nearly light anyway and there is no way we could go back to sleep after this, so we walk to the side of the freeway and wait for morning to thumb the next ride. This is a little unusual since we are not at an on-ramp, we are actually right along the side of the freeway itself, but it is early, a deserted stretch of Highway 101, so we decide to give it a try. *Qué puta noche.*

When I say there is no traffic, I am not exaggerating. After half an hour in which we could have laid down and slept *on* the freeway for all the cars that passed, the distant yet unmistakable toy-like sound of a Volkswagen engine signals the approach of a chance. It takes forever to arrive, and when it does, it is a hippie mobile – a Volkswagen van with flowers painted on the sides driven by a pretty, freckled young redhead wearing small, round, metal-rimmed granny glasses. She stops. We cannot believe our luck. We run up and pile in, no questions asked, before she can get a better look at us. Ben is in back and I am up front next to the driver, Megan. I have never known anyone named Megan before and I turn the sound of it over in my mind as we drive along.

"I can give you guys a ride as far as Santa Maria, she says." Megan doesn't seem to think it is odd that we are hitchhiking directly on the freeway at 6:30 in the morning wearing army camouflage jackets and carrying broken down, makeshift backpacks, so we don't provide an explanation. She is a nurse, heading to an early shift at a hospital in Santa Maria, which explains why she is on the road so early. *Led Zepplin* is blasting from the eight-track. It's a great way to wake up.

Ben and I keep exchanging glances behind the back of this beautiful, carefree, absolutely innocent young Paddy. We are growing increasingly uncomfortable and we know we are both thinking the same thought, but neither of us has the nerve to say anything to her. Besides, we don't want to scare her. When she lets us off, after we say a million thanks, just as we are going to shut the sliding door with a tinny *ca-tink*, and watch her drive off, it is Ben who gets up the nerve.

"*A ver*. Listen, Megan (he pronounces it MAYghan), uh, it was really cool of you to give us a ride and all, you know? We really appreciate it, but you know man, if I was your brother, I would tell you you're crazy, *wisa*. So, here it is - don't go picking up strange guys, especially guys who look like they slept on the side of the road, but any strange guys. It ain't safe. You know, there's lots a bad dudes out there, and well, we wouldn't want nothing to happen to you, *sabes?*"

Megan looks at us like she is thinking about what Ben has said, and also like she is seeing us for the first time. She says nothing. Ben shuts the door and we walk off, not looking back. Ben is shaking his head. We have done what we feel is right, it is up to her to heed the advice.

Santa Maria, before it becomes a wine mecca, is just a place that packs a remarkable number of rednecks into a very small town. We spend about three hours thumbing at the on-ramp where Megan left us, with no luck. People take one look at us as they approach the freeway and then speed up. As time goes on, we appreciate Megan's generosity even more.

"You think any *chavala* back home woulda done that?" I ask.

"Not unless she *wanted* to get raped," Ben answers. "Some chicks would maybe enjoy it."

"Shit, they could rape me and I'd be all happy about it," I say. "Any *chavala de aquellas* wants to jump my bones, she's welcome to it." We both laugh.

"So why'd she do it? You look like a fuckin' ax murderer, dude."

Ben laughs, "And you smell like the motherfucker I killed."

"No, seriously, man, why'd she pick our asses up?"

Ben shakes his head in disbelief at my naiveté: "She's Anglo, *carnal*. Think about it. She's a pretty, Anglo, college girl, *una enfermera*, for crissake, with a cool ride. She's probably ballin' some rich Paddy doctor. They'll get married, have a bunch of Paddy kids, and they'll all grow up to be rich *gabachos*, too. So what's she ever had to be scared of?"

While I am pondering this unexpected insight from Ben, out of nowhere two guys about our age, maybe a couple of years older, wearing worn out cowboy boots and wide-brimmed hats, walk up to join us. They are Mexicans, with the dark red skin and vaguely Asian eyes that say they carry a lot of indigenous blood. They speak no English and seem in a big hurry to head south, way south, back across the border. They do not say and we do not ask but it is clear they are running, and that means cops. It makes no difference to us. They treat us with respect, share their small stash of food when they hear we have not yet eaten today, and sympathize with our plight. We are all in the same boat – like the CCR song says, "Stuck in Lodi," except it is actually the *puta* town of Santa Maria.

Many hours pass and absolutely no one stops. It is clear no one is going to, not today, tomorrow, or ever, especially now that four of us have our thumbs out. About four o'clock in that long afternoon, Julio, one of our new friends, has an idea; the kind of bad idea that somehow makes sense at the time.

"There ain't no one going to ever pick us up here," he says in Spanish, stating the obvious. "We could sit here until our bones bleach in the sun and still no one is going to give us a ride." We all nod in agreement. "There's a Ford dealership across the street, and they got nothing but brand new cars sitting on the lot, each one with the key in the ignition, ready to go. Why don't we get our stuff together out of sight, then I'll sneak over, hop in one of those cars, and pick you guys up here at the on-ramp?"

As we weigh the offer for milliseconds it seems like a solid plan. We have no money, no food, and no other hope of ever getting out of Santa Maria. Plus, at any moment the cops might come looking for Julio and his buddy and when they start cracking skulls, or shooting – this is serious redneck country – they are not likely to be too careful about who is who. Balanced against that ugly possibility is Julio's plan. What could go wrong? So we assemble our stuff at a point just before the on-ramp, and wait for Julio, who walks off toward the Ford dealership, trying to look inconspicuous in his cowboy boots and hat, his dark red Indian skin, and his obviously being too young, too poor, and too Mexican to be looking to buy a new Ford today.

Five minutes later a new full-size Ford sedan – no plates, window sales sticker still intact– screeches to a halt in front of us. We pile in and off we go. At first it is a joy ride. The relief of moving again after nine hours, getting the hell away from Santa Maria and having such a nice brand new ride, drowns out all the doubts we should be having. Julio has good taste in cars; he must have picked out the biggest model on the lot. It makes sense: the jail time is the same for stealing a Pinto.

A few minutes pass and from the back seat I see that the fuel gauge is glowing a big sickening red. Of course, they never keep much gas in these test drive cars, maybe to discourage just this situation. I point out the problem to our friends in the front seat, who respond reasonably that we should pool our cash and buy ourselves some gas. I reflect that we may regret stealing a gas guzzler after all. A few moments of rummaging through pockets and backpacks turns up a total of forty-two cents among the four of us. My personal contribution to the pool is eight cents: three pennies, and my last nickel. It's enough to get us a couple of gallons.

Julio is unfazed. "Save your money," he says magnanimously, as Alfredo, his friend, pockets my eight cents. "We'll pull in, pump some gas, and then take off, what are they going to do, chase us on foot?" He chuckles. I have to admit that this new development seem as good as the initial idea of stealing the car.

We park at the self-serve pump. While Julio is filling the tank Ben turns to me in the back seat, suddenly very confidential. "*Órale, pues.* I can't get busted for this, I already got one GTA on my record, and if I get another, I am goin' to do time for sure." That Ben was a car thief before we started this day is news to me, and how in hell I didn't know about it, I cannot imagine, but we don't have time to discuss that bit of ancient history right now. The whole adventure is getting out of hand anyway so I agree to bailing out while we still can.

We thank Julio and Alfredo for the ride, shake hands, formally say our fare-wells — they are Mexican after all, from a country that still has manners — and set off on foot for the nearest on-ramp as fast as we can. They cannot believe we would walk away from a perfectly good ride, but they shrug, and being *Mexicanos*, mutter something about those crazy-ass *Chicanos*. Our last view of them is calmly pumping the gas they intend to steal.

Twenty minutes later Ben and I are standing at the nearby on-ramp when a Highway Patrol car flies past, blinding lights but no siren, headed toward the gas station. Another twenty minutes and it passes again, no flashing lights or siren, in the other direction. It is moving fast and we are keeping low, but both Ben and I are pretty sure we see two cowboy hats in the back seat on the return trip.

XI

Fix bayonets!

"Hey Johnny, you s'pose they leaving the carrying-wounded behind? I don't see any litters." Goldstein scratched his head under the helmet. It was 2200, time to flee the Dj as ordered. They were forming up to walk down the hill in two long columns, well apart and staggered. That would reduce the noise and prevent any individual incoming artillery round from taking out more than one man.

Russo looked around and confirmed that there were no stretchers, only walking wounded were leaving the Dj with the able-bodied. He knew of at least eight men hurt badly enough to be unable to walk, the result of the air attack when they first approached the Dj days earlier. The messenger from Division, who had taken the bullet from Lupe Perez, was also still hanging on. What would happen to them? He shrugged in reply to Goldie; then word was passed to cease all talking, smoking, and noise.

That last part was an impossible order. Before jumping off they had taped their dog tags together to stop them from clinking, but half a battalion of armed men cannot easily slink away in silence. Nine hundred pairs of boots creak, snap dead twigs in the dark, crunch the gravel underfoot, and scuff along the uneven trail. Half-empty canteens, which were numerous, make a *slop-slop* sound as a man walks. Ammo bandoliers, medical kits, rifle slings and side arms *flap* and *clang* against one another with each step. M1's have a mind of their own, both barrels and stock plates bang against things, metal to metal.

Goldstein and the other Jews had removed their dog tags altogether and buried them. The tags indicated each man's religious preference. "See that 'H' on there, Johnny? Stands for 'Hebrew.' If we get taken prisoner, that would not be a good thing to be wearing."

"I don' wanna be no Kraut prisoner eader, Goldie," he had answered. "And I ain't no Jew."

"You got a point, Johnny, let's just keep goin' and if neither one of us don't give up no matter what, we'll be ok, right?"

"OK Goldie, but you know, I just gotta say, dis is da shits." They both laughed the dark laugh of the combat infantryman in a bad spot, then fell in.

It was a pitch dark, moonless night. At least that much was in their favor. About midnight, three quarters of the way down the Dj they passed what sounded like some soldiers sitting in a poorly-dug hole at the side of the trail, not fifty feet away. One of them called out to them lazily in German, a greeting more than a challenge. Wayne shushed his men and pressed on. The German fell silent. An enemy listening post this close to their position was not good news, but a gunfight right now would be much worse. They got lucky. Apparently, the German was more interested in sleeping than in listening. The *Wehrmacht* command was not expecting the American prey to flee the trap it had gotten itself so conveniently into: so much for the military superiority of the master race.

A few minutes later they passed the truck, his very own, sitting right where he had left her. Jimmy Pete's body was buried just beside it, rifle stuck in the ground to mark the spot, right where they had pulled him off the truck bed before heading up to the Dj only a few days earlier.

Once out on the plain they had an exposed eight-mile walk to the nearest friendly position, if it was still there. Division might well be in retreat. Their only hope was that the enemy was more focused on finishing off Djebel Ksaira, which was putting up a last ditch, suicidal fight, and in pursuing the retreating American division, than in keeping an eye on the isolated force that was now slipping away from Djebel Lessouda. The sky remained moonless with eerie flashes emanating from the dozens of burning tanks, trucks, and halftracks, the only light along their way.

Russo saw from the wreckage that the outgunned American tankers had put up a hell of a fight. They passed an M3 and a German Mark IV *Panzer* that had apparently fired on one another simultaneously and at close range, so close in fact that the American's smaller-bore gun had successfully penetrated the *Panzer's* lightly armored side, even as its own sponson was obliterated. The two hulks sat just one hundred feet apart, the M3 smoldering, shredded like a paper bag blown full of air and then popped. The German tank was still burning furiously.

In the firelight from a dozen burning wrecks Russo passed the charred remains of GIs still sitting upright in their hatches, black specters under tanker helmets, with mouths, now fleshless, exposing jaws and teeth drawn in a rictus of pain and death as they tried in vain to escape. German infantrymen and a few tankers from both sides lay dead around them, the latter killed escaping their burning mounts. One man actually looked at peace, as if asleep, but most were contorted in unnatural positions – impossible for a living person – or were charred or dismembered beyond recognition as anything that was once human.

Despite all the combat they had seen since entering Tunisia, it was terrifying to walk through such a graveyard. A slaughtered tank company and half a battalion of infantry slinking away in the night like a pack of thieves: this was not supposed to happen to the liberating American army.

The plain itself was featureless, causing the wrecked and burning vehicles to loom larger than life. In the dark they resembled erupting volcanoes randomly scattered on the flat desert.

Even under the best of circumstances, without a *Panzer* division in their path, they would have a long, hard walk through the night to friendly lines. Even with plenty of food and water, even with their division waiting for them to come in to relative safety, rather than fleeing for its own life, it would have been a long odds bet they would hook up before the enemy found them. Given the circumstances tonight, with everyone carrying more ammo than water, expecting to be ambushed at any moment, having taken little food in recent days, it was a stretch to imagine that many of them would see dawn.

The wounded, Russo later learned, those who could not walk on their own, had been left behind with a couple of volunteer medics, relying on the good manners of the Germans. At this early point in the war both sides routinely cared for the other's wounded and put captured medical personnel to work in the closest field hospital. It was a tacit gentleman's agreement amid a conflagration. Brutality leavened by humanity. Still, sometimes someone shot a medic, by accident or otherwise. Sometimes wounded soldiers were bayoneted, or simply abandoned. It was better not to dwell too long upon things they could do nothing about, they told themselves. They simply could not have quietly carried out their most badly wounded men.

They walked on, keeping away from the light of burning vehicles, and eventually entered a long, flat infinitely dark stretch of the plain that they hoped would continue all the way to their destination. It must have been cloudy because when Russo looked up he could not see the stars. The darkness was so complete that when he stopped momentarily to adjust his equipment, which was chaffing his side, the man behind walked right into him.

In the deepest part of that starless night, off to the left, five hundred yards distant, a German machine gun spat tracers at them. It was a short burst and wild, recon by fire. The Germans, silent and stationary, blinded by the impenetrable darkness, must have heard what they thought could be a body of men moving across their front, so they fired blindly, hoping return fire would confirm their hunch. The standard response is to ignore it, don't give away a unit's position. Let the enemy think his mind is playing tricks on him. But that is easier said than done when someone is shooting at you.

A handful of exhausted, terrified GIs, ignoring fire discipline, training, and common sense, returned ineffective fire in the general direction of the German machine guns.

The isolated and brief American response brought a more focused and sustained German machine gun volley aimed at the muzzle flashes, killing one soldier immediately. Colonel Wayne quickly assessed the size of the German force from the number of firing points and the arc they fired from. He yelled for everyone to "break off and maneuver for the rally point," as they heard halftrack engines starting and several more machine guns joined the fire. Caught out in the open, with nothing to match the Germans' firepower, no cover, no armor or transport, and no visibility, Wayne knew his position was indefensible. They had to escape before dawn.

At first the German machine gunners aimed at standing chest height, but gradually they brought their angle down to ground level, where soldiers huddle under fire and most of the real killing in a battle is done. Mortar shells began whistling their way home as well, initially falling wildly around the half-battalion as the German mortarmen found their range by observing their exploding rounds. Wayne had only seconds to send his men on their way in small groups, but everyone instantly understood that he was on his own from this point forward. It was their only hope – evade and escape – they taught that, too, in Infantry school, although no American soldier ever seriously considered that he would have to put that knowledge to the test.

The mortar barrage lasted five minutes and mostly served to keep the Americans fixed in place, unable to flee while the Germans readied their attack. The screams of the wounded made it clear that the mortar shells had found the battalion. A man cannot run from a mortar barrage. Shrapnel flies up and out, the earth shakes, and the safest place – the only place, really – is hugging dirt at the bottom of a hole. The mortars effectively aborted the American attempt to escape, and only lifted as German halftracks, lightly armored but mounting heavy machine guns and trailed by dismounted infantry, advanced on the exposed Americans.

Russo and Goldstein sought what cover they could find behind a small shrub that fronted an even smaller depression, little more than a swale in the sand. They threw themselves down blindly and poured enfilade fire into the closest approaching halftrack, aiming just above the piercing headlights, hoping to hit the gunners. Their rifle fire may not have hit anyone, but it drew the track's attention. The German track turned in their direction, intent on either running them over or getting close enough for its top-mounted co-axial machine guns to fire down into their position.

As the track closed on the shrub Martinez and Whittier, two Charlie Company riflemen, flanked it, keeping it between them and its supporting infantry. As Russo watched in the intermittent flashes of light amid the developing battle they tossed grenades into its exposed bed. The explosions killed the driver and gunners, disabled the engine, and at least for the moment saved Russo's and Goldstein's lives. In the chaos that ensued they joined their two saviors in using the destroyed halftrack as cover, the beginning of a defensible position in the otherwise wide open desert. Russo and Goldstein crawled beneath the vehicle and fired from its hind quarters, between its tracks, lying back to back.

As German infantry approached the track with care they found themselves on the receiving end of withering fire from the four GIs. Martinez slid out from the front end of the undercarriage and climbed to the top of the track, losing his helmet in the process. He pulled the dead German gunner off a co-axial gun, checked that its action still functioned, and then turned it back onto the attackers. Even the small gain in elevation on the flat open plain provided a deadly advantage.

Russo found it hard to see. One moment it was pitch dark, the next a portion of the battlefield was temporarily lit up by rifle fire, tracers from machine guns, mortar shells or grenade explosions. His eyes could not grow accustomed to the dark because of the intermittent bright sheets of light, making the battle all the more chaotic. He was terrified, heart pounding, with a desperate need to urinate, but in the end he was simply too afraid to stop firing. In the green flash of a tracer round Russo thought he had a target, fired into the center of its mass, as he had been taught to do, but never knew if he hit it, darkness engulfing his field of vision once again.

Martinez fired the captured machine gun into the oncoming German halftracks and dismounted infantry with great effect until another GI, in the darkness and chaos, hearing the distinctive chatter of the German weapon, and seeing the helmetless gunner in the halftrack, mistook him for the enemy and tossed yet another grenade into the track's bed. The explosion took off Martinez's right leg at the shin, and he slumped to the deck beside the German he had killed, also with a grenade, not five minutes earlier. He soon bled to death. His killer never knew it was a "friendly fire" incident.

After the second grenade attack the battered halftrack began burning, its fuel tank ruptured and spilling diesel onto the sand. The fire light provided a great focus for both the attacking Germans and the defending Americans. Russo and Goldie now found themselves at the center of the fighting, which intensified in the semi-light as the two forces joined, emerging out of the darkness. A deep, hoarse rasp whose owner Russo immediately identified as Sarge was heard calling: "Fix bayonets!" The order sent a shiver of fear down Russo's spine as he recognized the battle's shift into a close, hand-to-hand struggle in the chaotic dark.

Instinctively following the order, while passing it along at the top of his lungs, from his position under the burning track Russo pulled the long slender blade from its sheath in his pack and tried to attach it to the end of his smoking rifle. His right hand shook so badly he had to use the left to steady it as he locked the bayonet in place. In addition to fear, he recognized another feeling welling up inside: anger. He was getting madder by the minute, first at those dumbasses who had fired back, starting this whole thing, and now at the goddamned Krauts themselves, who were threatening to overrun and kill them all. He had to kill them first.

As the sound of the fighting intensified around him, and the likelihood of a fuel explosion grew with each second, Russo reached the point where it was more terrifying to stay put than to move. Goldie spoke both their minds: "I don't want to burn under this motherfuckin' track. Let's get out of here," he shouted over the din.

Apparently, he was not alone in having just that instinct at just that moment. Russo, Goldstein, and Whittier, a lanky Texan carrying a BAR, the heaviest weapon the battalion had taken along on its flight, came out from under the burning track screaming like maniacs and firing from the hip. At the same moment in hundreds of seemingly independent decisions others rose to their feet, yelling and racing directly at the attacking Germans. Whatever else was happening in the larger battle, this particular group of American soldiers decided that if they could not evade and escape they would stand and fight. Thousands of rounds were discharged at increasingly short range as the forces closed in the dark, each side tearing gaping holes in the other with point blank fire.

The battle took on a medieval character when the combatants, too closely engaged on the intermittently light and dark battlefield to pause even to reload their weapons, instead began to use them as clubs or lances. When a rifle stock fractured while bludgeoning a man, or the weapon was torn away by a stronger enemy, a man used whatever was to hand in his desperation – side arms were fired, then used as cudgels, knives were thrust, helmets were thrown at approaching enemies, and bare hands were used to pummel, to scratch, or to strangle. Soldiers of both armies, trained in the arts of modern war, were reduced to kicking, biting, and gouging in a frenzy of mayhem and death.

Charging blindly in the direction of the oncoming German advance, Russo ran full tilt into a German infantryman facing ninety degrees to his left, firing at something, visible only from his muzzle flashes. Russo was upon the man before either of them knew it. The German turned at the last moment to face the threat, but not in time. Russo was running, the M1's muzzle three feet from the enemy's side when he saw him and instinctively fired. The force of the round at that range knocked the German to the ground. Russo abruptly stopped his headlong rush, stumbling over the fallen body in his path, and found himself standing directly over his enemy. Momentarily he froze in place. Always before he had fired at distant shapes that he could imagine as uniforms rather than men, but being this close made the whole thing seem like murder; it made the German into a man, not just another gray-clad target.

The German, a boy of about Russo's own age, was writhing on the ground. The bullet had passed through his shoulder before exiting his back. Russo looked down, his M1 pointed at the boy's unseen face, adrenaline pumping, panting like a sprinter at the end of a quarter mile. A grenade's nearby flash momentarily illuminated the pair. The boy looked up at him, was speaking, but in the darkness and the battle noise Russo could neither see the terrified expression on his face nor hear his plea for mercy. He began looking for other targets.

Then the boy grabbed desperately at Russo's pant leg with his good hand, begging for help, unheard in the din of battle. Russo felt the tug on his leg and reacted immediately. His face lost the last vestige of its humanity, which was replaced with a look that could only be described as "murder." He moved the rifle over the boy's heaving chest and rammed the bayonet home with all his bodily force. The blade passed the boy's outstretched arm, raised in supplication, a last futile gesture seeking mercy. It speared his spine, where the tip lodged between the vertebrae. At once the victim's upraised arm fell limply to his side.

Russo tried extracting the bayonet, but it would not budge. He had been taught how to deal with this situation – practicing on a sandbag suspended from a rope. He knew to pull the trigger while yanking the rifle outward, the recoil of the M1 helping to dislodge the blade from the enemy's ribs or spine. He pulled the trigger, but to no avail: the last round had been discharged. In the chaos of battle he had not seen the empty clip eject or heard the telltale ping.

Furious to retrieve his weapon, helpless and unarmed in the middle of the melee all around him, Russo placed one boot roughly in the center of the corpse's chest and pressed down, expelling quantities of blood from the wound and bathing his boot in crimson. But this time as he pulled, the bayonet came out. He immediately dropped to a knee beside the corpse and reloaded. His last view of the boy, in the flickering light of burning fuel, reminded him not of a wasted human life, but of a wild dog he had once driven over in Algeria.

The corpse was sickening, unnatural, and subhuman, all at once. The entire encounter had lasted barely twenty seconds.

The Germans, despite their superior firepower, were forced back by the spontaneous, ferocious, and unexpected counter-attack. But both sides knew their retreat would provide only a brief respite: they would regroup, reinforce, and return. As their infantry and tracks pulled away a safe distance the mortars and heavy machine guns resumed their work. The Americans seized the opportunity provided by the disengagement and fled. They had made the best stand they could and it was now time to evade and escape.

In the chaos of hundreds of infantrymen running across open ground with German machine gun fire pursuing them, Russo, Goldstein and half a dozen others found themselves alone, in a deep, quiet *wadi* they had been following more for the cover it offered than for the direction it took them. They had run as far and as fast as they could, had run for hours it seemed, knowing that when morning came the Germans would return and with the benefit of first light, would annihilate them.

Finally, they reached that point when the adrenaline rush of battle and flight ebbs, when wounds begin to hurt and over-used muscles to cramp, when the need for food, water, and rest can no longer be denied, when a soldier simply has no more energy and thus no remaining will either to fight or to run, when his fatigue exceeds his fear, his desire to live, even, and so he simply stops. The sun was just above the horizon and it was getting warm. They collapsed, unthinking, unseeing, along the sides of the *wadi*, not even posting a watch, and they simply and immediately slept.

It was mid-morning when they awoke, the sun in their eyes. They had slept where they had fallen for almost three hours, enough time to clear their minds, and also long enough to allow every strained joint to stiffen, every wound to throb; but not enough time to cure their exhaustion. They took inventory: eight dazed riflemen, all more or less able-bodied, most carrying half a canteen of water and little if any food. They lacked a radio, a precise fix on their location, and, without an officer to lead them, they had no map. After the intense firefight, they were also low on ammunition.

They quickly determined that Goldstein, a corporal, was the highest ranking man present, and he took charge. This was OK with Russo. Goldie was the kind of guy you wanted in command in a tight spot, whether it was in a bar in Oran filled with drunken French marines thinking to avenge their honor, or on a fucked up battlefield like this.

XII

The queers next door.

Almost everyone who lived in our immediate neighborhood, the Rivera side of Pico Rivera, was there for good. Individuals came and went but whole families seldom moved. One house, however, did not follow this pattern. It was right next to ours. It was a rental, like ours, and I cannot remember all of the people who moved in and out of that address, but the ones I do recall stand out vividly.

There was one nice family: a father, a mother, and two kids. They were Anglo, but the kids were really little, really cute, and Ernie's sister Val and Rene babysat them. We all hoped they would move out before those two little blonde boys got old enough to become targets for the *cholos* their generation was bound to produce.

The dad worked for TWA as some kind of cargo clerk at the L.A. airport. That was a pretty exciting job in our world. It got even more exciting when he brought me a present one day: an autographed picture of *The Rifleman* – Chuck Connors, the star of a popular TV show about a single dad raising his son in the Wild West. He doesn't carry a six shooter on his hip like most guys – he is a family man trying to set an example. Instead he walks around with a full-size Winchester rifle in his hand, specially modified for rapid fire. Despite his peace-loving ways, this paternal role model finds it necessary to kill people in almost every episode. After all, the show is called *"The Rifleman."* Now that's a dad!

They had been living next door for about six months, fitting in with the neighborhood pretty well despite their Jell-O molds and macaroni casseroles, when suddenly everything went wrong. We were asleep an hour or so before dawn, when I heard a racket outside. I got up and found Mom and Dad also climbing out of bed and heading in the direction of the noise. Both Gramma and Grandpa were half deaf by now, so they somehow slept through the whole thing. We couldn't see anything directly from our living room because the edge of our tiny garage stuck out between our house and theirs, but the reflected flashing of cop's lights on the street, and the barking of police radios, told us more than one squad car was out front. We heard voices, and a horrible tearing sound that reminded me of when Ben and I helped his dad demolish an old tool shed in his backyard with a set of crowbars, plank by plank.

Finally, we heard children crying and that was it. Mom pulled her robe tighter around her and headed out to see what the hell was going on. Dad and I followed. What we saw was shocking. Both the husband and wife were leaning over the hood of a police squad car with their hands cuffed behind them. She had on a flimsy nightgown; I could see her legs and underwear right through it. He was wearing only boxers and T-shirt. The kids, who were still toddlers, wearing those little-kid PJ's with the feet sewn in, were screaming for their parents, and two helpless cops were trying to comfort them. Mom stepped up and took over with the kids, bringing them back to our house. The cops seemed relieved; now they could get back to business.

It took another minute to register what the ripping noise was. Pieces of floor board started flying out the front door of the house. Everyone on the block was outside now, wondering aloud what on earth these folks could be doing that would make the cops want to tear up their floor in the middle of the night. Did they smuggle pictures of movie stars into the country, someone joked. Or maybe the mother was getting busted for putting too much fruit cocktail in her Jell-O molds. Someone noticed that in addition to L.A. cops, we had a couple of carloads of some different type of cop, and they seemed to be the ones in charge tonight. These cops were wearing blue windbreakers with the letters "F.B.I." stenciled across the back. I reflected that it must be serious to bring the Feds to Pico Rivera.

Eventually the cops inside the house stopped their work and, as a hushed silence fell over the crowd, we waited, cops and neighbors alike, for what came next. A couple of FBI came out of the house, each carrying what looked like a small sack of flour wrapped in brown paper and tied with string, one in each hand.

The tally varied widely depending on who you asked, but those nice neighbors of ours, between baking macaroni casseroles, raising their toddlers, and bringing autographed pictures of movie stars home for the neighbors, had accumulated between ten and twenty pounds of uncut heroin under their house. I guess working in the airline cargo business is even more exciting than I imagined.

—∿—

After the heroin dealers we had an unusual childless couple living next door. They were Anglo, just like the last couple. They were not young, maybe Mom's and Dad's age, and they had the same division of duties and roles as everyone else in the neighborhood. The husband went off to work in the morning, with his wife, wrapped in a pretty flowered apron, waving and blowing kisses from the porch. At the end of the day the husband pulled up in the driveway and the wife ran out to greet him, pulling off the apron as he comes. All that was unusual in this domestic arrangement was that they were both men.

Mom referred to them, without any prejudice, as "the queers next door." They were good neighbors. So far as I know they were not stockpiling heroin under the house. They had no children so they were quieter than most families on our block and they didn't bother anyone.

You might think that in a *macho* place like Pico Rivera a gay couple would not have an easy time of it. You would be wrong. I often observed a difference between our neighborhood and the more affluent places I have known later in life. In poor neighborhoods people tend to use impolite terms for groups of people, like *queer*, *paddy*, or *nigger*, but they also tend to treat individual people from those groups like they treat everybody else. Middle class folks, on the other hand, know better than to call people names, but they also tend, inadvertently of course, to avoid people who are different from themselves.

The Queers Next Door fit right in. The wife stopped in for coffee with Mom, and she and Dad treated them like any other couple. The kids on the block left them alone, and they were model neighbors. They were missed when they moved on only a few months later. The husband lost his job, the wife tearfully told Mom, because his boss discovered who he was. This has happened before, he says. We wished them luck finding a new place to live, in a new community, with a new job.

XIII

Why you helping me, *ése?*

I am sitting on the sofa waiting for Ernie to come out of the bathroom so we can play catch. He has been in there checking out his look and combing his hair in the mirror for the past ten minutes. I have my glove and my Dodgers hat, but Ernie has the ball. While I wait, Carmela teeters by in high heels, putting on lipstick. She sees me, saunters over with a big movie star grin, and plops her bony little ass down on my sixteen-year-old lap, just like that. She puts her arms around my neck, puckers up her cherry-red lips, and blows me a kiss from two inches away, then stands up and looks at my crotch. Satisfied, she goes on her way, giggling.

Rene, the sister who is my age, sees all this and rolls her big, sad, cow eyes. As she passes by, dragging her mattress on its way to air out on the back patio, I see the huge yellow stain in the middle and smell the reek of her piss. For as long as I can remember Rene has wet the bed. Her family's solution is to make her take the mattress outside each day, in front of her brothers and sisters and whoever else is around. This humiliation has not worked, obviously, or she would not still be doing it today. I am not embarrassed by Carmela in front of Rene, whose daily humiliation is complete.

Rene is chubby, with a face that never loses its baby fat, and she has the worst buck teeth I have ever seen, even in our orthodontia-free world. Her front teeth stick out seemingly parallel to the ground. Her hair is limp and damp and looks like she cuts it off with hedge sheers. She is unnaturally quiet, as if she is trying to be invisible as she moves around the house. I almost never see her at school even though we have been in the same grade since kindergarten. I seldom think of her. She is just there.

Then, one day I am walking to my locker late after school, having finished a detention for some minor offense, when I come upon a big commotion. I know it is a fight by the tight circle of kids yelling excitedly toward the action they have surrounded. But this circle includes as many screaming girls as boys. I try to peer over some of the shorter girls to see what is going on. Whoever it is, they are on the ground. From the high-pitched howling, I know it's a girl fight. That explains the crowd.

Eventually a teacher walks by; wimpy little Mr. Romero, the scrawniest teacher on campus, one of our first *Chicano* teachers. He is the one who gave me detention. It seems at first that he is going to pretend he hasn't heard or seen a thing, just keep on walking. Then he swivels his pencil-neck around in all directions, pathetically searching for another teacher, someone to lend support. Finally he realizes he is stuck with this one on his own. Reluctantly he forces his way through the circle of kids, then stops beside the tangle of girls on the ground like he is planted there, seeking a way to break it up without getting too close. No one offers to help him; this is almost as good as the fight.

Eventually the combatants tire and the crowd gets bored. The girls are parted, hair is pushed out of faces, and I see that one of them is Rene. What's more, the other girl has ripped her shirt almost completely off, I can see her bra, and as she gets up everyone is hooting at her. I can't allow it. After all, this girl is my neighbor, she's Ernie's sister, I have known her since we were five, and I can't just stand by and watch this.

She doesn't seem to have any girlfriends gathering around her. Being alone after a fight like this is too horrible to think about. Besides, it's dangerous. Before I realize it I have taken off my jacket and put it on her. She is a little stunned so I have to help her slip her arms through the sleeves like you would a kid, then I have to zip it up for her. I gather her books and papers. The crowd starts breaking up but some of the guys, seeing me help her, begin calling out "*Wisa!*" and "*Heina!*" which means she's my girlfriend. Only they know she's not, they're just being a pain in the ass. I would be doing the same thing in their place, but still, it pisses me off.

The other girl is still spitting, calling Rene names so fast I can't catch them all. *Puta, Coña, Beech*, all come though clear enough, but not some others. This girl is new, from Ensenada I have heard, and maybe they have some words all their own down there. She may be new, but she is surrounded by some of the hardest girls in the school. Hard girls wear too much eye makeup, which is really saying something, put their hair up to enormous heights and twist it in incomprehensible swirls, wear black warm-up jackets with fancy pink lettering on the back that proclaims their gang affiliation, and they are always pissed off. These girls are helping the new girl put herself back together while hissing toward Rene who, despite having grown up here, is all alone. I don't like the looks those girls are shooting over at her and since I am heading home anyway I'll walk with her, just to be on the safe side.

In all of our years of going to the same schools, we have never walked together, not once. We rarely acknowledge each other's presence, even when we find ourselves in the same room at her house, or at the table eating a family dinner, so I feel like I hardly know her. But then I also feel like I know everything about her, from her bedwetting to her alcoholic father to the unusual way she holds her fork between her first and second fingers, not at all like the pencil grip everyone else uses.

Rene is not much of a talker. I cannot remember her ever laughing, or even smiling, and her words are usually the minimum necessary – like when she answers the door and tells me, mumbling, eyes downcast, that Ernie isn't home. She always seems terribly sad and alone, even in her big, loud family. Once we get away from the crowd at school she starts crying. I think maybe she has been trying to be tough, to live by the same rules boys have to, but now that we're alone she can't keep it up. I don't know, I have no sisters, and girls are a total mystery to me. She is still not speaking, just whimpering, but she lets me point her toward home with a gentle pressure of my hand on her back.

More calls of "*Wisa! Wiiiisa!*" followed by laughter. I am going to pay for this, I can see it, I tell myself, shaking my head. But it has got to be done.

"Fuck you, alla you," is all I can say, shouted back over my shoulder while giving the finger as we walk away, the laughter trailing off.

We reach the curb and pause for a passing car before leaving campus. While we wait Rene starts shaking all over. It is not really cold outside, and besides she is the one wearing the jacket, but this often happens to people after a fight. It's the shock effect or something; you start shaking, your teeth chattering.

I can't help it: I put my arm around her. She kind of leans into me, the car passes, and we start off walking like that, not talking. It will take fifteen minutes to get home. She keeps crying and I feel funny just standing there, with my arm around her, slowly walking along, so I decide I have to say something, but what?

"Rene, what started that *pleito*, some girl shit?"

More crying.

"Looked like you got her pretty good, eh? I didn't know you could throw such good *chingazos*."

More crying. This approach might cheer up a guy in a similar situation, but complementing her fighting ability it is not going to do much for Rene's mood right now.

"Are you any warmer now?" She has stopped shivering.

"*Simón*, thanks."

Ok, now I got her talking, two words.

"You gonna catch it for the *chingazos*, or for your shirt gettin' ripped up?"

"Depends on if Ma's home." That makes sense. Marta would skin her alive for fighting, and for ruining a perfectly good shirt she probably bought at the thrift store a few years back for one of the older girls for a quarter. But if Marta is gone when we arrive maybe her sisters could clean her up and the torn shirt could go missing in the mountains of laundry that enormous family seems always to have lying around waiting to be washed, ironed or folded.

Out of nowhere, she asks: "Why you helping me, *ése*? Your friends are gonna give you a really bad time."

She is right, of course, and we both know why. If she were one of the pretty, popular girls I would have had to fight my way in to help her and to lend her my jacket and every guy at school would have wanted to be walking home with his arm around her. OK, she is not pretty. Well, of course she knows that. But it's worse than that: she knows she is such a non-entity that it is actually embarrassing for a guy to walk home with her, even to be seen talking to her. How do you live with that? Still, she is waiting for an answer to her question: why am I here?

"Rene, we've known each other since we was kids, right? We got to stick up for each other, ain't we?" That's all I can say.

In the fifteen minutes it takes to walk home it has begun to get dark. I look up at the big street light we are passing under, the one that has been burned out for as long as anyone can remember. It is a neighborhood landmark, a nighttime meeting place for purposes romantic or larcenous. We know when we reach this spot, the pall of darkness stretching between two distant working lights, it is only a minute before we will reach our block. By unspoken agreement we stop.

She smiled at my last comment, which makes me feel a lot better. I finally said something right. Then, out of the blue, she takes her hand out of the jacket pocket and slips her arm around my waist, which makes it easier to walk together, and she lays her head more firmly against my shoulder. I can feel her body relax as we resume our walk; she is letting down her guard. I also sense that she is exhausted. And I recognize an unfamiliar feeling in my own stomach. I tell myself it's not anything like that, but it is something warm all the same, something that makes me a little sad that we have turned the corner onto our block. As we reenter the artificial yellow glow of the next functioning streetlight it is about to end; this time that we both know will never come again.

Thank God Val is home when we reach Ernie's house. She is a couple years older than us, a year older than Ernie and a year younger than Carmela, and sometimes I think she is the only grown up in Ernie's whole family. I tell her what has happened. She thanks me, like she means it, then she takes Rene off my hands, literally, and I leave, without my jacket. I'll get it back some other day.

Ernie sees me and comes outside. He asks about Rene and I tell him he needs to keep an eye out for her, she has some serious enemies. He knows what can happen. While he is talking I start to wonder what I was feeling on the walk home, because I was feeling *something*. It was the kind of thing a guy feels for friends; that makes him watch out for them. We show our feelings toward other guys by punching them on the shoulder, by calling them names, by wrestling or sparring, or by coming to each other's aid. With girls it is all about getting something, about how much and how far they will let you go. Feeling or friendship doesn't often enter into it.

This was different. Rene was helpless, she needed me, she was in danger, and I stood by her. It cost me so little – a few taunts at school for a day or so, that was all. It just felt good, like I was on the right side for once. I did not understand all this very well at the time but I did recognize that some things I would not turn my back on.

—◊—

We take to the front lawn of weeds, where a dozen kids are gathering for the daily after school football game. It is fairly dark but we have maybe another half-hour of play time. The group grows to fifteen kids, boys and girls, all ages. It's usually not much of a game, with all the girls and the little kids, but it is still a lot of fun. We take it easy so the little ones don't get hurt, and sometimes, as a result, we have a spectacular play, like when Jaime, Mario's little brother, who is barely seven, jumps up and snatches a pass someone has deflected, making the world's youngest interception. It is so perfect, and he is so determined to score, that no one even seriously tries to catch him. Instead guys stage-dive and miss all over the field as he runs it in for a touchdown.

I keep trying to delay the start of today's game: "We sure everybody's here?" I don't know why I am doing this, but I keep looking up to Ernie's house to see if Rene is going to come out and join us. This is crazy, after what she has just been through, and especially since she has never once played with us before. People get impatient, telling me we have to get on with the game, it's getting dark, what the fuck am I doing, and I give in.

Here is a first: Carmela, her cherry-red lipstick laid on with a trowel, joins the game, and somehow winds up as quarterback for our team. On the first play she has no idea what to do, so, with a lot of flailing and screaming, she finally runs the ball up the middle amid a flurry of grabbing hands from the homeboys on defense. When the pile gets up, Carmela's blouse is torn open, buttons popped off everywhere, revealing a shock to us all – a red bra – something never before seen or even imagined, at least among the boys. She giggles and makes a half-hearted attempt to cover herself. Suddenly a car door slams so loud it sounds like a gunshot. A couple of the guys who don't see it actually duck to avoid the bullet. Marta, mother to Carmela and Ernie and Val and Rene, and all the rest, has driven up just in time to see this scene unfold. With great dignity she walks purposefully over to our game; the kids part for her.

"Carmela," she says with solemnity, "*Ven aquí*." That is the end of her football career, but not of her red bra. It also marks the only time in my whole life that I have seen two girls – let alone sisters – with their shirts ripped open on the same day.

—ᴍ—

One afternoon soon afterward no parents are at home but Ernie's house, as usual, is full of kids. His brothers and sisters, and their friends, roam and clump from room to room, the little ones playing and the bigger ones just hanging out. Carmela comes to us in the backyard where we are shooting baskets against the net-less garage hoop. With great solemnity she declares that she will allow one of us lucky boys to go into the bathroom – the only room in the house with a door that locks – all alone with her for exactly five minutes. She'll set the alarm clock, no cheating. She has it in her hand, is waving it around like some kind of aphrodisiac, and it works. We don't want to appear eager, but we are. In the end she picks Armando, a tall kid from down the block who at nineteen, is about her age. He is home on leave from the Marines, having recently finished boot camp, and has not yet appeared in public without his uniform. It attracts the kind of attention a guy wants, the female kind. I have nothing against the Marine Corps, but this particular Marine, Armando, whom I have known from way back, from as long as I can remember, has always been a dickhead.

They go into the bathroom, the door lock clicks. We can hear giggling and bodies bouncing off the glass shower stall doors. Three minutes later – we're counting the time on half a dozen wristwatches – the little bathroom window opens and a uniformed arm flings a red bra at us. Ben and I look at each other with a mixture of envy of Armando, and shame for Ernie, who thankfully is not around to witness this.

XIV

I don't get you.

Armando is out on the street bragging about what he has done with Carmela. To hear him tell it he is a pretty quick worker because he accomplished an awful lot in his five minutes. Ernie is still not home and I feel I have to defend his sister's honor, even if she has none. Maybe it is really Ernie I am standing up for.

"You're bull-shitting, *ése*," I say confidently, not really believing I am challenging Armando like this. Ben looks over at me like I am completely out of my mind choosing-on the Marine. He could do it, sure, but me? Everyone knows where this is headed – an ass kicking, my ass – but what can I do now?

I remember Mom's admonition, *"Don't ever be the one to start a fight, but if someone else starts one with you, be sure you're the one to finish it."* OK, well here is my chance to both start and finish one, except that the other guy is years older than me, half a head taller, and oh yeah, he is also a trained killer for chrissake, a United States Marine.

Armando responds at once: "*Órale*, Fuck you! Go home to your mama or I'll bust your *pinche* head open."

That comment really pisses me off, especially the part about going home to my mama. I am sensitive about being an only child, and also about having an over-protective mother. I don't want anyone to get the idea I allow any actual coddling. But what else do I expect from Armando? I have challenged him in public, chose him on in front of a crowd on our own block, kids who have known us both forever, kids who know where we fit into the neighborhood pecking order – he's a *cholo* turned Marine, I am a spoiled only child – and now he has challenged me in return. He has to, or he is going to get a serious reassessment in everyone's eyes. I must seem an easy mark, a kid he can beat the shit out of without ruining the crease in his uniform.

On my end, the comment about my mother is a no-way-walk-away challenge. You never, but never, mention another guy's mother in a situation like this, even in passing. There is no good way for this to end. We're in a mad-dog confrontation, where anyone who walks away is considered a pussy for the rest of the summer or, in my case, a lot longer. Neither of us can take that, especially the Marine, in his uniform, with all the neighborhood girls around watching. Many more bras can be removed before he ships out in a few weeks, but not if he lets a spoiled, younger, smaller only child choose him on.

If I let him intimidate me I will be inviting every asshole in town to mad-dog me. My life will become a series of humiliations. But if I stand up to him and at least get in a punch or two before I hit the pavement I will earn some much-needed respect.

I remember then, in the instant I have left to live, my grown-up cousin. Ronny is a biker, the Hell's Angels type: jeans, large scuffed work boots, jean jacket with motorcycle club decal on back, long Elvis sideburns. He served a few years up at Folsom for aggravated assault, and he has the prison tats to prove it. Not the Mexican kind, of course, but Aryan-themed. He now works as a bouncer at some dive bar in Reno. Ronny is actually of Irish extraction, a genuine Paddy, but he married my cousin, a daughter of one of my father's numerous brothers, so I guess that makes him part Sicilian.

The reason I remember Ronny at this critical moment is that he understands this type of situation better than any adult I have ever known. Once, when he and my cousin Jeanette were visiting, he took me out in the backyard to show me his 9MM pistol, which he kept tucked in the back of his belt, even for a family visit. Then we had a nice little talk.

"If you get into mad-doggin' with some o' these Meskins, man, realize you ain't gonna get out of it without a motherfuckin' fight. Just accept that as a fact right off the motherfuckin' dime. An' once you know you're gonna be in a goddamn fight, it's better to be the dude to throw the first motherfuckin' punch. That gives you what you call the motherfuckin' 'initiative.' These Meskins, they fight dirty, so you gotta be quick. But remember, you don't win no motherfuckin' fight by throwing that first sucker punch – you win it by throwing the last one. Motherfucker!" He laughed at his little joke, then showed me how to fight for real, how biker's do it on the street, and I assumed, in the yard at Folsom Prison.

Ronny looked me over. "You got a ring?" He asked doubtfully. I didn't. "A ring is good," he showed me his. It must have weighed a pound, a thick band with a many-faceted non-descript stone set in it.

"Make sure this motherfucker is turned stone-side-out. When you hit some poor Meskin it'll mess the bastard up real good. Hey, never mind you got no ring," seeing the disappointment on my face. "You're a strong kid, built real solid, just remember its best to catch the motherfucker by surprise, put all your motherfuckin' weight into it and once you start whalin' on him, don't never stop punching and kicking until he is down, and I mean down, down for motherfuckin' good. It ain't like in them movies where you throw one candy-ass punch and wait for the motherfucker to get up so you can hit him again. No way, man, them motherfuckers would be dead meat fightin' like that. Motherfucker!" he screamed in delight.

Then he told me what to do with the other guy *after* beating him senseless: "You drag the motherfucker over to the curb, if one is handy, and if he ain't too much of a lardass for you to move, and you stretch his motherfuckin' mouth over the edge of the curb." He demonstrated with his hand against our curb, thumb on top of it, fingers down the front. "Like that, get his motherfuckin' jaw open if you can, that's the best. Then stand the fuck back and stomp the shit out of the back of that mother's head. That'll bust up his motherfuckin' teeth and maybe spring his jaw." Ronny was nothing if not thorough.

Remembering Ronny's advice all in a flash I get very clear on the reality I am facing right here, right now. I wait. I realize now that the words issuing from Armando's mouth are just show; they are part of the mad-dogging ritual, the buildup to the only important thing, the fight itself. If Armando doesn't also realize this maybe I have a chance of surviving the next five minutes. One thing is certain: I have to fight like I have never fought before. I have to fight like I am trying to kill him or I am going to get my ass kicked but good. Briefly I wonder if they teach the mouth-on-curb routine in Marine boot camp. Probably not. There aren't too many curbs in the jungles of 'Nam. I now find that feeling welling up from somewhere deep inside of me, like I summoned it just by needing it so badly. Anger, hatred, fearlessness all combine in a desire – even a determination – to kill this *pendejo* bastard dickhead Marine who is taunting me. I don't know where this stuff is coming from, but I welcome it.

The mad-dogging means nothing to me now. It's all on his side, I am only waiting. I have calmed down, quiet while he rages on. I can feel my breath slowing and I realize I have been hyperventilating, but now no more. I am waiting. I have become vicious. He is no longer Armando, the loudmouthed asshole I have known all my life, he is just a target.

The other guys have spread out a bit to give us room to air our differences, and to get a good view of the *chingazos* scheduled to erupt at any moment. They're taking sides, yelling for one or the other of us to beat the living shit out of the other.

Ben, of course, is yelling for me. "Fuck him up, *ése*, fuck him up good, *carnal*." That's a nice sentiment and I appreciate it, but I am not really listening. In the back of my mind I know that if things go badly Ben, *El Mero Chingón*, who weighs a good two-twenty, will not let Armando actually kill me. He'll step in and stop it if it gets out of hand, but that is only a backstop, insurance. I put it out of my mind. I plan on murdering the guy.

If he stopped running his mouth for a minute and just looked into my eyes he would see that he is no longer dealing with a frightened kid. I am psyched for the fight; at this point I would be disappointed if we didn't fight. I would have to find someone else to beat the shit out of. I am amped and ready. He keeps raging but it is like watching television with the sound off: I don't hear his words. I am in my own world, where my senses of sight and touch are heightened, my awareness of his movement keen, and my other senses, especially hearing, are turned way down.

He continues, "Come on, *cabrón*, let's do it." He's puffs out his chest and balls his hands into underhand fists at his sides, classic *cholo* style. His chin is jutting out. He bounces his fists up and down at his sides as he rolls back and forth on the balls of his feet, one foot slightly forward, the other slightly back, taunting me. I notice everything and wait. Then he reaches out to push me, hard on the shoulder - just the move I have waited for.

This move leaves him open, leaning forward, off balance, his right arm outstretched. He expects me to back up, so he can keep pushing me back before actually starting the fight, the better to intimidate me and establish his dominance before the first real blow. It's standard *cholo* strategy, you can observe it at school or on the street any day of the week, but it isn't going to work this time. Instead, as he reaches forward to give me that first push I lean into him with all my weight: my arm, my shoulder, my whole torso down to my hip come forward behind my fist. I do it while he is off balance and leaning into me, also coming forward. I lead with my left, my dominant arm. I aim for his nose, but he is quite a bit taller than me and I am coming with everything I have so I sacrifice control for force. I catch him six inches lower than planned, square in the throat. His Adam's apple bows under my blow and he staggers back. It feels like my fist has actually penetrated his flesh.

Instinctively following Ronny's advice, I don't hesitate or pause to appreciate the damage I may have caused. I have the initiative. I follow up with a flurry of punches to the face but after the first two or three they mostly hit his shoulders and then the side of his head as he is bent forward, doubled over, hands on his throat, making a bizarre animal sound, gasping for air. I stop punching, since my only target is now his bent back. Instead I take advantage of his posture and knee him as hard as I can in the face, snapping his head back. I quietly register the distinctive crunch that signals his nose is probably broken, and he drops unsteadily to his knees. As he falls I kick him hard in the gut a couple of times, until his hands come away from his face, to protect his body. Then I step back slightly and kick him in the head. He goes over on his back, all the way down.

Quickly I close in to stomp him, but Ben and his big brother Jorge are holding me back, saying, "*Chale, basta ése,* you wanna kill the motherfucker?" They say it with a respect, almost an awe, I have never felt before, from them or anyone else.

I let them hold me but my adrenaline is still pumping and if I can't hit him I can at least yell a string of taunts: "*¡Pinche cabrón! ¡Aquí estoy!* Then I slip out of my friends' grasp, turn and walk away. Ben and Jorge, and everyone else on the street, are left looking at my back as I walk, maybe even strut, into my house to wash the blood, his blood, off my hands and clothing. The Marine is gasping for air, his face a mass of bloody mucus. He is down. I want to call cousin Ronny, but it is long distance to Reno.

—m—

That summer I became the kid who nearly killed a United States Marine, in uniform, in front of Ernie's house. Talk about recalibrating my status! It is a story that kept me from having to fight many other times over the coming years. For a while nobody wanted to mess with a Marine-killer. Someone would start up mad-dogging me at school or on the back lot, and his friends would say, "*Órale, ése*, don't choose-on that *vato loco*, that motherfucker'll kill you." More often than not he would find a way to save face and walk away from it.

Ernie was away buying pot while all the excitement was going on at his house. Over the weeks and months that followed we occasionally referred to the fight with Armando, but we never talked about its cause. Ernie must have known early on what his oldest sister was like, but it was undeniably confirmed when she turned up *embarazada* less than a month later. She didn't talk of marrying the guy, who was never clearly identified anyway, and little Carlitos joined Ernie's enormous family in due time. What was one more kid in that madhouse? Carmela had long ago dropped out of school, no great loss for either side, and between occasional efforts to raise her baby, she continued her ways. Strange thing was, that baby, the *bastardo* Carlitos, damn if he wasn't the cutest little guy any of us had ever seen. The kid grew up with no father, and with Carmela for a mother, but he had a couple dozen aunts, uncles, and friends on the block who treated him like the last Chinese emperor. We carried him everywhere, fed him, played with him, and generally vied for his attention. He had that kind of personality – everyone loved little Carlitos, the *vatito*. The little dude.

Al is drinking again, and calling Marta a *puta*, which is really hard for the kids, especially Ernie, who is old enough to want to protect his mother. It is early on a Saturday evening and, from across the street at my house, we have been listening to the growing *borlote*, the ruckus. The *Huapango* Mexican country music gets turned up loud, then back down, then more yelling and more music, louder still. Finally, the kids come trooping across the street in a straggling line. This has never happened before. Sure, one or two will get scared and run to Mom for comfort, but never the whole group. I can't help thinking of them as rats fleeing a sinking ship. It's a phrase I heard on television, and it seems to fit. This is the only time I have ever seen them all in one view, out in the open: nine kids in all, six girls and three boys, plus little Carlitos, who is being carried by Val, the thin studious sister, now the grown up seventeen-year-old. Mom opens the door to them and they pour into the living room like refugees crossing a border into a safe haven, refugees from a war in which they are loyal to both sides, a war that is endlessly fought and refought for a reason no one remembers.

Val, with tears in her eyes, speaks the obvious: "Daddy is really going crazy on Mama, can we stay here? I don't want the little ones to see it." Carmela acts like she is the aunt here, not the mother, like Carlitos is Val's kid, not hers. She lights a cigarette at the ashtray beside the couch and is instantly absorbed in the movie Dad is watching. She asks Rene, who has plopped down on a chair with a dazed look, to move aside so she can see the TV better.

"*Arrestilu* John, *po assassinarla chista volta*," Mom says to Dad, in Sicilian so the kids won't understand that she's told him to go save Marta before Al kills her. Except they do understand, Spanish has pretty much the same word for "murder."

Dad walks out without a word. We all watch him: Mom, me, Ernie, Carmela, Valerie, Rene, Adrian, Debbie, Maria, Dario, and Margarita, even little Carlitos, we all watch his broad, straight back as he crosses the narrow street. He has never stepped in between Al and Marta before, never before been the center of attention in any situation I can recall; I can hardly believe what I am seeing. As he approaches Ernie's house, Marta comes out on her front porch. Her housedress is torn and her hair, usually kept in a tight bun, is wild. Al flings the screen door open and grabs her arm. She screams. I hear Dad, still a ways off, raise his voice: "Al!" his deep baritone calls. Al turns to look at Dad, but even from a distance I can see that he can't make him out, he is too drunk, and maybe Dad is too implausible in this new role as mediator.

Dad keeps walking toward him, "Al, go sleep it off, let her alone. *Lasciu star,*" he says the last bit in Sicilian for some reason. He says it all with surprising force. We can hear it from our house clear across the street. He walks as far as the edge of the porch, right where the stairs begin. There he has a back-and-forth with Al while Marta stands by looking like she is in shock, either from her beating, or from seeing her neighbor rise from his eternal stupor. Al still has her by the arm. We all strain but we can't hear the words now being exchanged between the two men.

Suddenly I recognize that I am proud of Dad. It's an unfamiliar feeling but I try to acknowledge it. It keeps slipping away like it doesn't belong to me but I keep bringing it back. I have never seen him take such initiative before. For all any of us know, Al could pull out a gun and shoot him right on the spot. After all, if Marta is a *puta* in his drunken mind, then maybe Dad's her man. But Dad doesn't seem afraid. He is calmly talking to Al about God knows what.

Al lets go of Marta's arm and moves to pull something out of his pocket. Oh my God here comes the gun, he is going to shoot Dad or Marta, maybe both of them. Mom must have been thinking the same thing because she sucks in her breath then releases it, right when we all do. Al uses the handkerchief to wipe the sweat from the back of his neck. He looks like he is going to turn around and walk back into the house. My pride soars. Dad is pulling it off! At that moment, when things could have turned, a siren sounds in the distance and from practice we all strain to hear where it is going. Al stops too and listens. At first it does not occur to me that they are headed for us; the cops almost never come to our neighborhood, we always joke that's because it's too dangerous. Except tonight, for some reason, they decide to help. It must be slow, or maybe the donut house over on Passons ran out of coffee.

Time seems to stand still as we listen and wait, suspended like characters in a play waiting for some off-stage technical business to be done so the next scene can begin. The siren grows louder and the squad car turns the corner and pulls up in front of Ernie's house. What the hell are they doing here? Two enormous Anglo cops emerge; it is amazing they fit in that Crown Victoria, which groans and then rises visibly on its suspension when they climb out. One is slightly taller, well over six feet, and has a blonde crew cut; the other looks like he could pull a tractor, he resembles nothing so much as a bull. They holster their night sticks, eye the adjacent houses warily, and walk slowly up to the porch, keeping ten feet apart, standard operating policy in "the field" which is how I once heard a cop refer to our neighborhood.

The Bull roughly forces his way past Dad, jostling him aside as he climbs the three little stairs up onto the porch. I expect the concrete to buckle under his weight. Crew Cut motions for Dad to move off. Dad backs away a few steps, thinks to say something, hesitates, then shakes his head and trudges back toward the curb. He doesn't entirely leave, but he gives the cops plenty of room. That makes sense; he doesn't know what they are going to do.

The Bull questions Marta, whose face is bruised, lip bleeding, hair wild and housedress torn. That, plus the smell of Al's breath and the slur of his words, tells a familiar story. The cops look down at Marta and Al from their enormous height, asking their questions and writing down answers that are not answers at all. Crew Cut keeps an eye on Al while the Bull gets the story from Marta, which is not easy since, in addition to being badly beaten, she speaks only a little English and is even more terrified of the huge cop than she is of her husband.

They decide they have enough evidence, which was plain the moment they drove up – Al is drunk and Marta's taken a beating, anyone could see that. They cuff Al's hands behind him and, as his entire brood grimly watches from the front windows of our house, and the rest of the neighbors from the street, where they have gathered in the twilight and the slashing red light from the cops' cherry top, they lead him down to the squad car. Marta is quietly crying from the porch, holding the railing as she watches her husband being led away. She doesn't know if she will ever see him again. From my perspective, next to Ernie and behind some of the smaller kids, who are on their knees at the window, I can see that an awful lot of neighbors have appeared out of nowhere to watch this scene.

Just before he reaches the squad car, for reasons known only to himself Al turns out of the cops' loose grasp and kicks Crew Cut hard in the balls. The Bull backs off a step, unsheathes his stick, and, while Marta cries, the kids at the window wail, and the neighbors swear, he beats Al around the shoulders, the back, and the hips. The Bull dwarfs Al, and he is as powerful as his namesake. Each of his blows can be heard, practically felt, all the way across the street. It is like a baseball bat being repeatedly smacked against a mattress, or something softer. The Bull works hard at it and his wide pink face turns red the way some really White people's faces do when they exert themselves. Each blow seems it must break the night stick, or Al's spine.

It is strange how hard it is to fall down with your hands cuffed behind you. Even drunk, Al wobbles and wavers for quite a while. Then he collapses like a rag doll, lying on the ground unnaturally, with his hands caught behind him. Dad stands frozen to the spot, just a few yards away. The crowd, as if by magic, grows larger, and gets louder too, catcalling the cops, *las chotas*, in a mixture of *Chicano* and English curses. Chaos erupts in my living room as the kids scream for their father's life. Ernie makes for the door but Mom stops him firmly with a hand on his chest, which is level with her face. He backs off only reluctantly, out of respect and deference toward her.

Crew Cut recovers quickly from Al's stupid but accurate kick. He stands over Al and returns the favor with his heavy boot, connecting with Al's head; once, then again. His pink face is red, like his partner's, with exertion and anger.

Dad still keeps his distance but seeing this, yells, "*Enough!*" in a commanding voice that it takes me a moment to register is his.

He is facing the cops, and his single word is instantly translated, seconded, and repeated by a growing number in the crowd: "*¡Basta!*" and then "*Que chinga la chota.*" Fuck the cops.

The Bull motions for everyone to back off and we have a tense moment when it is unclear what the neighbors will do. Then, from the porch, Marta comes running down to her husband. "*¡No lo maten! ¡No lo maten!*" she screams. Don't kill him! "*¡Tiene hijos!*" He has children! She kneels beside Al, pointing to the sea of faces in the windows across the street.

The cops don't understand a word she is saying, but they look around at the dangerous crowd of housewives, laborers, and kids on bikes that has nearly surrounded them. They stop the beating, for now, throw Al roughly in the back of the squad car and flee as the neighbors fling obscenities, and a couple of inaccurate rocks, after them. As they turn the corner I see Jandro, Mario's dad, step out onto his porch with his shotgun. The cops left just in time.

In my living room everyone is crying, even little Carlitos. I mean *everyone*, including me, although I am hiding it pretty well in the chaos. Everyone, that is except for Mom and Ernie. Mom is comforting the kids, her second family, as she calls them. She is amazing, helping Val, who, through her own tears, is trying to be strong for the little ones. Across the street, Dad is walking over to Marta, who is now on her knees, alone, and sobbing into the spot on the lawn where Al made his suicidal stand. He hovers nearby but doesn't know what to do, and I, for once, don't fault him for that.

Ernie turns to me, dry-eyed, and whispers, all seriousness: "Someday, *ése*, I'm gonna kill those motherfuckin' pigs."

I believe him, and I want to help. I hate cops, all cops, but especially those two big *gabachos* with their sticks. What were they doing in my neighborhood anyway? Dad was taking care of business alright without them. We had it under control. And why don't we have any Brown cops, or cops who speak Spanish, anyway?

Later that night at Ernie's house we have finally gotten everyone settled down. The little kids are in their beds. Ernie and Val are giving Carlitos a bath, with Dad standing behind them, wearing a big smile, hands in his pockets, just watching. Carmela has gone out somewhere, and Mom has patched up Marta's face and is now helping her straighten up the living room. In the kitchen I have finished washing out a dish rag I used to scrub Marta's blood from the living room carpet, and I find myself standing next to Rene at the sink. The house is nearly quiet. We can hear Carlitos splashing in the tub, laughing his head off with Ernie and Val. It is cheering, that little guy, having a ball after all that has happened this night. There is nothing more to do, no chores to distract us from the fact of Al's arrest, or from the certainty that his beating continued once they arrived at the police station. None of us wants to stop what we are doing, to go to bed, now or possibly ever again. We don't want the dreams or the restless alone time waiting for sleep.

I am exhausted, like I have played a full game of very bruising football – on the losing team. Rene looks like I feel. I wonder when she last tried to comb her hair. It has been wet at some point with sweat, tears, or dish water, and has dried, sticking to her forehead and to one cheek. For some reason it strikes me as one too many humiliations in a day and a life already filled with them. I reach out. She flinches, like she thinks I am going to hit her, then catches herself and looks up at me. She half smiles in embarrassment for a second, before lowering her big cow eyes to the floor. Using the tips of two fingers, trying to not actually touch her, I push her hair out of her face, but it falls back limp, worse than before now that it is unstuck from her cheek. I attack it with greater commitment, running my hand through her hair several times, pushing it back behind her ears. It sort of works, her face is at least visible.

Slowly she looks up, silently watching me as I continue to push and smooth her hair. I pull it away from her neck and try to flatten that part out as well. When I think I am finished, I don't know what to do with my hand, so it hovers for a second around her head, until she takes it in both of hers and slowly brings it back down to waist level between us. She doesn't let it go, and I don't mind. Her hands are soft and warm to my touch. It is that same old feeling like

I had, what was it, over a year before, after her fight with the *chola*, a feeling that this is how people should act and feel together.

"I don't get you," she says so quietly that I am not sure if she has spoken or if I have imagined it.

"*Tampoco*," is all I can think to say. Me neither, I don't understand anything.

When we finally arrive home, Gramma has laid out bread, peppers, eggplant, and *coppa cola* for supper, but that was hours ago and she has gone to bed. Dad and I are too tired to eat, but Mom insists we have something. It would be bad for our health to go to sleep on an empty stomach. Dad and I share a look, such a rarity I cannot remember it ever happening before. We silently submit to her will, but at least we do so together.

While Mom is making the sandwiches, I ask Dad, "What were you gonna say to them cops, when they came and then told you to back off?"

He looks at me like he doesn't know what I am talking about.

"I could see on your face, you were about to say something, then you backed off."

Dad gives me another, different look. He looks at me like a man looks at another man, not at a kid. Finally he says, low enough so Mom won't hear, "I was about t'ask 'em why dey gotta be such fuckin' assholes. Den I remembered youse and didn't do nuttin'."

XV

Teresita.

"**P**lease go to the office," pimply Mr. James tells me when I enter his classroom two minutes late for first period English. Kids make noises indicating that I am in trouble, kind of a "wuhuuu!" sound. On my way across campus I wonder what it is this time. I have not been in a fight, I have not cut class, I have not mouthed off to a teacher. For once I worked hard to prepare for last week's U.S. Constitution test because I heard that if you fail it you are held back the whole year. Even Mom has noted my unusual diligence. I practically memorized the Constitution, and did in fact memorize the Preamble, for extra credit, not taking any chances on being held back. I am confident I got at least a C.

In the office I meet with Miss Hickman, my white-haired history teacher who smells of dust, and Mr. Birney, our portly, wheezing, balding principal. They are very serious. I cannot imagine what the two of them have to say to me.

"Young man," Mr. Birney begins, "how do you think you did on the constitution test?"

"Did I pass?" is all I can think to say. How the hell am I supposed to know how I did?

"Did you get any special 'help,' anyone who might have known something about the test?" Mr. Birney continues.

"Help?" I ask. Then it hits me, they think I cheated. I must have passed the test, but they know me well enough to question that result. "I studied every night for weeks, I even memorized the Preamble," I explain.

"I see," says Miss Hickman, doubtfully. She knows the quality of my work, and this ain't it. "Could you possibly recite it for us, now," she asks, confident she has caught me in a lie.

I could, I liked the way it sounded, and memorizing it had not been very difficult. But I am not going to perform for her like some circus animal. "I didn't cheat," is all I say.

They are both momentarily silent, then Mr. Birney retrieves my test paper from the top of a pile on his desk. "We wondered how you might have pulled it off." he says, with a bit of a wheeze and a half-smile. I look at my paper, which is marked "110," but then it has a big red question mark drawn next to the score.

In my confusion Miss Hickman jumps in. "You made a perfect score on the test itself, one hundred points, plus the ten points extra for memorizing the Preamble, which means," she pauses, "that you received the highest score among nearly a thousand students throughout the district." Her white face is red with anger but her voice remains calm and even. "I knew you cheated as soon as I graded your paper, but tell me, how did you do it?"

"I studied real hard, for weeks. I didn't cheat," I repeat.

They go on to ask me about my reading habits and, learning that I have none, they are further dismayed. "I just studied the textbook, it's all in there." I say. But they are not listening.

Miss Hickman takes my paper from Mr. Birney's hands and rips it in half. "I don't know how you did it, but you cheated. Of this I am certain. You will retake the test in my classroom, today, during detention after school. Unless you do equally well under my supervision we will consider it proof of your cheating."

"Why don't you consider this proof that you're a fucking cunt?" I scream in reply, getting up so quickly that my chair falls over, extending my middle finger by way of farewell, and walking out of the room.

I will say nothing about this to anyone. It will be easier for people to believe that I am just in trouble again, and after my parting shot it is only an hour before I am suspended, for cheating, or for telling off a teacher, it doesn't matter. It's fine. The last thing I need is a reputation as a history nut. The test score was a fluke, but an honest fluke, I did not cheat, but that doesn't stop them from giving me an "F."

On my way back to Mr. James' room, through a neighboring classroom window I see Teresita, my new next door neighbor, seated at her desk, and all thoughts of the test, and of Miss Hickman, instantly evaporate. Linda recently broke up with me; her mother insisted that I was the wrong type of guy for her. That is not likely to be a problem with Teresita.

—∞—

For a period of nearly two years a nice big Mexican family from *Michoacán* lives next door, in the rental that has seen a lot of turnover through the years. It now finally feels settled. Among all the kids is this very dark, very pretty girl: Teresita. She speaks decent but stiff English and is more comfortable in Spanish. Because she really wants to improve her pronunciation it's a great excuse for me to spend time with her. Not that I speak such great English myself and she sometimes asks questions about grammar that I have no idea how to answer. Still, we talk a lot.

Teresita is almost a year younger than I am, but seems to know, in the way teenage girls do, so much more about boy-girl stuff than I do. I am hopelessly in love with her from the first day, the first time she smiles at me when we meet. I think about her constantly, and I replay over and over any little snippet of conversation that I can somehow stretch or twist into a coded expression of her feelings for me.

I spend an entire weekend ruminating over a brief conversation we had at school. I had placed myself so that I would "accidentally" run into her in the break between second and third periods, even though it meant sprinting across campus as the bell rang. As I rounded the corner of the science building I caught sight of her heading my way with a couple of girlfriends. I slowed to a walk and worked desperately to get my breathing under control. I planned to walk up to her, not noticing her at first, like I just happened to be over here on this end of campus. Then, at the last minute I could look up and – surprise – how funny running into you here. Except that she saw me first and called out my name before I even looked up.

It wasn't supposed to work this way in my careful plan; I was caught off guard. I didn't say anything, just stared at her like I had never seen her before.

Then one of her friends, with a knowing look and a sly grin, stage whispered to Teresita, "Don't look like *he's* happy to see you, *chica*."

"But *I* am hap-pee to see *heem*!" Teresita shrieked, and they walked on, giggling and looking back over their shoulders at me.

First I play the conversation, if you can call it that, since I hadn't uttered a word, over and over to be certain I have the words exactly right, and the intonation, and the body language. When I am sure I have a faithful rendering of the encounter I begin psychoanalyzing it in earnest. This is what takes up most of the weekend.

Did she mean it sarcastically, like "why would *I* be happy to see *him*?"

Or did she not really mean anything at all, just didn't know what else to say in an embarrassing situation with her friends?

Or, if I dared to consider it, could she have meant exactly what she said: that she was really glad to see me? Which, of course, could just mean she's my neighbor, and we practice English together, and our families are close, and she likes me "as a friend."

I fall so deep into my ruminations and analyses that I forget to meet Ben when I promised. I certainly can't ask Dad for help, he won't even talk to me about baseball, let alone girls. I would rather die than mention it to Mom. What about one of my friends? No way. While girls apparently chat endlessly about boys – this I know from my cousin Linia – guys do not discuss this kind of thing. Our talk relative to girls is focused on the, often imaginary, physical side of things.

Wait a second – Linidu. I should have thought of her earlier. Throughout my life Linia has been my 4-1-1 on girls. She is popular, knows all the popular kids, goes to all the popular parties, has gone out with lots of guys, and has a serious boyfriend.

I call Linidu on Sunday afternoon, after a day and a half of beating my head against the impenetrable wall of girl thinking. As usual, she is more than willing to talk about what she calls, generously, my "love life."

We meet at the playground, the usual place, and sit on the same swings we used to play on only a few years earlier. Being an only child is much better with Linia around. She is more like a sister than a cousin. We are only a few weeks apart in age, and we literally grow up together.

"Alright," she says in her best mature voice, "What happened?"

After I tell her my story, in exact detail, with a verbatim rendering of the conversation between the two girls, rounded out by a complete description of facial expressions, she ponders for only a brief moment before responding.

"You ran all the way over to see her, and then, when you actually did see her, you didn't say anything?" She scolded. "Oh, man, you really don't know anything, do you?"

I have to admit she is right, shaking my lowered head in acknowledgement.

"Who was the girl?" she asks.

"Teresita, I told you!"

"Not her, the other girl, the one who said you didn't look happy to see Teresa." Linia always uses people's formal names; she hates nicknames, although everyone in our family calls her Linidu, a habit begun by the grandparents when we were little.

"I don' know, I seen her around, but don' know her name." Our class has over a thousand kids, three thousand in the high school, and I doubt if even Linidu knows them all by name.

"What'd she look like?"

"I don' know," I say. "I was lookin' at Teresita."

"Try to remember, it's important."

I go back to my mental picture of the interaction, where I have inscribed every detail, at least I thought I had until now. I see Teresita walking along with a girl on each side, but the focus is all on her. I sort of shift the camera to focus on the girl who spoke, as she says her single line: "Don't look like *he's* happy to see you, *chica*."

Suddenly she comes into better focus. "She is taller than Teresita, with long black hair that is kind of stringy, and she had on a lot of eye makeup." I stop, proud of my amazing powers of recall.

"Great, you just described most of the girls at school. Taller than Teresa — that's not hard, she's my size, barely five feet tall. Long black hair: that narrows it down a lot! And Cuz, have you ever noticed that all the girls wear tons of eye makeup — look at me for Chrissake!" She mugs, turning a mascara-laden eye to me so I can get a better look. Then she gasps in exasperation. I have to admit she is probably right to give up on me.

"Well, what else could I tell you?" I ask, pathetically. "I can see her but I don' know what to say 'bout her. Oh, she had big, uh. . ." My voice trails off as my outstretched hands mime the rest of the message.

"What did her voice sound like?" Linia says, ignoring my crassness.

"Her voice?" That is going to take a minute. "When she said it, she sounded like she knew everything about everything."

"You mean she sounded self-confident?"

I have never heard that term before, but I figure I know what it means. "Yeah, *simón*, like she was totally self-confident."

"What was she wearing?" then she adds, "Aside from a pea coat." She is right. All the girls seem to have pea coats this winter. But that is just what I was going to say, so I am stymied again. Then I remember something else, maybe it will help.

"Well, it was funny, because it was kinda cold that morning, and she *was* wearing a pea coat, but she was also wearing *huaraches*. Seemed kinda odd to wear a coat and then sandals, you know."

Linia's eyes light up. "Wait a sec. There's one girl I know, why didn't I think of her? She's famous for always wearing *huaraches*, no matter what. Like she thinks it is sooo cool." She thinks for a moment. "And she is real curvy too. OK, it must be her, Rita. She's a close friend of Teresa's, so it really makes sense."

"Why's it important to know who she was?"

"Because, *pendejo*, what she said is only half the story. The other half is what she meant." Getting only a dumb look from me in response, she plunges on.

"Rita is Teresa's friend, so you gotta figure if she likes somebody, say, *you* for instance, although I cannot imagine *how* that would be possible, you're such a dolt, but then, *all* guys are dolts, so maybe it is possible." She seems to have lost her thread for a moment, but only a moment.

"Anyway, if she likes somebody she is gonna tell Rita about it, that's pretty sure. And Rita, if she had never heard of you, like from Teresa, probably would have ignored you totally in the hall that day. Girls don't talk to or make cracks about guys they don't know, not in front of them anyway. But you said Teresa called your name, so Rita knew who you were, the name must have clicked, and that's because Teresa must have already told her something about you. And so when you didn't say anything back, she figured you didn't like Teresa, so she decided to make fun of it, like a good girlfriend will always do to her friend, to make her feel worse."

My head is swimming in this sea of feminine logic. I need a translation. "So, that means?"

"It means Teresa likes you, or else Rita never woulda said what she said."

"Are you sure?" Linidu is usually right, but I am going purely on faith here.

"Yes, I am sure. Besides, I ate lunch with Teresa last week, and she kept asking me all about you, like did you have a girlfriend, and did you like anybody, so yes, I am sure."

"Why didn' you tell me she was askin' bout me?" I ask.

"Because a girl doesn't want to let a guy know she is interested first, right *cugino*?"

I want to ask why not, but instead: "So what do I do now?"

"Oh my God, Cuz."

XVI

I love you.

I have taken Linia's advice to heart, thought it through, and I am ready to act. If this makes me sound somewhat less than romantic, that is because romance is pretty far down my list of concerns. First, I try to act natural when I feel anything but natural now that I know, or at least think, relying on Linidu, that there is the possibility of something developing between Teresita and me. I am equal parts excited and terrified. This is much harder than my relationship with Linda, whom I did not love. Second, I need to make some sort of move to let Teresita know how I feel about her. In my ruminating way I plan out various approaches, but as opportunities come and go and I don't act, I am getting desperate. After all, she lives next door, so I see her every day, which means lots of chances to approach her, or to ignore her. In my nervousness I have stopped talking to her even when I run into her. All I can do is smile and turn away. She must think I don't even want to be friends anymore.

In desperation I talk to Ben about this. He tries to help. Although his advice is about as lame as my own ideas, at least he understands my position.

Once again Linidu comes to the rescue. Assuming that hell will freeze over before I make a move, she organizes a party at her house. She has a big double car garage that my uncle Jimmy long ago turned into a kind of unheated den for the kids. It is a popular hangout, especially since my aunt likes to think of herself as only a wee bit older than us. She dresses in hippie clothes, tries to talk in the latest slang, listens to Santana, and lets Linia throw parties.

She has lots of parties, but I usually don't go. Her parties are by and for the small group of popular kids, most of whom I barely know. The kind of party I go to usually ends up with fights, property damage, and the cops. I don't want to bring that kind of trouble to my uncle's house. But this is one party Linia is hell-bent on getting me to.

"You're coming, right?" she asks after school on Friday, the day before the party. "You'd better come."

"Linidu," I use her nickname since she hates it. It is the only weapon I have against her superior knowledge across all social fronts. "You know your friends don' like me, why make trouble? Who am I gonna talk to? And if I come with my guys, you know it's gonna get outta hand."

"No, dumbshit, you don't bring that pack of *cholos*. Just you. I'll have someone special here. I'm sure she's coming. That's the whole point." She smiles mischievously. She loves this kind of thing, the intrigue, the secrets, holding other people's fate in her hands.

My heart starts beating through my shirt as it dawns on me what is going on. That's why this party was organized and why it is so important I come, and without my usual friends.

"But. . ." I have nothing else to say. It is the moment of truth.

At the party, as expected, I know no one very well. It is all the popular kids, maybe sneaking a little beer in the backyard, listening to *Crosby, Stills and Nash*, then to *Chicago*, making-out in corners with the lights down low. This is not my kind of party but it feels kind of safe and relaxed, and I don't have to worry about getting jumped, not by these kids. I try walking around like I am going somewhere, all the way to the other end of the garage, where my friends would be, but when I get there, and no friends are waiting for me, I can only turn around and wander back in the other direction. It is amazing how hard it is to look natural in a large group when everyone else is talking in animated small groups. I imagine that I stand out like a sore thumb, but it's more likely that no one even notices me.

Then I catch Linia's eye, and she motions with her head toward the big old console TV pushed against one wall of the garage. Sitting in front of it, talking to another girl, is Teresita. I look back at Linidu, who shoots me a look that says: *Get your sorry ass over there now, or deal with me later!*

I walk over and, not knowing what else to do, I kneel down in front of Teresita. Her friend – it is Rita, I recognize the *huaraches* – sees me approaching, smiles at Teresita, stands and wanders away, immediately picking up another conversation. "Hi," is all I manage to say, but with the music so loud, conversation is not really possible even from this distance, so she scoots over a bit, making room, and I sit down next to her on the garage floor, which is covered by a scrap of carpet that smells like my Aunt Claudia's poodle, *GiGi*.

We sit side by side, not talking much, but with our hips and arms touching, for what seems an eternity. We watch people pass one way and another in the garage; we laugh together when a guy who is not watching where he is walking trips over a girl who is lying on the floor and nearly falls into the table that has all the cokes on it; and we listen to the music: Santana, singing *Evil Ways*. I am happy as things are, because I now know for sure that she likes me, otherwise she would have gotten up and left. Besides, she keeps her hip and arm pressed up against mine.

The music stops. While another stack of records is cued up on the turntable, Linidu walks over. She looks at us, sitting like two manikins, like catatonic Siamese twins, leaning against one another for support, and says, "Cuz, I think Teresa's shoulder itches, why don't you scratch it for her?" Then she turns and walks away.

Teresita blushes. Although it is hard to see against her dark skin, I recognize it in her eyes. I lift my arm and slide it around her shoulders, not to scratch, of course, but to squeeze her gently. Then the strangest, most magical thing happens: Teresita kind of melts into me, leaning and scrunching herself into a comfortable position like a cat, half on my lap. I can smell her hair, which is right under my nose. We stay like that for what seems hours. It might have been, because, when she looks at her watch and suddenly gets up, saying that she needs to get home by eleven or her father, Little Louie, will kill her, I find that my arm is numb.

"I'll go home too, it's right next door," I add lamely, like she doesn't know where I live.

"OK, you can walk with me to home," she says simply, in her sweet accent and unique syntax, making it official – we're together.

We leave the party holding hands for all to see. I think she initiated that as well, but it feels natural. When we get outside I put my arm – the one that still has feeling – around her, and we slowly walk home. Now that we are outside and it is quiet, we can no longer just enjoy each other's company and listen to the music. We have to talk. I have prepared, with Linia's help, a few suave things to say on such an occasion, comments about how nice she looks, about how smart I think she is, about how lucky I am that she moved in next door. But when the moment arrives nothing comes to my lips except, unexpectedly, "I love you."

I instantly regret making such a direct, corny, and un-cool statement. After all, this is the first meaningful sentence I have spoken to her in weeks, ever since our English-improvement sessions ended in my nervousness. I expect her to remove my arm from her shoulder and give me a look like I have said a bad word. I expect her to tell me never to speak to her again, like I am some kind of pervert.

She does in fact stop, right in the middle of the street, under that perpetually burned-out street light, a block from our houses, in the total darkness. And she does take my arm from her shoulder. But instead of turning away from me she holds onto my hand, with both her smaller ones, the fingers covered with silver rings, the wrists gently clanging with a million bracelets, and then she does the most unexpected thing – she kisses my hand, a simple kiss, the brush of her soft lips against the back of my hand. She looks up at me. I manage to lean down and kiss her, on the mouth, clumsily at first, but then better. If the lights of an approaching car had not forced us to move out of the street, I don't know that we ever would have stopped. We walk on a bit, it is getting close to eleven and I know her father's strictness. At the sidewalk in front of her house, under the yellow light of a working street lamp, I look into her eyes deep, completely black eyes, and kiss her briefly again.

Then she runs, laughing, up to the door to make her curfew.

XVII

I'll show you what trouble is!

I begin seeing less and less of Ernie, at school and at home. Until recently we were still together every single day, at lunch or between classes, and even as that gulf between freshman and sophomore and then between sophomore and junior grew larger, we still talked out in front of the houses and hung out on weekends. After a while I start to think maybe he has moved out, because his old white Chevy van is not parked in front of his parents' place. I hear he is living over in Pico with his cousins, but I don't understand why.

Ernie and two dazed hard-ass *cholos* walk into Western Auto on Whittier Boulevard, where I have the world's shittiest after school job working for a crazy cheapskate *gabacho* named Ed. No one in my family has ever had a good job, and we specialize in abusive bosses, so I am just following in the family tradition.

When Ed hires me, he asks if I want one or two of the Western Auto shirts we all wear. Two is better, he says, I could have one to wash, so I take two. Then I see my first paycheck – Ed has deducted, including taxes, nearly twelve dollars for the two shirts. This leaves me with only a few bucks for my first month's work, at $1.25 an hour. At this rate I won't be able to put enough gas in my croaking Mustang to get to the job.

Ed stops me while I am sweeping the floor in the hardware section. The store gets so much action that you have to sweep twice a day to keep it any kind of clean. Ed must be raking in the money, the place is always packed. "Look what you have there!" he bellows, pointing at the floor in front of me. I look down first at the broom but soon realize he means the small mound of dirt that I have accumulated by sweeping. Ed dips his hand down into the pile and extracts a thin, metal washer. It must have been dropped by a customer and I swept it up from the floor.

"Do you realize what you are doing?" Ed booms.

By some job-preserving miracle I don't answer with the only reply that comes to mind - "sweeping?" – so he goes on.

"Do you have any idea how much these things cost?"

Actually, I do. Ed gets them wholesale for under a dollar for a box of five hundred. "If you keep sweeping out the merchandise you'll have me in the poorhouse!" He shakes his head in that disgusted way of his and walks off, tossing the washer back in the bin. As soon as he is gone I lean over, pick it out of the bin and slip it in my pocket. I'm going to keep it, on my key chain, a reminder of a very early lesson about bosses.

The washer is the first thing I steal from Ed, but not the last. I take spark-plugs for tune ups on my Mustang, sodas from the machine, aviator sunglasses, and assorted oil, STP and other car consumables. Ed steals from me so I steal from him.

Each night, at precisely nine o'clock, closing time, we are all ordered to punch out, but that doesn't mean we close. After clocking out we continue to help any last minute customers, then clean up, count the cash, and lock up, all on our own time. Once a month Ed calls for a store meeting after closing time. This gives him an opportunity to tell us what worthless pieces of crap we are, also on our own time. I figure I put in about ten to twelve hours a month unpaid.

—⚡—

I hated that job. But later I also treasured it. I learned everything I would ever need to know about work, and especially about bosses, from that *gabacho* bastard Ed.

—⚡—

This particular day, after not seeing Ernie for a few weeks, and not having really talked to him for a couple of months, he walks in with his new friends looking to buy one of those little steering wheels, about eight inches across and made of shiny, chromed, welded chain link. They are really hot with low riders. I would like to have one myself but I can't afford it, and Ed would definitely notice if one of these babies disappeared and then turned up on the steering column of my car. Ernie's hair is long and unkempt, which is not like him. He has always taken pride in his look, but apparently that is no more. He feels different to me, and when he doesn't even seem to know me, it actually hurts. At first I assume he is spaced out, focused on the steering wheel, and hasn't recognized me in my Western Auto shirt. I mess with him:

"*Órale. Aquí, estoy, y qué?*" I say it in my best choosing-on voice, but then a smile cracks on my lips. Missing the joke, one of Ernie's friends, a small, thin guy with a *pachuco* hat over the bandana tied around his forehead, starts like he is going to come at me, a hand reaching toward his waist band, where I see the handle of a revolver under his shirt. Ernie puts out a restraining arm. Then he looks up from the little steering wheel. He gives me the nod, the short, upward tilt of the chin, just one, no smile, that in our world signals recognizing a friend, and he asks me something about the wheel. I wonder, did he recognize me all along? I don't get it. I have a hard time picturing this choice little wheel on Ernie's enormous and ancient Ford van, but maybe he is fixing it up. You know, tassels in the rear window, shag carpet on the deck, fuzzy dice hanging from the mirror, lights in the wheel wells, little moon hubcaps, hydraulics so you can adjust the height of your ride, eight-track tape system with extra speakers all over the place, and now, the little steering wheel to top it off. That's how I would do it, anyway, the way I dream of fixing up my battered and paint-challenged Mustang, if I had the money.

Later, while his buddies are looking at two different wheels, Ernie leans forward across the counter. I think he is going to say something, make some joke, reconnect like it's still him and me, which was only a few months ago. He lowers his shades and I can see his bloodshot eyes. The motherfucker is high. He whispers, "You think you can walk one of these outta here tonight, *ése*?" Just then Ed comes up, doesn't like the look of Ernie and his friends, and kicks them out.

"Stay away from those guys," he warns. "They're only in here to shoplift. Like all them Mexicans." *¡Qué gabacho!* Except for Ed and his drunken, sadistic, good-for-nothing son, who occasionally struts around the store, everyone working his ass off in this shitty place is *Chicano*, and whatever I am.

—⟶—

I am walking from my locker at the end of the day with my Geometry book under my arm. I am close to flunking that class and I figure I better study and see if I can finally "get it." Math has never appealed to me. I never saw the point of it, beyond adding and subtracting, but I don't need another "F." Someone comes up quietly from behind and slaps the book out of my hand. It lands with a plop in the mud puddle caused by a broken sprinkler filling the ring around a tree. I turn around and it is a punk named Jorge who was passing on his bike and thought it would be funny to knock my book loose. He meant no real harm, wasn't aiming for the mud, I can tell, but still, I am pissed. He sees my face and starts to ride off, but I am on him in a second, dragging his ass off the bike, and I start pounding him.

I don't realize that he is with a group of guys, also on bikes, until it is too late. They pull me off of Jorge and before everyone settles down my nose and lip are bleeding and a tooth is loose. Jorge apologizes, says he didn't mean for the book to go in the mud, as he dabs the blood off his own nose. He cleans up my book as best he can, and we shake hands. It is just another misunderstanding in the neighborhood.

—⟶—

A few weeks later its August 29, 1970, a Saturday, and East L.A. is on fire. The Moratorium, a *Chicano* demonstration against the Vietnam War, a heavy-handed police response, and a frustrated, cop-hating public, the whole place starts to burn. I first notice something is wrong when I smell smoke while at work at the Western Auto. Carlos, the manager, points out to the street, where a fine rain of ash is gradually covering everything. The mid-day is growing weirdly dark.

We have no trade, not a soul in the store, the first time I can remember that happening. Ed is worried. He goes for a radio while some of us drift out into the street to see what's up. Looking up Whittier Boulevard toward LA I see nothing but black smoke. When I get back inside Ed has the earpiece of a transistor radio glued to his ear. He announces, "The fuckers are burning their own homes and businesses down; they're working their way down the boulevard. Get out the guns."

Western Auto sells a lot of things: car tires, bicycles, generators, all manner of tools and hardware, and guns, both pistols and rifles. To my knowledge no one has ever actually bought a gun from us. Serious hunters go to one of the gun shops, where the selection is bigger, the prices better, and the salesmen more knowledgeable. Everyone else buys what he wants on the street: *un cuete*, no overhead, no paperwork, and often no serial number; a simple handheld grinder takes care of that. The store's meager supply of weapons is kept in two locked, dust-filled cases on the wall. They never change. We have a Winchester, a couple of little .22's, and a 12-gauge arrayed in the rifle case, and an assortment of small, cheap pistols in the other case.

Ed finds the right key when Carlos, normally docile, develops some backbone. "Hey boss, this ain't right. We're not gonna die defending the store. Let's lock up and get the hell outta here while we can." Ed hesitates, the key is about two inches from the lock. We're all watching, what will Ed do, and then, what will *we* do when he starts handing out guns and ammo?

"Ed, they're a bunch of kids here," says Carlos, pointing at us. "Don't tell 'em to do this." Reason prevails and we get out, amid the gathering smoke, before the trouble reaches us. I'm glad. I don't want to shoot people I don't even know and who have done nothing to me, and I certainly do not want to do it for Ed for $1.25 an hour.

The riot ended quickly, but the aftermath was felt for a long, long time, especially in the form of hard feelings with the cops. A community that fears, or worse, hates, its police is going to be unsafe for everyone. Eventually our continuation high school was renamed Ruben Salazar High, a dubious honor for a respected *Chicano* journalist who was shot in the head with a tear gas canister the cops fired blindly into a building where he was interviewing people. Salazar died, but his name lives on at a continuation high school in Pico Rivera. *¡Qué Viva la Raza!*

It had never been a friendly-cop kind of community but after the riot, after Salazar's and the other deaths that August day, and after so many other beatings and shootings, it grew openly hostile. If you called for an ambulance because your grandmother had fallen and broken her hip, they would take an hour to come, and would arrive accompanied by two squad cars for protection, presumably from Grandpa. If you reported a gang fight on the playground after school they wouldn't come at all.

―∞―

I hear a car screech to a stop out front then raised, angry voices in Spanish, followed by the sound of metal on metal, and something squishier. It's the house across the street, next to Ernie's. This family has two teenage sons who are covered with street gang tattoos, like their dad, whose tats include prison gang work. We are friendly, neighborly, but they make Mom uncomfortable. "Those kids are trouble," she sums it up.

"Everybody is trouble," I answer, the man of so much wisdom and experience.

"You stay away from them or I'll show you what trouble is!" she responds.

We look out to see what the commotion is all about. A car full of *cholos* has pulled up in front of our neighbors' house and attacked the father and two sons, who are working on a Chevy parked on the front lawn. The attackers have baseball bats but the neighbors have wrenches and tire irons right at hand. Mom goes to the phone on the kitchen wall, dials the cops, and says: "I want to report a fight, there are a bunch of kids beating each other with bats and clubs, and there's a cop in the middle of it."

I look out again, up and down the street. I check the curbs all around for a squad car. When she gets off the phone I say, "Mom, there's no cops around."

She smiles and says, "I know, but you want them to come, don't you?" Sure enough in record time three cars squeal onto the scene, and six cops join in the head bashing. So that's how bad it has gotten, you can't rely on the cops to come save someone's life – except another cop's. We're pretty much on our own. After the "help" they brought when they arrested Al, that's fine with me.

―∞―

I come home from school and know at once something is wrong. It is way too quiet, like a John Wayne western before the Indians attack. As I let myself in the slamming of the screen door behind me resounds like a gunshot in church. I walk into the kitchen and find Gramma, standing at the counter, crying like a baby.

"*Che c'e, Nonna,*" I ask. From the weight of the air around her I know someone has died, and I guess, from his absence, that it is Grandpa. "*Cu é mortu, eh?*" I want her to say the name "*Nonno*" so I will know, and it will be over. I am surprised to find myself choking up. I never gave grandpa much thought, he was just always there, like the house, but now, dead, I realize how much I like having him around. He is so full of life, how can he be dead? I look again to Gramma, but she is too distraught to speak. As tears form in my own eyes, thinking of my poor old *Nonno* lying dead in his bed, drinking his last syrup bottle of wine with lunch, taking his last afternoon nap, and then not waking up, he walks into the room. It takes me a minute to realize he is not a figment of my grieving brain. Then a worse fear still, if Grandpa and Gramma are both alive, it must be Mom or Dad.

"*Cu é mortu, Nonno, dimmi,* please, *piacere*" I beg. He shakes his head, raises a hand from the elbow and rotates it slowly back and forth like a beauty queen waving from a float. This is one of his gestures. It is very expressive but it has no specific meaning beyond "the world is *Pazzu* – nuts." He is very old and his eyes, which have seen much sadness, and caused more than his share, are heavy and tired. He nods toward the front door.

I walk back outside expecting to see my mother's body lying on the front lawn. Maybe I walked right past it without noticing on the way in a minute earlier. Instead of her, I see what I had in fact missed. Being alert to your surroundings is a survival skill we all learn from an early age and I have generally excelled at it, but not today.

Two strange cars are parked across the street. They each have the circled "E" of an official car on their license plates. Although they have no markings, one has a cop's cherry top tucked into the rear window. I cross the street and walk into the house without knocking. Mom is holding Val's hand as they both cry and baby Carlitos sits on the floor playing with some wooden cooking spoons. If Mom is crying it must be bad.

I know at once that Al has not finally beaten Marta to death because I see her alive, sitting with the cops. It is something else, but I am so confused now that I don't know what to expect. Someone, maybe Ernie, is going to have to tell me. Marta is at the table with three plain clothes cops – two Anglos with short hair wearing dark suits with high water pants, and one smaller guy who looks *Chicano*. Al is out of town driving long haul. I wonder if these cops know Crew Cut and the Bull, the assholes who beat the hell out of this woman's husband in front of her and all their kids.

The *Chicano* cop is talking very quietly to Marta in Spanish. I piece the story together from the fragments I catch. I cannot very well interrupt to ask a question.

Ernie was discovered a few hours ago sprawled across the front seat of his old white van. The window had been rolled down, like he had been talking to someone he knew, except this guy didn't come to talk. Instead he fired two bullets into Ernie's face at such close range that, in addition to the damage done by the bullets passing through his skull, they left powder burns on his nose and cheek.

The cops are thinking drugs but have no suspects, no leads, and other than Ernie's body, the van, and the two slugs that went through him and dug into the upholstery, no evidence. They assume that a dead *Chicano* kid equals drugs. There is no investigation; no arrest, no prosecution, just another funeral Mass with the church full of high school kids in mourning.

That's the way it is. It happens, but who cares? His mother, his father, his brothers and sisters, his little nephew Carlitos, the neighbors who have known him since he was a little boy, and his friends, that's all.

Ernie has a closed casket. It is not possible without going to a great expense Al and Marta cannot afford, to fix him up well enough for a family viewing. But it does not seem right, does not seem like you can really say good-bye unless you can see him, touch his face or his hand as you pass the casket. Anglos and Protestants find it creepy, but Latin Catholics understand how to say good-bye to someone they love. They know you have to look upon his dead face in order to know in your heart that you will never see him again in this life.

Ben and I sit together in stony silence at the funeral. After the service we carry the casket out to the hearse. It is amazingly heavy. This is the tradition, exercised far too often: when a high school kid gets killed the pall bearers are other high school kids, his friends. Except those two *cholos* who came into the Western Auto with Ernie are not among the pall bearers, they are not even at the funeral. It is Ernie's friends from childhood – Ben and Dave, Mario, Ernie's brothers Adrian and Dario, and me – who carry the casket.

After the funeral at the church and the burial at Rosemead cemetery we go back to Ernie's house to pay our respects. It is almost Christmas and neighbors have made *tamales* for the meal that must be offered to visitors after a funeral. Normally I love *tamales* and make a point of being at Ernie's house on Christmas Eve to get them hot out of the steamer. It is Mexican tradition to make them the night before Christmas – the women and girls in the kitchen all day, and the men and boys in the living room drinking beer, watching football, and waiting for the call to eat. Today I don't feel like eating. The food smell is nauseating. The smell of *tamales,* the *masa* and pork and red sauce, somehow reminds me of Ernie's death, his decaying body. Maybe it is because of the closed casket, the fact that I can't say a proper good-bye. Or maybe because the last time we spoke he asked me to steal for him, and I didn't. Maybe if I had kept closer to him this could have been prevented. I cannot eat at all. Ben, on the other hand, has his usual shipwrecked sailor's appetite and stuffs his face. Why not? It makes no difference to Ernie.

Maybe a hundred people are milling around the house and yard, the whole neighborhood and the extended family from other parts of town. It starts off somber but pretty soon, when you get that many *Chicanos* together, with plenty of good food and cold beer, it turns into a kind of bittersweet party. Later the *tequila* comes out, then the coats and ties come off, and it's a for-real party. That's okay with me and I am sure it would be fine with Ernie. I just can't seem to take part in it. I keep seeing people I want to talk to, people who maybe were closer to Ernie than I was over the last few months. Maybe they could tell me what really happened to him, both on the day he died and during the time that led up to it. Maybe that could help me to stop feeling like I let him down; that if I had made more of an effort I could have helped; that I could have been by his side when that guy walked up to the van; that I could have saved him. The whole time I am looking around the party for the two *cholos* who were with him when they came into the Western Auto to steal the steering wheel but they are not to be found. In the end I talk to no one. I don't dare unclench my jaw for fear of the wail that will come out.

I have been wandering around the house and out into the yard, ruminating in an endless cycle of what-iffing. The little house and patio are so packed you can hardly move. I see Carmela, laughing with her newest boyfriend. And Marta, looking worse than she ever looks after Al beats her: looking dead in fact, vacant, a woman who has lost her oldest son. Mom, talking to Adrian, Ernie's little brother, and a budding *cholo* in his own right. Val, with Carlitos in tow. He looks so much like Ernie, the shiny black hair and wide build; the big, sad brown eyes in his dark face. Al, with that fighter's brow he got during his six months in the County lock up; he walks over and holds Marta's hand.

We are all there: Ben, Dave, Mario, Gilberto, and me, and our families. Everyone on the block and relatives and friends from the whole of town; everyone except the one we all want to see walk through the front door one more time, flip off his shoes, push back his hair with a careless hand, and pop open a beer.

Dad is nowhere to be seen, he went home right after the church, skipped the cemetery. I had such hopes that he would change somehow after that day he stood up to the cops in front of this house, but he didn't. It was a moment of crisis when he rose to the need. It's hard to believe, but he did it, and I won't take that away from him. But as soon as the crisis passed he fell right back into the hole where he normally lived.

I find myself alone in the boys' room, empty and quiet. I sit down on his bunk, the choice lower one beside the window where we once sat making all those damned B-29 airplane models Al had boosted for our recovery. How long ago was it? A few years from a kid to, to what? I think of his body in that casket, still carrying that appendix scar, in the place where Jesus, too, was pierced. I look up at the crucifix on the wall, and feel for my side, finding my own scar. Jesus is still there too, and still crucified.

I start to ask a question in a low voice, only for myself to hear, just loud enough so I know I am alive, beside the cross, near His suffering. I can't put it in words but I want to ask God if Ernie is with him or if he is just the body in that box we put into the ground. With my elbows on my knees and my head in my hands, the words die on my lips. Suddenly I can smell those damned tamales from the kitchen and a great sour nausea rises in me. I start to get up, maybe some air will help, but I feel pressure from a hand on my shoulder, gently but firmly pushing me back, making me sit. Then another hand is on top of my head, pushing fingers through the stubble of my buzz cut, and I know who it is, even though I can't see her, with the tears that have suddenly filled my eyes and are pouring through my hands, clamped over my face.

"I know you loved him too," she says softly.

XVIII

Why the hell would someone drive a tank into church?

Sitting in the *wadi* the little band of survivors looked to Goldstein for direction, for what to do now that they were lost and alone, and a new day had finally arrived. "OK, we move our asses, now!" Goldie said, rousing the group to its feet. "We ain't gonna get any water or food jus' sittin' here, and it's a fair bet no one's gonna come out lookin' for us. Not with all the shit that's goin' on out there." He indicated the direction from which they had come, the battlefield from the night before.

"Hey Goldie," whispered Russo while they were loading up their gear, "how do we know we ain't gonna find ourselves runnin' up da backs a doze goddamn *Panzers* chasin' after Division?"

"No guarantees in any of this, Johnny, 'cept stayin' here we die. *That* is for sure."

"Managgia!" was Russo's only response. He shook his head and hefted his rifle. He was complaining, because that is what soldiers did, but he gave no thought to what came next. If Goldie said they had to move out, then they just had to do it. Goldie was his friend and a good soldier whose skill and judgment he trusted. For now at least, Goldie was also the senior man on the scene and so, by the way the United States Army worked, Corporal Goldstein was in command.

"That about says it all, don'it *paisan*?" Salve, a fellow Italian who had somehow lost his helmet during the night, added to Russo's comment.

Their only chance was to force on through to the rally point, which they hoped still existed, while the Germans were kept busy securing Dj Lessouda. When they attacked, they would find it abandoned except for the medics and the wounded. No one wanted to ask what the Germans would do when they set off the booby-trapped supply caches waiting for them. The men left behind would pay a heavy price for those small annoyances. But Colonel Wayne could not leave weapons and ammo for the *Wehrmacht* to throw back in his teeth. It had to be done.

Once the German commander on the scene decided to pursue the fleeing American battalion, the fast-moving advance units of his *Panzers* would quickly catch up with the exhausted, disorganized, and dismounted GIs, and would dispatch them on the open ground in broad daylight without so much as slowing down.

The *wadi* where Russo, Goldie, and their little group were sheltering provided cover from the enemy on the open plain, but it seemed to veer, judging from the morning sun, too far to the west to take them where they needed to go, back toward Division's last rally point. They had not spotted any other survivors since the initial split up after the battle last night. Where the hell had they all gone? Could it be that this little handful of lost soldiers, led by a corporal, was all that remained of the battalion, nearly 2,000 men? It was best not to ask that question either.

They left the relative safety of the *wadi* and using their watches, the sun, and dead reckoning, headed by the shortest and straightest route to where they thought the rally point should be, the point Division had indicated in its message, some thirty hours ago. Once out in the open they trudged on for hours, rifles slung at their backs, canteens emptying quickly in the cold winter desert, seeing not a sign of life, human or other. A half hour before sunset they spotted a dust cloud on the far horizon and instinctively fell to the ground to lower their silhouette.

"Could jus be a san'storm," Wilson, a young Texan, offered hopefully, shielding his eyes from the sun and squinting for all he was worth.

"Or could be our guys 'round the rally point," Salve countered, not sounding convinced, or even all that interested. They had nowhere else to go. And without a radio they would only find out what was waiting for them up ahead when they arrived.

"Hell," Goldie said, "could be *Panzers*, chasin' Division's tail, like Johnny said. Maybe we're behind the Krauts." No one spoke after that. They got up and kept walking toward the dust cloud, still miles off in the distance, stopping every hour for five minutes of rest. Each time they stopped it was more difficult to get moving again. As it darkened they took final rough bearings, pinpointing distant hills to check their progress against in the morning, if they were still out in the morning. At this point Goldie decided they would just keep walking, without further rest stops. He feared that if they stopped in the dark, sat down for even a moment, he would never get them, or himself, up and moving again. Having long ago finished their water, their food, their cigarettes, and their questions, they just walked.

"Hey'all," Wilson drawled in a parched and cheerless voice from the middle of their little column. "It's 2200. Been twenty-four hours since we left the Dj."

Two or three "Fuck you's," were the rasped reply.

"No," Wilson continued, "I mean was only s'posed to be eight fuckin' miles to the rally point, remember? And we musta walked what, twenty-five miles, as the crow flies, by this route. So we musta passed *that* rally point a ways back, and no one was home."

"Division musta fallen back a bit, makes sense," Goldie offered, if only to keep the men's spirits from falling any further, below the level at which they would continue. They had to keep moving, to stop was to die. Wilson shook his head and fell quiet.

As he trudged forward Russo was lost in a reverie that kept changing its subject. One minute he was dreaming of Coney Island, a hot dog, and a tall glass of cool lemonade. He could smell the fresh bun and the pungent sauerkraut. Next he was sitting in a brand new shiny Ford coupe with Gina at his side, waiting for a light to change, and what struck him most about this scene was that he was wearing civvies. The very next moment he was sleeping in a nice comfortable Army cot back at Fort Dix. He could smell the clean, antiseptic smell of the Army sheets. Now he was at early Mass, standing in line for his turn to kneel at the altar rail and take communion. Who was shouting from up ahead? Didn't they realize not to yell like that in church? Father was going to kick someone's ass if he spotted who was making all that racket. But the yelling only got louder, and then he heard the unmistakable sound of tank tracks, the bogey wheels whining as they turned. *Why the hell would someone drive a tank into church?*

—ᴍ—

They walked, dazed, asleep on their feet, right into a picket line of Stuart M3's extended in front of the new defensive line. It was miles from the original rally point, which Division had abandoned, falling back to this new thinly defended line it would now try to hold. The dust cloud they had spotted before dark had been the tanks digging in. Luckily the tankers were alert and their OPs noticed the straggling line of infantrymen as they approached in the pre-dawn, walking upright, with no attempt at concealment. They tracked them through their gun sights until they were so close that their uniforms and identity were unmistakable, then went out to bring them in. If the tankers had not been so alert, and if other small groups of survivors had not passed through their position over the past few hours, they might have gotten shot right at the moment of their salvation.

The Germans had broken off the pursuit after the initial killing on the plain the previous night, licking their own wounds from that unexpected and unexpectedly fierce firefight, content with digesting their victory at Faid Pass. Thus they violated the most basic and enduring rule of war from ancient Sparta onward: remain in contact with a retreating enemy and exploit his weaknesses; don't give him time to regroup; continue the attack, and annihilate him.

The tankers offered the stragglers what they had: chocolate bars, cigarettes, and water. An ambulance came up to provide transport for the exhausted men, who piled in for the short ride to the bivouac area. Stragglers had been reporting in all night. Colonel Wayne himself had come in several hours ahead of Goldstein and Russo, half dragging his three surviving HQ staff members. He was filthy, dehydrated, and mad as hell.

The back of the ambulance was dark. It stank of excrement and something worse, which they all recognized, unsaid, as burnt human flesh. It was too dark to see the black pools on the floor, but the acrid smell of spilled blood was overpowering. Still, by the time they had driven for five minutes they were an unconscious heap that had to be physically dragged out of the fetid ambulance by orderlies at an assembly area near the newly-dug artillery emplacements.

XIX

Are you hurt kid?

My Western Auto days come to an end along with the East L.A. riots. The store does not burn, but it closes for a time while the neighborhood is cleaned up. The Boulevard gets a lot less business after the riot as people find other areas to shop. Meanwhile, I still need a job.

Hearing this, a kid named Steve tells me he works as a bagger at a liquor store in the industrial area of Montebello, one city over. The official job title is Bottle Boy, and it pays fifteen cents an hour more than Western Auto, making this a great career move. The store sits amid warehouses, truck depots, and factories making I don't know what. It is located in a strip mall along with a donut shop, a taco stand, and a storefront five and dime that seems to sell whatever the owners have been able to steal in bulk that week. It is a busy street and after each shift lets out a flood of guys from the warehouses and factories comes in for their daily pint of Smirnoff, quart of Colt, or six pack of Schlitz. It also sells a few grocery items: milk, eggs, candy, canned goods, and toilet paper. But these are extras: it's the liquor that draws them in.

Steve is a very mellow guy on account of smoking prodigious quantities of *yerba* every day, so we get along fine. He gets me in with the boss and this is a great job. The owner is a prosperous *Chicano* named Sam who has a string of liquor stores in busy locations around East L.A. and is seldom at our place, which seems to run on its own quite well. When he *is* around, like when we do a big inventory of all the stock, he turns out to be a really nice guy, the kind of boss who treats us all to lunch at the taco stand and makes us laugh with his dumb jokes while we work. And we work hard for him. Sam's Number 6 is a success.

The clerks have to be over twenty-one to sell liquor and two of Steve's older brothers hold those jobs. They are also nice guys and it makes for a relaxed work environment, maybe too relaxed. Because it is a job with a very special fringe benefit given that Steve and I are high school students – the presence of an unlimited supply and variety of liquor. Many big parties –

the wild, drinking, doping kind I go to, not the nice, popular-kid parties at Linidu's – benefit from my employment at Sam's. Steve and I start a little business on the side, taking orders and selling liquor out of the back of my old Mustang after school. We have no overhead so our prices are low, and we sell exclusively to high school students. Fridays are big for us as kids stock up for the weekend.

How did we feel about stealing from Sam, the boss who treated us all so well? We never discussed it, stealing presented no moral dilemma, only a practical one if we got caught. Sam was a nice guy, but he was still a boss. He must have been making a fortune, while we had very little. Steve and his brothers stole food for their parents, who needed the extra help. In our minds it came under the catch-all self-justification category of taking from the rich.

This wonderful job had only one major drawback – at least once every couple of months we got robbed, always at gunpoint. The robber needed to bring a gun because this was Montebello. If he walked in unarmed and demanded money, the way some guys rob banks nowadays, we would have laughed in his face then kicked his ass. So in a way a gun was a necessity, for his own protection. As a student I worked part time, so I put in six months before we finally got robbed on my shift. I was warned about this before starting at Sam's by Steve and his brothers, but still, the first time I stared down the barrel of a pistol I was more scared than I can ever remember.

The robberies fell into a predictable routine:

First, a lone guy or a pair of guys walk in when the store is otherwise empty, preferably late at night. He pulls out his gun and starts yelling for money, and we put our hands up. The clerk, who is usually stationed behind the counter, opens the cash register and hands over all the money, including a wad of ones with a twenty on top held together by a roach clip-like device that is wired to our silent alarm system. Eddie, one of Steve's brothers, invented this little gizmo himself. The robbers don't get much money because aside from the booby trapped stack, which is mostly ones, we slide all the other twenties, as they come in from customers, into a narrow opening in a safe set into the concrete floor. None of us has the combination. While the cops are hopefully rushing to the rescue we are always forced into the walk-in freezer, where the milk and beer are kept cold for customers. The handle of a broom that we have conveniently left nearby is jammed into the lock, securing us inside. We want robbers to have an easy time of it locking us in. The quicker they feel we are taken care of, unable to call the cops, the quicker they will leave.

This became such a routine that we actually kept old coats on hooks in the freezer just in case. Being locked inside the walk-in was not really much of a problem. If we got tired of waiting for the cops we quickly unloaded a shelf of milk onto the freezer floor and squeezed out through one of the service doors.

Despite the inherent risk in this situation we took it in stride. We knew that people who rob liquor stores are not real bright, and are nervous as hell, so there was always a chance of someone getting shot, if only by accident. But only once did I come close to getting killed on this job. Given the unending string of robberies the odds were, sooner or later, that something like this was going to happen.

It is my third robbery, and my last. One night, it is maybe midnight, I am in the store room in back, behind the freezer unit, stacking up a load of candy boxes to restock the shelves out front, and helping myself to a Fifth Avenue bar, my favorite. I am thinking how they always seem to taste better at work, where I don't have to pay for them.

When I walk out into the store itself I see a lone robber leaning across the counter, pointing a revolver across it, eager to take a handful of money from the clerk. Tonight it is Bill, Steve's oldest brother. I freeze. The gunman has not yet seen me. I don't want to startle him and get myself or Bill shot. I just want him to grab his money, lock us in the freezer, and go. I can see he has the silent-alarmed wad of money in his hand, so the clock is ticking on the cops' arrival. Tonight they are very quick; they must have been at the donut shop next door. In fact, that must be it because I do not recall hearing a squad car pull up. So the cops hoofed it over, dusting powdered sugar off their uniforms on the way. One of them is holding a shotgun, so unless he carries it when he goes in to buy a glazed, maybe they stopped at the squad car first. Now I can actually see it: an LAPD black-and-white is parked directly in front of the liquor store.

Suddenly, out of the corner of his eye, the robber sees the cops coming through the double glass doors out front. We already know he is a total fucking idiot, because he is robbing a liquor store with a police car parked out in front. Any doubts about his smarts are dispelled when he tries to run for it, right into the back of the store where we have, for this very reason, no exit. I happen to be in his way, holding stacked cases of candy bars, with the end of the Fifth Avenue bar sticking out of my mouth. He runs right into me, money in one hand, pistol in the other. I bounce back a step but don't otherwise move. I am trying not to provoke him, so I am being totally passive, but we are in the narrowest part of the passageway. Seeing he is going to have trouble getting over or around me, and feeling the cops closing in on him – they are right behind him, yelling like crazy for him to drop the gun – he makes his last bad choice of the night. He turns, pistol out in front. The two cops, Bill, and I, all yell "No!" The remains of the Fifth Avenue bar fly out of my mouth, splattering onto my candy boxes.

As his arm begins to rise both cops fire. They are standing five feet from him, and they really have no other choice. The sound is tremendous, deafening. The shotgun blast hits him full in the chest. From that distance the double 00 load is still in a tight pattern that strikes with such force that it throws the robber into me like they had swatted him with a bat. I am directly behind him and the full force of his body knocks me to the concrete floor, where I hit my head and am briefly stunned. The single bullet from the other cop's .38 also plows into the gunman's chest. The poor guy is dead before he lands on top of me, my candy boxes wedged between us.

I feel the heat and force and wind of the shotgun blast. I smell the gunpowder. Despite the close range stray pellets are everywhere – in the walls of the passageway, in the freezer case glass, and, I am sure, in me. When the cops finally roll the corpse off of me it's a bloody mess. Candy bars, shredded cardboard, the guy's entrails, and about a gallon of blood are smeared and sticking to both of us. I am unconscious and no one knows if I am dying along with the robber; it is one big, sticky, nauseating mess.

The cops are standing over me, hands covered in red, muttering, "Oh shit, are you hurt kid?"

I come back to earth but still do not feel a thing. All I can say is, "I don't know." But I remember thinking this is the first time I have seen a cop show any concern for me, and it took him blasting me with a shotgun to bring out his soft side. My dazed reaction convinces the cops I am mortally wounded; they radio frantically for help.

A single ambulance takes both me and the dumbass corpse to the hospital, lying next to each other on two gurneys. While the paramedics try to determine the extent of my injuries, with each bump in the road I see the dead guy's arm flopping out from under the bloody sheet they used to cover him. We pull up at the emergency room and nurses in operating scrubs cut open my clothes using those funny scissors that are blunted on the end. They peel off my shirt and then even my pants, and swab away the blood and muck, looking for wounds. This is difficult, because bits of various kinds of candy bars and wrappers are stuck to my face and neck by the powerful adhesive force of drying blood and entrails. It is amazing how much blood this guy had in him – and it is everywhere.

My parents are called to the hospital, but are only told, in that helpful, official manner of bureaucrats everywhere, that I have been shot by a police officer during a hold-up. With Dad driving hard and Mom increasingly hysterical, they arrive in record time. The nurse meeting them says that I have a nasty concussion, a half-dozen superficial pellet wounds, and that is it.

Despite this incident, it was still a great job, but I had to cave in to Mom's insistence that I quit.

XX

Teresita has a boyfriend?

For the next several weeks everyone is in a flurry over the robbery and my "being shot." Teresita plays Florence Nightingale. Not that I need any special care. My concussion results only in a small lump on the back of my head and a few days of nasty headaches. Still, it is a good excuse to spend time together. Her parents think she is being a good neighbor, we're just kids after all, but they give us access to each other like never before. I loll around in my bed and she ministers to me. Instead of English lessons, we now practice "French," and I am the pupil. Teresita is far more experienced in these matters than I thought.

We keep it from our parents because we're neighbors and our families have gotten close. As friends we have easy access, as *novios* we would be closely watched. Once I recover we mostly meet after school at the picnic benches behind the library, but sometimes we find a quiet moment at one of our houses. One such day she takes me to the room she shares with her three sisters, opens the dresser drawer belonging to Maria, the oldest, lifts out a couple of bras, and shows me where Maria hides her rubbers. She sneaks one and we try it out. Then another, and another...

—⌇w—

As Teresita's birthday approaches, plans are made for her *Quinceañera*. A traditional Mexican *Quinceañera* has a lot in common with a wedding. The girl wears a fancy white dress with a *mantilla* on her head, the parents spends money they can't afford renting a hall and feeding everybody in town – not to mention the beer and tequila – and it distracts the entire family from the misery of their real life for about six months. It is also mandatory, like a big Mexican wedding, no matter how poor the girl's family.

One day I notice Lupe, Teresita's mother, is over having a cup of coffee with Mom. They get real quiet when I pass by so I know they are either talking about me or about something they don't want Lupe's kids to hear of through me. Naturally I am curious. I wonder if they know about Teresita and me. Mom finally gets tired of my hovering and tells me to go next door and play with Teresita. Poor Mom doesn't realize that playing with Teresita is exactly what I want to do. She refuses to recognize that I am sixteen and growing up.

Lupe and Mom often have long conversations in the afternoon – about what, I am not sure; sometimes I think even they aren't sure. Lupe speaks a total of about ten words of English, so she yammers at Mom in Spanish, and Mom answers in Sicilian. With the hand gestures, the facial expressions, and the common problems of husbands, kids, and money, they seem to communicate just fine. Today they seem particularly conspiratorial. I begin to wonder if they have indeed learned something of Teresita and me.

Later that afternoon Mom wants to talk to me. She is not very subtle, which is a good thing. You always know what she wants. No guessing required.

"Honey," she says – thank God we're alone – "Lupe and I had a real nice talk today. She needs an escort for Teresita at her *Quinceañera*. Her boyfriend's a really poor Mexican and his family can't afford to rent him a tux. So Lupe asked me if I would ask you to be her escort. We'll rent a tux, although it's a lot of money, and the party will be fun for you. Besides, you'll be doing Lupe and Little Louie a big favor. If you don't do it, they're gonna have to pay for that boy to rent a tux, and you know this whole stupid thing is already costing them an arm and a leg. So, I told her I had to ask you, but I said I didn't think you'd be selfish about it. What do you think?"

"Teresita has a boyfriend?" is all I can manage to say. "Where is he, I've never seen the dude."

"I think he's been away, actually," Mom says plainly. "But he'll be back by the *Quinceañera*. He'll come and can dance with her and everything. You won't have to be her date or nothing, just her escort for the church part." This is getting better by the minute. "You can even invite a girl as a date."

"Oh, I get it."

"Then you'll do it?"

So this is how I find out that Teresita is also studying French with some other guy. It must be a correspondence course since he's "away," common code in polite company for locked up. Where else would he be, we don't have exchange students? I'm stuck with this commitment now, though, and I have not the slightest idea who to invite as my "date," other than Teresita.

I alternate between wanting to kill this new rival I have never seen, wanting to scream at Teresita for doing this to me, and wanting to forget it all and just grab her and kiss her. We keep seeing each other and she seems unchanged in her feelings for me, but I cannot get this rival out of my head. I am also totally unable to ask her about him.

The big day arrives. I am wearing a powder blue tuxedo with my head almost completely shaved, making for a nice look – a mixture of *cholo* and James Bond, I like to think. Teresita is wearing what can only be described as a First Communion dress – white, lacy, high neck, down to the ankle, a little lace doily *mantilla* for her head. We process into church like we're getting married. For some reason it's held at the little Mexican church way over in Los Nietos, across from the Southern Pacific tracks. The whole ceremony is in Spanish – this is post Vatican II and this parish went right away for turning the altar around and hearing Mass in their own tongue. We kneel at the altar steps and then it's over and on to the Los Nietos Veteran's Hall, where the party will be held.

While I have not managed to ask her about her boyfriend in the weeks leading up to this, now that we're in the back seat of her father's old boat of a Chevy being driven to the hall I can't put it off any longer. I didn't see him at the church, but then I don't know what he looks like, maybe I missed him because I was looking for a guy in an orange jumpsuit. Teresita seems immensely happy today, which makes her coal black eyes shine even more deeply than usual, but she remains totally mute on the topic of greatest interest to me. What the hell is she thinking I am going to say when she starts dancing with this guy who is just getting out of lock up in time for the party? Maybe she hasn't told him anything about me either and he is going to wonder who the hell *I* am. I have to find out.

"*Oye, Teresita,*" I start out, real softly so only she can hear. "*Dicen que tienes otro novio. Dime, ¿de verotas?*"

I am real quiet, and it is easier to ask in Spanish. Still, heads from the front seat turn at the sound of my voice trying to be quiet, so she answers in her best halting English, giving us a measure of privacy. "I have a boyfriend before, but he go away. So now I have you." She smiles so sweetly it almost melts my heart right onto her lap, but somehow it doesn't answer anything.

"But I heard he got out and he's going to be at the party, that he's your date tonight."

"Well, he *is* coming to the *fiesta*," she says with her wonderful lilt. "I make to invite him, but I am with you." She looks at me like she is saying *Remember what we do together?*

This statement of where she stands raises my temperature a couple of degrees but still somehow it doesn't add up. What am I supposed to do, cross examine her? *Chavala!* Instead I leave it alone. As we are pulling up to the Los Nietos Veteran's Hall, a dilapidated once-white hulk of cracked stucco that makes halls I have been to in Pico Rivera, Montebello, or East L.A. look posh, I have to ask: "So what was this dude in jail for?"

Little Louie, Teresita's father, comes around the car from the driver's side and opens the door for her. He takes her hand and as she steps out of the car, holding her dress up high to clear the sewer she needs to cross in order to get to the curb, she turns back over her shoulder and whispers to me: "*matando a un tipo.*" Then she turns back to her father and straightens her dress in an elaborate manner, clearly intended for my benefit.

I am left sitting in the car, a little stunned, as she walks off with her parents toward the Veteran's Hall. I think maybe I have not heard right. Quickly I go over it in my head: *tipo* is dude, ok so far. *Matando.* No way around it; the verb is *matar* – to kill. Great, he's a killer, he's also her ex, he's been locked up for God only knows how long without female company, and now, like she says, she's with me. I can't wait to meet him.

—⁓—

At the start of the party Little Louie dances with Teresita to the tune of a wild-ass *Mariachi* band. *Mariachis* are *always* wild, but these guys must have started drinking before the sun came up. They seem to have set a good example though, because the crowd, most of whom arrived before us as we dawdled at the church taking pictures, is already well on its way. Little Louie barely comes up to little Teresita's nose as she is wearing heels. She is absolutely beautiful, with her thick, wavy black hair held off her face by the doily, a real Spanish-style *mantilla*, and those immense, and immensely dark, luminous black eyes that are like empty holes that I want to fall into and never come out again.

Little Louie motions for me to take over from him on the dance floor. I walk up in front of everyone, afraid I am going to trip over my own feet and fall on my face. I dance slowly with Teresita around the floor, trying not to step on her new white shoes. We have practiced this part a couple of times in the past week, but I am no dancer. At least, holding her, I no longer fear falling over. Little Louie grabs Lupe and comes out to join us. We are all four dancing like they're my new in-laws. Mercifully, everyone else soon comes out onto the floor and we're just another couple. I could even start to enjoy this.

After the first dance, a tall, thin guy, *un flaquillo*, we would call him, a scarecrow, with scars from terrible acne, wearing someone else's suit, approaches. I can tell from Teresita's expression that this is Ray, her boyfriend. He asks me politely, even shyly, if he can have the next dance. I don't see any way to say no, given that he's a convicted murderer, but more than that, I don't feel threatened by him, he's acting so meek I almost feel sorry for him. That's confusing. I very much want to hate him.

After the one dance Ray formally returns Teresita to me and fades away. We start to dance again, but not for long. All her male relatives, and that is a lot of guys, have to dance with her. She'll be busy for an hour at least. I figure this is a good time to grab *un trago*. I am digging open a Schlitz with a very rusty beer can opener when I bump into somebody standing next to me at the drinks table and, of course, it is Ray. We have met, sort of, and I can't just walk off. So I introduce myself. We both say *"mucho gusto"* and he shakes my hand, the old fashioned way, none of the Bro' shakes popular among some of the guys who are trying to imitate Black Power culture. I figure maybe he's been away a long time.

"Órale, Thanks for taking care of Teresita," he says warmly. "Her folks asked, but we didn't have ten bucks to spare for the fuckin' tux." He seems sincere.

"No problem, *ése.*" I say easily, like ten dollar tuxedos are a way of life for me. Then, because I don't know what else to say, and also because I am a total idiot, I ask, "So how'd you end up killin' some *malnacido* motherfucker?"

Ray looks at me like his command of English is slipping for a minute. Then a small, evil smile comes to his face: "He danced with my lady."

As sweat starts to break out on my nearly shaved forehead, Ray reveals himself, the prick! A big smile crosses his face. "*Órale, pues*, Teresita told you I wasted somebody?"

I nod.

"*Chingado*! That's like her, *carnal*, she's just messin' witchu. *Puta madre.*"

"So what happened," I try not to squeak as I say this but I am not one hundred percent certain I succeed.

"I was down in *Mehico*," he says, enjoying this. "My grandmother broke her arm and needed some help so they sent me down for a few months to do shit work for her." Ray smiles. He's not a murderer, he's a boy scout gone to help his *abuelita* in *Michoacán*.

For the next hour I hardly see Teresita. She is taken up with her endless family, either dancing with the males or being preened and fussed over by the females. Once or twice I catch her eye and she smiles at me like she means it.

Ray and I drink another beer, then grab a bottle of tequila, a salt shaker, a cut-up lime, and work our way outside to the parking lot, where it is cooler and a lot quieter. After a while a twelve year old we call Webber comes out to puke at the curb but it is otherwise peaceful. Not for long. I start to hear yelling between songs, not the kind of yelling that happens when someone wants the band to play their favorite tune, but the kind where someone is promising to kick someone else's ass. Could be brothers, or cousins, or best friends – it's a party after all. Ray and I sit on the hood of Little Louie's big ol' Chevy, our feet propped on the massive chrome bumper, listening to the growing trouble inside. We drink tequila shots right from the bottle in the traditional way. First, you lick the back of your hand between your thumb and forefinger, then pour some salt on the wet area where it will stick. Suck on the salt, take a gulp of the tequila, and then bite into the lime for a chaser. Repeat until you run out of tequila, salt, lime, or until you can no longer remember the sequence.

"You want to go back inside, *ése*, see if we can help out Louie with *este puto borlote*?" I ask without much enthusiasm after several rounds.

"*Chale, no carnal*, I don't really want to get in the middle of that family when they start drinkin' and throwin' *chingazos*. They're fuckin' *loco*."

I have to agree. I have no stake in this fight. Unless Little Louie is getting his ass kicked. He's a nice guy. But he's got all his brothers with him, and I am wearing a nice, rented, $10 tux, and, come to think of it, neither Ray nor I are in any shape to move off this fender at the moment, so we keep sitting, drinking more shots.

Two squad cars from LAPD show up, Los Nietos doesn't have its own cops. They walk right by us sitting on the hood of the Chevy drinking tequila, I am sixteen and Ray, I have learned, is seventeen, but they don't even seem to notice. The music stops at once, like the cops killed it by their mere presence. A few moments later the guests start pouring outside and this party, like most I have been to, including weddings, other *Quinceañeras,* birthdays, baptisms, anniversary parties, and more than one funeral, ends early.

Carefully, like we are descending Mount Everest, we manage to get up off the fender as Teresita and her parents approach. I say a heartfelt tequila-enhanced good-bye to Ray, who reciprocates; we're now *carnales,* of the flesh, friends for life. This often happens to guys who drink tequila together. He gives Teresita a chaste kiss on the cheek before disappearing unsteadily into the crowd of departing partygoers. Teresita, her parents, and I, start to get into Little Louie's Chevy. Louie is seriously drunk, to the point that he either can't find his keys or he can't get them out of his pocket once he has located them. Hey, it's his party, it's costing him a fortune, so he should be able to get drunk, right?

Lupe doesn't drive so in spite of my impairment I open the front door, help Little Louie back out onto the sidewalk where I can get at him better, and start to dig around with my hand in his pants pockets to retrieve the car keys for him. He picks this moment to start being ticklish, accusing me of feeling him up, all sorts of stuff, in front of his wife and daughter and half his family, who are also in the parking lot, shit-faced, trying to locate their cars. I don't get offended, in fact I start playing along. I remember the old rhyme "one tequila, two tequilas, three tequilas, floor," and translate it for Little Louie, who thinks it is hilarious, even though it doesn't work at all in Spanish.

We get into a damn funny – to the two of us anyway – game of grab-ass out in the Veterans' Hall parking lot. I am laughing so hard I start to cry, and so does he. Then we both need to take a leak, right now, so we unzip and piss right on the asphalt, which inspires a half-dozen other party-goers to join us in a ragged line, pissing along the parking lot median. Eventually I get the keys away from him but as soon as I do and hold them up to show Teresita I did it, she snatches them away from me. Louie and I stand mute, like two kids caught with their hands in the cookie jar. Teresita and Lupe push us into the back seat, Lupe gets in front, and Teresita, who at barely fifteen has no license, gets behind the wheel.

We must make quite a site with little Teresita in her white dress, her head covered by a flowing *mantilla*, the only part of her that would be visible above the door, driving that big ol' Chevy while her dad and I are still playing grab-ass in the back seat. But at least we get home in one piece.

XXI

Only in the leg, man.

T he one thing my school excelled at was football. A few years before my time we were named the top high school team in the country after a 13-0 season. We could pack in ten thousand people to see a home game on Friday night. I played because, like the school, it was the one thing I was good at. I could block, tackle, and run. My nearsightedness didn't really matter. I only needed to see the color each side was wearing. I loved the physical contact, "sticking" the other guy, the uniforms, the gear, and the attention. In fall, football was my top reason for showing up at school: *miss school, miss the game*, was one of our most effective high school rules. But football was a contact sport in more ways than one.

Physically, we were a small team, far smaller than the teams we played – mostly Black kids from South Central. Being small was a big disadvantage in this game of muscle and force, but it was what you got when most of the players were *Chicano*. Coach McKee liked to say: "I can always find a fast Mexican to carry the ball, what I really need is some big Paddies or Russians to block." Years earlier we were promoted out of our local league. Other than pre-season tune-up games, we largely stopped playing other Brown teams. Instead we went up against the big, tough Black schools in the ghetto. That is how we thought of it – they lived in the ghetto, while we lived. . .I don't know, it was my home. To make up for the size disadvantage they were stuck with, our coaches followed Vince Lombardi's creed: *Winning isn't everything, it's the only thing*. The path to victory was paved with extreme mental and physical toughness. So, in preparation for the season we worked ourselves to an emotional and physical edge that would impress a Navy SEAL. We ran, we lifted, we stretched, we hit, and we ran some more. It was weeks before we even saw a football. We built muscle and we built speed.

It got a little out of hand. Like the drill where we paired up with another guy and carried him on our back as we ran up and down the stadium bleachers. Up was hard, but down was terrifying. If a knee failed to hold our combined 350 to 400 pounds two guys tumbled down the steps. Once we finished a circuit, we traded places and did it again.

Practices were tough but even during games our rules of engagement set us apart from our opponents. If we were hurt we walked off the field. No one was helped off – except once when Trinny Segura broke his femur, which was really an exception that had to be made, because he was unconscious. We never sat on the bench; when not playing we stood on the sideline and cheered on our teammates. We never took our helmets off – I bent that rule once, during a time out, when I took off my helmet to scratch my head, and a guy from the other team walked up and punched me, breaking my nose. We never relaxed during time-outs – while the other team was drinking water we did loud, enthusiastic calisthenics. This *did* intimidate opponents, especially in the fourth quarter.

By tradition the first game of the pre-season was always against St. Peter's, the local Catholic school where Colleen and Linda were students. Billed as a friendly scrimmage among neighbors, it was in fact an organized slaughter. I don't know why St. Peter's even agreed to play us. We tore them up, they never got on the scoreboard, and we left them broken and bleeding before their real season even began.

On the first defensive play from scrimmage during our St. Peter's game my sophomore year I line up against the center and realize he is not wearing a cage. As soon as he moves to snap the ball my forearm flies up into his face, between the brow of his helmet and his little chin bar, smashing his nose. He fumbles, we recover, and I get to play the rest of the game against the second string center, with his teammate's blood on my arm. It doesn't get any better than this.

In our homecoming game against a solid Black team from Compton, all our training and conditioning pays off and our aggressive pursuit is impeccable:

we gang-tackle the ball-carrier at the line of scrimmage. Three or four guys hit him at once as he tries to make it around end on a failed sweep. When the pile clears he doesn't get up. After a few minutes of impatient delay, his mother running down from the stands screaming, an ambulance is called. The wait is killing us, we want to play. Coach McKee, his patience gone, grabs a shovel from the equipment shed and marches out onto the field: "Bury him here and let's get on with the game!" he yells. We all laugh.

Late in the same game we are up by three when Jorge Arras, our quarterback, throws a rare bad pass that is intercepted. The defensive back has speed and an angle on the sideline that takes him past Jorge, the last possible tackler. The crowd is throbbing with anger on our side and excitement on the far side of the field. From my position on the offensive line all I can do is watch as it looks like we are going to lose our lead in the fourth quarter, something that has not happened in at least five years. Then suddenly the ball carrier goes down like a rock. Guys on the field are asking what happened since no one was around when he crumpled. He is writhing on the ground, maybe a torn Achilles tendon, someone suggests, but then where did all that blood come from.

I notice a commotion along the sideline where they saw the gun and heard the crack of a shot. We missed it out on the field. Some *cholo* in a varsity jacket, enjoying the homecoming privilege of a former player to stand on the sideline with the team, decided to make the tackle we all missed and shot the ball-carrier as he ran by only a few feet away. "But only in the leg, man" he tells the cops, and later the newspaper, like he showed real restraint. The rulebook is silent on this situation. If one of the players had fired the shot, then you would have unsportsmanlike conduct at the very least. But this was a fan. The Compton defensive back probably would have scored but who knows, he had thirty yards to go and he could have fumbled, or dropped dead from a heart attack, an act of God. In the end the referees decide to call the game. They can guess the shooter is not the only fan who is carrying. Since we are ahead at that moment we win.

The coaches are committed to winning at any cost. After a game we lose by one point in the closing seconds, to a team that outweighed us by fifty pounds a man on the front line, a game that I played every minute of, offense, defense, special teams, the works, the coaches line us up behind the gym. The fans, the cheerleaders, everyone has gone home except us – It is late Friday night and we are spent.

The coaches, however, are full of a fury they reserve for us on the rare occasion of a loss. They come down the line insulting each of us in turn and backing up their words with a kick in the behind or a smack on the helmet hard enough to make ears ring. We run punishment sprints for forty-five minutes, until most of us are puking and dragging. Then they line us up again and tell us that we have another thirty minutes of sprints to run and does anyone want to quit? I realize right then that I do in fact want to quit. I love the game, but not this bullshit. The thought unsettles me. Football is all I have to hang on to.

Even the injured do not escape the coaches' wrath. While recovering from my broken nose, I spend two weeks in a special PE class for injured athletes. We are not treated like wounded heroes, more like prisoners of war held by people who have not heard of the Geneva Convention. The coaches view us as malingerers despite the bandages, stitches, casts, and sets of raccoon eyes. One afternoon, we are out next to the pool. It is hot and the guys are looking forward to swimming for PE – except for me, since I can't swim. The coach who has drawn this duty today is "The Turtle," because he has no neck.

The Turtle is pissed off about something, or maybe that is just his way of showing he cares. In the blistering heat he has us get into the push-up position around the pool and then hold it for an eternity. This is not too hard, since I have been doing hundreds of push-ups daily for months, although the pebbly non-slip surface digs into my hands, and the concrete is blazingly hot. Next to me is Steve Andreas, who is recovering from a broken ankle. This is his first day back on the road to active duty. He whispers to me – "Órale, I thought we were going to the plunge. My leg is killing me, how long is The Turtle going to keep us up here?"

"Tell him man, remind him about your ankle and he'll let you off," I offer. Bad advice, it turns out.

"Coach," Steve calls out to The Turtle and politely says something about his recently-broken ankle. The Turtle strides over without a moment's hesitation and kicks Steve in the gut. This throws him off balance so he falls over the edge into the pool beside him. With his wind knocked out he starts to drown. "Don't you ever jawbone me when you're in the position," The Turtle says as a couple guys pull Steve out.

—ᴍ—

One day near the end of practice a *cholo* walks across the field smoking a cigarette. The coaches yell at him to put it out and to get the hell off their field.
We're all watching, so what is he going to do? He flips them off. Bad decision.
They chase him down and drag him into the gym office. Practice is now over
for sure so we head in for showers. From the coaches' office I can hear yelling and then what sounds like someone throwing furniture around the room.
Pretty soon Coach Mazzoff, the meanest bastard of them all, one part Russian,
three parts Hulk Hogan, comes out wearing a sick smile and that special swag-
ger he affects when he has some particular evil in mind. He grabs a few towels
and heads back to the office. As he slips inside he says with a smirk – "He
attacked us." Later, while I am dressing, I see the bloody towels in the hamper.

Two days later a fire nearly burns the gym down. Someone has thrown a
Molotov Cocktail through the window into the coaches' office. Only the building's cinder block construction saves it. So it goes, tit for tat.

The game I love has become just another place to catch shit. The coaches,
who never have a positive word for anyone until and unless the championship
is won, the punishing physical regimen, the abuse, and the wild ass games,
which sometimes end in free-for-all brawls, including the fans, it all starts to get
to me. It is not fun anymore.

The coaches are sadists, but they are not unusual. From junior high on,
nearly every teacher has a large wooden paddle like a cricket bat displayed
prominently by his or her desk and uses it to enforce order. Swats, they're
called. This is how the general student body is treated, so it is only a small step
to the greater discipline and bizarre rituals in use with the athletes.

One September, at a team meeting, we settle down for game films from the
previous season. Except the first thing up is not a game film. It is grainy, low
quality porn: a naked Black guy with a dick that would not look amiss on a race
horse is in the center of the picture, getting a blow job from two blondes. The
room goes quiet. After about three minutes of this the sequence ends and they
switch to the actual game film, "Now that we have your attention," the Turtle
says with a sneer.

Later that year we play a team in South L.A., what we used to call Watts.
They are a rival for the C.I.F. championship and we beat them last year at home

due to a questionable call that went our way. This year we have fights before and during the game, as usual, and we expect worse when it's over, especially if we win again. Near the end we are ahead. It's been a hell of a game. Close, back and forth, hard-hitting on every play; so many fights that the refs have threatened to stop the game if the coaches don't get control of their players. But we are wild dogs after raw meat, so the threat does little good.

Then it looks like we have it locked up – less than two minutes to play, we're ahead by six, we have the ball – and the home-town crowd is getting uglier by the minute. They are throwing shit at our sideline, bottles, rocks, that sort of thing. Coach Mazzoff looks worried. It takes me a moment to realize this since I have never before seen him express any emotion quite so human. No one has forgotten the game where one of our people shot an opposing player. This is a community whose fans are at least as well-armed as ours.

Word is passed that when the game ends we are not to go to midfield for the traditional handshake with the opposing team. We are to keep our helmets on, grab our gear and run – not walk – for the bus, which will have the engine running. Anticipating such a scene we arrived for the game in uniform, so we don't need to enter their ratty gym to shower and change.

At the closing horn all hell breaks loose in the stands and we, both players and coaches, run for our lives. None of our fans was dumb enough to come watch this game, and we left the band and cheerleaders at home for their own safety. We pile aboard and fold ourselves into our seats using good duck-and-cover technique as the crowd comes after us.

Rocks ding off the sides of the bus. The driver doesn't need to be told to get the hell out of Dodge but as we race along the back of the stadium for the safety of the nearby boulevard someone throws a big scrap of lumber at us, a nice six-foot-long four-by-four. It flies like a javelin right through the windshield, misses the driver, but nearly causes us to crash anyway as he freaks out and starts over-steering.

Only when we are safely out of range, approaching the freeway, do we all breathe a little easier, raise our heads, dust the broken glass off the driver and the front rows of players, remove the four-by-four from where it hangs half in and half out of the windshield, and kick back for the ride home. No one speaks. Amazingly, despite all that has happened, the whistling of the wind and traffic noise coming in through the gap in the windshield, and the fact that I am wearing a filthy, sweaty uniform and pads, I fall asleep.

—⚒—

After two years of the game as we played it I'd had enough. The abuse, or discipline, whatever you want to call it, got to be too much for me. I knew I needed out, but I couldn't just walk away. So I told Head Coach McKee that I had to work after school, my family needed the money. It happened to be true. I left the team and with it a way of life.

This did not end up being a positive move. To my former teammates I became invisible; I ceased to be a part of the team in every sense. Without the rule "miss school, miss the game," I started to cut class. Then I got myself thrown out of English and into study hall, where I met The Truly Bad Kids and decided I must be one too. We cut some more school. We did things during school hours that were usually reserved for weekends, but no one seemed to notice or care. No one called home to tell Mom I had been missing a large chunk of the school day for the past three weeks, and no parental note was required to return after an absence. The school didn't care anymore than we did.

XXII

Defilin' da house a God.

Here is a story I used to hear the grown-ups tell. Old *Abuelito Tomás* walks down the Boulevard with a bucket full of live crabs. He sets the bucket down on the sidewalk so he can shop for produce at a stand. A passerby asks – "*Señor*, aren't you afraid those crabs are going to escape?"

"No way, those are East L.A. crabs. If one of them tries to get out, the others will pull him back down."

This is how I end up in study hall. I have this *gabacho* English teacher, Mr. Seaman, who thinks he is too cool. He has longish hair, wears mod shirts with bellbottoms, and grows mutton chop sideburns like the later Elvis, but he's still Anglo and too old and it doesn't work. One day Mr. Seaman decides to play some rock music to help us appreciate it as poetry. I like this idea; it has never occurred to me that songs are really just poetry set to music. He plays *Lucy in the Skies with Diamonds* and then asks us to interpret it. As I said, I like this idea, so, very uncharacteristically, my hand goes up and I say: "It's about dropping acid. LSD is Lucy – Skies – Diamonds." I am proud of myself, but Mr. Seaman seems to think I am pulling something.

"This is not about drugs, this is about imagery. . ."

"Uh, it's about an acid trip." Now I am a music critic, not to be denied. The other kids are giggling, enjoying the show.

Mr. Seaman does not like the laughing, and he is not going to let some dumbass kid argue with him. "That is the stupidest thing I have heard in a long time," he says, putting an end to the matter, at least in his mind. He should not have said this. Everyone is looking at me because they know, even if Mr. Seaman does not, that I have to respond. He has practically mad-dogged me, chose me on right in class!

I should point out that Mr. Seaman has no fingers on one hand. The story is that he was tuning up his lawnmower a while back and had an accident. This is an important detail because, in response to his insult, I say, "At least I'm not stupid enough to put my hand under a lawnmower while it's running." And that is my last day in English and is how I get to be in study hall with The Truly Bad Kids for the rest of the semester.

One of those kids is Art Bolero. He is one of a kind, a very bad kind. He is short, built like a fire plug, has greased black hair, and is perpetually looking for trouble. More than looking, he is a prospector mining for trouble, an explorer seeking landfall at the next big fight. I imagine at least once he really found it, because he has a glass eye, which only adds to his badass rep. Art is a bully. He is also a member in good standing of a local social club known as the Pico Boys. They have jackets, tattoos, and a bad attitude toward life. Art likes to pick on weak kids; it must make him feel tough. We are destined to cross.

Before school one day I see a group of kids, the usual circle watching a fight, and in the middle of it is Art, trying to get something going with a weak little Paddy named Walkin. You know the kind of kid who has never lost his baby fat and is condemned forever to look twelve years old? That's Walkin. I don't especially know him or care about him, although I have gone to school with him for ten years. Mostly, it just pisses me off when someone pulls that crap, so I step in and say, "If you are looking for *chingazos*, *ése*, try me. *Aquí estoy.*"

He gives me that look, the one that says, "*¿Y qué?*" It's a challenge right back at me. Well, pretty soon we are both in the vice principal's office. Mr. Balenciaga wants us to "put this behind us," but he knows as well as we do that we will not, that it is not our way to shake hands and move on. He is just going through the motions and so are we.

Like it or not, Art and I are going to have study hall together, so we are going to have to ignore each other, I figure, in order to get through each day.

But it doesn't quite work out that way. Over the next few weeks we have so many run-ins that some of The Truly Bad Kids are starting to say that if Art and I are going to fight so much we might as well get married.

Study hall is presided over by a teacher who is never named, and whom I cannot remember very clearly. He usually spends the period reading the newspaper. His only rule is "don't bug me." So long as we keep reasonably quiet this teacher is OK with whatever we do. For a while we play poker. But we soon discover that the easiest way to be really quiet is to leave the classroom, and the campus, altogether.

The Truly Bad Kids include three guys I begin to hang out with on these trips off campus: Steve, Arturo, and Billy. Steve and Arturo are Brown, *cholos* with impressive tattoos and long histories of troublemaking. Billy is Russian, tall and blonde, a drinker and a fighter. That any of them was still in school, even study hall, is remarkable. I have study hall for just the one period – English. These guys have study hall for four or five periods, they basically live there. Steve, Arturo, and Billy, for all their faults, are actually pretty nice guys, at least to me. My reputation as "the guy who nearly killed the Marine," probably doesn't hurt. So is the fact that I stand up to Art Bolero, who everyone else seems to give plenty of room because of his Pico Boys connection. It's not that I lack a full appreciation for what it means to cross a member of a street gang. I do, it's just that I don't give a shit.

Study hall has several good-looking and none-too-bright girls and we spend a lot of time trying to get in their pants. During study hall, out in the parking lot, or at someone's house, we have sex, drugs, and rock-n-roll all around. My single period with The Truly Bad Kids doesn't seem long enough to do all the stuff we want to do, so I start cutting additional classes to make an afternoon of it.

Study hall is located away from the rest of the school, on our Continuation campus – now called Ruben Salazar High School – across from the parking lot, which makes the coming and going a lot easier, if anyone cares to check on us, which they do not. Study hall is actually not so bad. It isn't school, no books or lessons; it offers an opportunity to make new friends, which I need; and it has its share of surprises, like the day Arturo suggests we break into Art Bolero's car when we see it in the parking lot. We take some eight track tapes and, in a really nice touch, Arturo pisses on the front seat before we leave. Art might have guessed it was us, but we play innocent and he had no way of knowing for sure. He has plenty of other enemies. Still, this incident adds to the strain between my group of The Truly Bad Kids and his much larger gang. It is a feud that starts in study hall and just gets uglier.

Art drops out of school, which at this point is only a formality. We have not seen him in study hall for weeks. He leaves with a really bad taste in his mouth, so one afternoon he returns to campus with some friends, carrying lengths of heavy-gauge winch chains. They walk into random classrooms throughout the school swinging these around their heads, lasso style, doing some real damage to people and property. Windows get broken, lab equipment is smashed, and people get hurt. The teachers rally, chasing Art and his pals across campus. I am coming out of the gym, late for my next class, when I see my favorite Spanish teacher, beautiful Miss Luna, chasing Art Bolero across the quad.

It's an odd sight, because Art is in such bad physical shape he can barely keep ahead of her, even though she is wearing a tight skirt and high heels. It is also a very compelling sight because, in a word, Miss Luna is hot. She is the only female teacher under twenty-five, and she drives a little Fiat sports car with the top down and her hair tied up in a kerchief like a movie star. She treats me like I am somebody you can talk to, a real person, a guy even. She laughs; she wants to know about our loves, our sports, and our families. She is hands down the best and most popular teacher at school. So, of course, I want to help when she pants – "Stop him," and points at Art. Frankly, I can't believe my luck. I have been given permission by a really hot teacher to beat the living crap out of a kid I hate. Context is everything.

I chase Art down from behind, which is not difficult, he has been running for a while. I throw him to the ground, and start pounding. He is so winded all he can do is gasp: "Pico Boys are going to kick your *puta* ass."

To which I respond, "*A ver*, I am kicking yours right now, asshole." And keep wailing on him. Eventually a couple of the coaches come and actually thank me for my efforts before they yank Art to his feet and take him over to the main office. Miss Luna gives me a look that I spend the rest of the day trying to convince myself means she thinks *I'm* hot.

I go to my locker to get stuff for class. Inside I find someone has already slipped a long folding hunting knife through the air vent. I take this to mean I have a friend who is trying to warn me that I need to watch my back. I drop the closed knife into my pants pocket. I also take from the locker a slender chain, not the big heavy type Art and his boys have just used to tear the flesh off a kid's arm and to break a girl's jaw. Mine is more the kind of thing you wrap around your fist, a poor man's brass knuckles. Still, it is contraband. Just then Mr. Balenciaga walks up and says he and the cops want to talk to me. Talking to Mr. Balenciaga has never been a good thing in my life and it takes me a minute to realize that in this matter I am a witness or something, but not a suspect.

All the kids around my locker catcall and make rude noises, like we all do when someone is in trouble, only this time, I am not. We walk into the school office where I see the cops with Art, all puffy and bloody from the pounding I gave him, his hands cuffed behind his back. I realize I have the knife and the chain – weapons – in my own pocket and I get worried all over again. But Miss Luna is there thanking me, making me feel older and cooler.

It is amazing how giving someone a beating can be either a bad thing or a good thing depending on who asks you to do it.

A few weeks later we have a minimum day and my friends, the new ones, The Truly Bad Kids from study hall, plus Ben and Mario from the old days – decide to walk over to the Alpha Beta to get a Coke. On our way to the market we walk along the main street on the Rivera side of town, Passons Blvd, and past our parish church – St. Marianne de Paredes. As we pass the church we cross ourselves like good Catholics. Then we see Art and his Pico Boys across the street.

They have already been to the market and start heaving their half-empty soda bottles at us across the two lanes of intervening traffic. We are not looking for a fight, but we live by one simple, inviolable rule: Do not let anyone challenge you and get away with it. It is only going to encourage him to move from small challenge to greater challenge to confrontation to humiliation. Better to die on your feet than to live on your knees, someone once said. Maybe he lived in a neighborhood like mine.

We run as one into the street; the little knot from Pico meeting us halfway. This means we have our *chingazos* right in the middle of the street, stopping traffic. Drivers wave their fists and honk their horns but we are too busy to bother with the complaints of motorists right now. As punches and kicks are thrown, yells and curses mix with squealing brakes and honking horns. Then, all at once we respond to a strange presence with an instant and universal hush. I look up from my position half way down on the street trying to grab the leg of a boot that keeps kicking me, when I see the cause of the interruption: old Father Treble. Shit!

He is the last of the old Irish priests at St. Marianne's. He must be seventy, with wisps of white hair around his temples, but he is thin, wiry, and ornery as hell. When he is gone they will turn the altar around, not before. Then, we will get Mass in English and Spanish rather than Latin, and the bishop will assign a *Chicano* priest who can "relate" better to us. We'll get Vatican II, like they have over in Los Nietos and apparently the rest of the world. But right now what we have is the Old Testament, in the person of Father Treble, carrying a baseball bat, and he is not looking for a pick-up game.

We shake ourselves loose from each other and stand, each of us breathing hard and looking down, in total silence and fear at what the old priest is going to do. We have all been to confession with him, and have suffered his displeasure with our sins, which is sometimes shouted out loudly enough to violate the sanctity of the confessional. We have all seen him stop in the middle of Mass to name a person who has walked in late. We have endured his stern lectures on the temptations of sex when caught daydreaming or staring at a nice-looking girl in Catechism class. So we are afraid, alright.

He raises his voice enough to be heard, but no more, so we have to lean a little ways forward to catch what he is saying.

"Defilin' da house a God. . ." he gestures up toward the church with the bat, like Babe Ruth pointing to left field. "Sinnin'. . ." and then "Get da hell outta 'ear or I'll crack yer mizrable skulls open." This intervention breaks off the fight for the moment but doesn't end the war. We go our separate ways, and quickly. As we leave I turn around in time to see old Father Treble directing traffic with his bat, trying to restore order to a messy world, at least in front of his church.

Ben, Mario and I tell the rest of our old buddies, Dave, and Gilberto, what is going on, but they have their own troubles and all we can do is watch out for each other when the opportunity presents itself. It doesn't occur to us that we might be viewed as a sort of Rivera-side gang ourselves.

The next day we learn that Miss Luna has totaled her little sports car on the 405. With her dead I have one less reason to go to school, on a growing list.

XXIII

That ain't the army I signed up for.

Russo lay where the ambulance had dumped him and Goldie and the rest of their little group the night before. They had unloaded, found a nice soft piece of ground nearby, and collapsed right there. Now he awoke to the sound of artillery being fired directly over his head. He found himself lying on his back, a stiff arm thrown up over his eyes. He turned over, cursing as he rolled on top of his rifle, and propped himself up on one arm. Goldie was staggering to his feet a few yards away, carelessly unzipping and then relieving himself right on the open ground where he had slept. Russo followed suit. Then they gathered up their weapons and gear and joined a growing wave of worn out, disheveled men headed toward what they hoped would be a chow line. They didn't speak, couldn't really, as the big howitzers, just twenty yards behind them, hurled volley after volley aloft. The smell of cordite quickly became choking thick so they moved a little faster.

He was not quite sure where he was, or for that matter how he had gotten there, but the presence of friendly artillery was more than welcome despite the earsplitting sound and the flashing fingers of fire reaching overhead to scorch the air as the heavy 155MM shells headed out. Inaccurate German counterbattery fire soon began to answer, the shells landing far enough away to allow the exhausted men to pursue a meal, but not far enough to be entirely ignored.

"Dat's enough ta wake da dead," he yelled, indicating the row of working howitzers, as they approached a smoking chow wagon, finally far enough from the artillery to be heard if they yelled.

Goldie leaned close, "One helluva 'larm clock," he smiled, his face cracking in age lines that he was too young for, as he shrugged back in the direction of the big guns.

One by one, orphan troops from the battalion's various companies got chow. It was a kind of chili stew – thick, greasy, more beans than meat, but burning hot and welcome for breakfast, or was it lunch? Once they had a mess plate in hand they slipped over a small hill to avoid the worst of the noise. Russo and Goldie sat among a group of some twenty strangers eyeing each other warily like stray dogs taken to the same pound, as if to ask, "Where the hell did you come from?"

Goldie, as usual, broke the tension. "So, where the fuck are we?" he asked, looking around. A few hundred yards away they saw what looked like a bombed-out city, except the buildings were made of stone and looked incredibly old.

"Some shithole called Sbeitla," was the answer from a PFC with a stiff new splint and bandage over his right hand that made it hard to eat. More tension, more silence followed. His name was McIntyre, Mac. He had been with them through the long awful walk from the *wadi*, but he had hardly spoken ten words the whole time. Mac was a rifleman from Able company so Russo knew him only by his unit insignia. No one had noticed until now that he had a broken arm. The medics must have set it while the others slept.

"Them's ancient ruins, from Roman times, I read somewhere," another voice offered.

Then, "Sbeitla?" another stranger perked up. "That must be thirty-five miles from the Dj, I saw it on a map!" The tense silence continued as they sat and ate, listening to the artillery, both incoming and outbound.

"Yeah, I *thought* it was a helluva long walk," came an unidentified voice.

At this crack Russo gave an involuntarily chortle, his shoulders rising and falling once, jerkily, as he shook his head, still chewing. It just struck him as a funny thing to say. Then, slowly, others began to giggle, first one or two, hiding their faces in their sleeves while they continued chewing, until the contagion spread to the whole bedraggled group. They laughed like madmen, like drunks, tears streaming from their eyes, food dribbling from their mouths.

"I *thought* it was a helluva long walk," and "Thirty-five fuckin' miles, can you believe that!" they repeated. If they began to recover, they only needed to catch one another's eye to begin again. They laughed and shook their heads in disbelief, reborn as warriors in that moment of hysteria.

Just then Sarge appeared on the crest of the hill, his left forearm wrapped in a dirty bandage, the Thompson cradled in his right. He stopped and looked hard at the men, bloodied, filthy, exhausted, and for all that giggling like a pack of school girls. When they saw Sarge even those who didn't know him stopped their laughing and looked up at him, suddenly serious. All except Goldie, who tried but only managed to partially suppress his fit.

Sarge's face had been frozen somewhere between exhaustion and anger when he first appeared above them, like Moses come from the Mountain, carrying a sub machine gun. Then, he relaxed.

"Crazy motherfuckers," he said without apparent malice. "We move out in five." He must have figured that people who could laugh after what they had been through were just crazy enough to follow him. They were still soldiers, not beaten, still able to follow orders.

Sbeitla was an ancient town, dating at least to the Romans. It had been a Byzantine settlement until it was sacked by the Caliph in 647AD, and it had since survived for nearly thirteen hundred years without a comparable disaster. A small, poor, mud-brick farming community consisting mostly of one long, winding, unpaved main street set in an undulating plain; it was adjacent to one of the largest Roman archeological sites in North Africa. In more peaceful times archeologists and rich tourists had traveled to admire its tiled floors and partially standing temples. This day, however, its time was up. Stukas rained bombs on it, German artillery pounded it, and now a disorganized American army tore it limb from limb while passing through in an increasingly panicked retreat.

Sarge informed the group as they walked streets choked with civilian and military traffic – moving and dead – that they were now part of his squad, whatever the hell platoon or company they came from, because those units most likely didn't exist anymore.

"Besides," he said, "it's just as easy to fight in one unit as another."

The Germans were probing American defenses around the edges; they did not seem to know that the center had collapsed. Had they pushed through, following the retreating troops, they could have ended the battle that day. Timidity, lack of fuel, or overconfidence led them to slow down, giving the Americans a chance to regroup or at least to escape. It wasn't much of a respite, and more misery was still to come, but for the moment the *Wehrmacht* had slowed its advance, a godsend for the Americans.

The withdrawal was chaos, a mad rabble in headlong retreat. A young officer drove up to a fuel depot, passing Sarge's squad, and fired pistol shots into a dozen fifty-five gallon diesel drums. Then he hopped back into his jeep and drove off, toward the rear. He was followed moments later by a platoon of tankers, led by an even younger officer, headed in the opposite direction, toward the advancing Germans. They must have passed the first officer less than a hundred yards up the road. They cursed heroically and worked frantically to salvage every drop of fuel as it poured into the sand, loaded what they could save into their thirsty Stuart's, then headed out to join the rear-guard fight.

As the withdrawal continued, the fleeing men's stories of disaster grew desperate. Sarge, leading his men against the tide of retreat, toward the enemy, was stopped by a small group of disheveled soldiers, without rifle or helmet, who grabbed him, eyes wide, and screamed "Run, run, they're right behind me!"

Sarge pushed them away like beggar children and kept moving forward. "Never believe a straggler or a casualty," he yelled back over his shoulder to the men. "These mutts think Rommel himself is chasing them."

"Maybe he is," Russo whispered to Goldstein. Goldie raised an acknowledging eyebrow.

They were forced to dodge American trucks escaping three abreast down the narrow street. Russo looked at the beat up deuce-and-a-half's like a lovesick schoolboy gaping at his sweetheart's picture. One fleeing truck nearly lost control at a sharp turn and clipped the edge of a house. It kept going as half a dozen Arab women and girls raced out into the street, like rice pouring out of a torn sack, screaming revenge.

"Hey Sarge," Mac piped up. "Where the fuck we headin', if you don' mind my askin'? Seems the party's in the other direction."

Sarge stopped, turning around to face his little group. "That," he said with a look of disgust, pointing with the Thompson held in his good hand toward an overloaded jeep careering toward the rear, "That ain't the army I signed up for. I came over here to kill Krauts, not to run from 'em. I figure there has got to be something left of the fightin' army up ahead, the way them tankers headed."

He paused and looked at the gaunt faces of his men. "Anybody wants to run, go on, you got plenty'a company. But I'm leadin' this group of *soldiers* back to the front, wherever the hell it is."

With that he turned and walked off, leaving the rest of them staring at each other, feeling suddenly foolish and lost. The Army never gave soldiers a choice about where they were going or what they were going to do when they got there. The sudden freedom was unnerving. So were the consequences of their choice.

They knew that twenty riflemen were not going to make a difference against an endless column of German Tiger tanks. They also knew that they had a much greater chance of staying alive if they did just as Sarge suggested and ran for it, like everyone else. But they were still soldiers: they had been whipped once and didn't care for it, much less for the prospect of it happening again. Most important of all, they discovered, through their exhaustion, that they were mad, fighting mad. Mad at the Germans, of course, and mad at the whole of North Africa for being such a fucked up place. But mostly they were mad at the Army, their army, for being in retreat, for getting beat; they were embarrassed. All the talk about the Army's proud traditions, the grand victories of the past, the inherent superiority of the American fighting man, it all rang false as they beheld a full division in headlong retreat.

So they stood, common sense and self-preservation fighting within each man's breast with his anger. Then Mac called out, "Hey Sarge," and he stopped and turned again to look at them. "We're gonna need a lot more ammo if we're gonna kill all them Krauts."

Sarge pondered that for a moment then looked about. "Well, there's plenty of ordnance lying around, look for something we can use" he replied, indicating crates stacked behind an abandoned stockpile of mortar shells. The men began to search, looking around like kids on an Easter egg hunt, turning up food, water, medical supplies, weapons and ammo in the wreckage and refuse of a retreating army.

"Hey, take a look at dis," Russo yelled to the group, holding up a dozen pairs of those ladies stockings that they had heard made the crossing with them. "They made it all the way to the front."

"Not my color," Goldie replied, and the group laughed again. "Besides," he added, "yesterday at this time this was the *rear.*"

A group of stragglers crossed their path on its way toward safety. The squad descended upon them, stripping them of everything they might need to fight, and doing it with more bravado and scorn than any of them would have thought he possessed.

"You won't need that B.A.R. where you're headed," Goldie told a blank-faced private as he lifted the man's weapon from his unresisting grasp and relieved him of his full ammo bandoliers. He patted him down for rations and found a pack of cigarettes.

"Goldie, dis is fuckin' nuts," Russo said later as they ransacked a house whose wall had been torn open by a shell. "We coulda just walked outta here, like da rest a dem."

"Yeah, we coulda." Goldie replied simply, lifting a hunk of moldy cheese off a tabletop in an adjacent courtyard and brushing the dirt away from its surface. "But we didn't."

XXIV

I fought them off.

I am now a senior. Ernie has been dead for nearly a year. I can walk by former football teammates who do not even notice me. Teresita has moved back to Mexico with her family. I get a card from her at Christmas but that is not much to go on. My hair is long, bushy, dirty, and wild. I don't have a girlfriend to speak of. Ben dropped out last summer and went into the Marines, leaving Colleen grieving. My only friends are The Truly Bad Kids: Steve, Arturo, and Billy, and older guys I meet hanging out with them on the weekends. We're still stealing, fighting, and always getting wasted; the usual trio. I just go along. I don't initiate, but I always follow. It's what I learned from Ben. And I don't really care what we do. None of it seems to matter, it's just one more day and then one more again.

In a few months school will be over, and everyone is talking about their plans: going into the service or getting a job at the huge Ford plant, if it doesn't close down first. I wonder what Ernie would be doing if he were alive – probably not much different from what I am doing.

My grades are abysmal. I have failed Geometry and English (no surprise from fingerless Mr. Seaman) and I am well on my way to an F in Chemistry. I hate the teacher, a scrawny old Anglo with some crazy ideas. He puts a piece of pig iron on his car bumper to attract the rust, so the rest of his shit-can car won't get any of it. That seems about as useful as putting out an ear of corn at a picnic to attract all the flies. Anyway, I am pretty sure that trifecta of failure – English, Geometry and Chemistry – will prevent me from graduating in June. I am getting into the frame of mind where I actually want that to happen, I want to flunk out, just to show them – although who "them" is, and what I want to demonstrate, is a little vague. But that's how I feel, just – *Fuck 'em all!*

Then one day we have an opportunity to cut class "legally" to attend a presentation by some college recruiters. "Recruiters, you must be messin' with me, *ése.*" Mario says as we walk over to the auditorium. "Likely to be from the College of USMC."

"*Chale*, whatever it is, it's better than sitting in that fuckin' chem. class."

It turns out the University of California's new campus down at San Diego is starting a program for "minority" students, which is us. The recruiters are Brown Beret types, *Chicano* activists, and I like their "no B-S" approach. The leader is a tall young *Chicano* with a seriously pissed-off attitude and a simple pitch: "College is full of *gabacho* assholes and it is time we got our share. So you apply, you take the tests, and we'll get you the fuck in."

"What about grades?" a girl with a huge beehive sitting down in the front asks, the very question I was wondering about myself.

"*Entiendo.* We know how it is here, *hermana*, just apply. That's all you gotta do, *sabes?*"

"And what about it costing?" Another girl asks. We all murmur about that, no one has money for college.

"*No problema*," he says with a sneer, "the man pays for it all." We like the sound of that.

They hand out brochures with pictures of strange looking concrete buildings, a beach, and more good looking blondes, both female and male, than I have seen in my whole life. So I take the application and I fill it out. I apply, even though I am not Chicano. I guess they just assume everyone at my school is Brown, so no one ever asks. I have no idea why I am doing this. I wish Ernie were around so I could ask his opinion on this crazy thing. In my "personal essay" which asks about my "future plans" and how college will help me fulfill them, I say that I want to go to college so I can get a better job than my dad, who slogs cases of paint all day, and so I don't wind up with a bullet in the face, like my buddy Ernie. That's about the extent of my aspirations.

Early on a cold Saturday morning I get up and drive out to Whittier College to take a test called the S.A.T. I had no idea Whittier had a college, only a Boulevard, and I have no idea what this test is going to be about, but I go, I show up, I bring a couple of #2 pencils, as directed, and I do my level best. This is not like the U.S. constitution test. I cannot study for the S.A.T., which seems kind of unfair, but I do the best I can with the unfamiliar material.

I get a couple of teachers, including the *gabacho* who gave me that F in Geometry, to write recommendations for me. I know, it takes *cojones* to ask a teacher who failed me – with good reason, I never did any work for him – to write me a college recommendation, but he somehow seemed not to hate me, so I ask, and he does it. I wish Miss Luna was still alive, she would write me a great letter, telling how I helped her bust a gang member who was terrorizing the school.

At the same time I am playing at going to college, I keep spending more and more time in study hall, which is to say, cutting. I am waiting for the word on whether I am going to college, and yet I am doing everything in my power to get thrown out of high school before the end of my last year.

It all comes home in one bad coincidence, the usual coincidence – being in the wrong place at the wrong time. My car isn't running so I am walking home from school late and alone. It's later than usual because I spent serious time trying to talk to yet another girl who has no interest in me. It's going nowhere, like all the rest, except for Teresita, who is gone. It's getting dark early these days although it is only six, and I am not paying attention. All my life I have had a sixth sense, street smarts, whatever you want to call it. I know what is going on around me in a room, at school, and especially out on the street. But for some reason my radar is malfunctioning tonight.

I am walking along in the dusk, passing under that perpetually burned-out street light, wondering why I can't get this girl to go out with me. Then I am thinking about Teresita, how we first kissed right about here. I wonder who she is kissing now, down in *Michoacán*. Then I am thinking about Ernie, who once ran me down with his bicycle less than a block from here. I can't walk this street without thinking of him; our childhoods are one in my memory and it all happened right here. Then I am cataloguing my faults: some Mt. Etna sized zits, two long-ago broken off front teeth, chewed up finger nails, amazing stupidity, my talent for scaring most girls off, and most guys too, with my reputation as the Marine killer.

I stop and look up at that street light. I cannot remember it ever working right. Yet in its shadow I have lived some of my most intense moments with people who are special to me. Even Rene, that day I walked her home after her fight. I am turning this over in my mind when out of nowhere a car pulls up and three *cholos* quickly get out. It is Art Bolero and two of his Pico Boys, Manny and Trinny I think they are called. I could run, tear ass between the houses and across the backyards where the car can't go, and get home – but under our code that is only allowed if you are being chased by the cops. I could go up to the nearest house with a light on, pound on the door and scream for help, I know the people who live around here, this is my neighborhood – but that would be wrong, a pussy move. So I stand alone in the dark of that broken streetlight where it is just them and me, a confrontation that has long been inevitable. I decide to pretend that *I* have the upper hand, not them. They're a sad group of pussies, anyway. I call out, "*¿Quieren algo conmigo, putos?*" I don't have my knife or my chain on me, but I convince myself I don't need them.

They laugh. "*Demos chingazos, carnales,*" Art says casually to his buddies, and he walks up, with those big boots of his, and tries to kick me. I see that move coming from a mile away and grab his leg, lifting it high; he goes down on the asphalt. Then I back up a step and wait. Art gets up and they jump me, all three of them.

I am a strong, tough fighter, and I really hate Art, but it is three on one. I start swinging and kicking and hope for the best. I land a really solid punch to Art's face, the kind that could break the cheek bones, but it also breaks some little bones in my hand. The pain makes follow up punches with my dominant left hand all but impossible. I am going to have to take the beating so I curl up and try to protect my head.

Hey! As I go down I see a long, slender bayonet-like blade coming out in the tangle of bodies. That changes everything. I try to wriggle away from them and get some room. We're all mixed up arms and legs and I don't know what they're planning. Then I feel the sharp spreading pain in my side and know I have been stuck. I am no more than two minutes from home, on a street I have walked nearly every day of my life, in the perennial dark of a burned out street light, and I have been stabbed. It happens again, and again, my back, my side, as I try to turn away.

They pause and somehow on pure adrenalin I manage to pull myself slightly up from the pavement. Manny and Trinny see all the blood, grab Art by the collar, push him into the car and drive off. I can still see the bloody blade in his hand as the door closes. *"Chavalas!* Pussies!" I yell after them.

I can stand up fine. In the movies a guy gets shot or stabbed and he goes down, just like that. In real life unless the bullet or blade strikes a major bone, severs the spinal cord, or if it's a headshot and your brains get scrambled like what happened to Ernie, you stay standing until you gradually faint from blood loss. That can take a while. So I walk home, still too proud to seek help at a neighboring house. After a few steps the initial shock wears off and it starts to hurt. I get a cramping feeling in my gut on top of the obvious pain from the torn flesh and I can feel something poking out from a wound that is maybe six inches long, like a slash, so I press my ripped shirt down over it. Maybe it's just the rough edge of the split skin, or maybe it's actually my guts, I don't know. I can feel blood running down my back from the other wounds but he must have missed my kidney because I know that would hurt a lot worse. Right now I don't want to know how bad it is, I just want to get home. I keep pressure on my gut from my good hand and keep walking. Blood is pulsing out with each step, dripping down my shirt and my khaki pants front, but I am more concerned at the moment with my broken left hand, which is swelling up and hurts like crazy.

I get home and find the house empty. Both Mom and Dad are gone. It is only six, still work hours at the shoe store for Mom, and Dad probably caught some overtime. Grandpa and Gramma are visiting my aunt Claudia, Linia's family, a mile away. I decide to call Mom at work, because as I start to feel woozy, I realize I need to get to the doctor.

As I lift the receiver I remember once, when I was little and Ernie's dog was sleeping on the front stoop of his house. I came out without looking, just a kid laughing and talking to his best friend. I stepped on the dog and he turned and bit me, hard. Mom had to take me in to the doctor for a tetanus shot. I remember how mad she was, at the scare I had given her, and at the expense of the doctor – she had smacked me good and hard for that. So I put the receiver back. I think maybe instead I'll go across the street and see if Ernie can help, but then I remember. I have a fleeting thought that maybe Rene or Val are home, they would know what to do. It would be closer still to go to Teresita's house next door, but they have gone back to Mexico and the newest family over there is still strangers.

Anyway, I am so tired now I don't care about any of that. I really just need to sleep. Maybe that will help. So I find the couch and ease myself down. I am going to make a mess but Mom's plastic sofa cover will catch most of the warm blood flowing out of me. It is still pumping, a strange feeling, throbbing around my fingers. Whatever is sticking out of the opening in my gut is hurting worse, cramping, but then the pain is getting duller and duller. I try pushing it back in. Maybe it's getting better. I'll sleep for a bit and everything will be alright. I'll try to elevate my broken hand. . .

—m—

Dad found me. He came in from work a few minutes after I passed out and saw me lying on the couch soaked in blood, looking white as a sheet and dead. If I had been conscious to see it I would have been amazed by how quickly he got over his shock, stuffed my protruding intestine back in the gaping hole, and used a clean dishtowel and his belt to put a pressure dressing over my wounds, which were in a band around my waist. Then, despite our being the same size, he carried me "like a baby" to his car. He laid me out on the back seat and drove like hell to the emergency room.

Mom arrived while I was in surgery. They gave me three units of blood, repaired my perforated bowel, fixed the herniated abdominal wall, sewed up the jagged cuts and shot me full of antibiotics. They told Mom and Dad that after the loss of blood and the drop in pressure the risk of infection was my biggest worry.

"I hope he has stopped leaking blood," the doctor tells them, "but with internal injuries, you never know, we'll just have to wait and see."

For three days they never left my side, either of them, and a constant parade of friends and neighbors, including Al and Marta, who lost Ernie not too long before this, came to sit with them, and with me. That night I dreamt it was Ernie, coming to visit me after my appendectomy, only this time I know he is going to get it too, and I am looking forward to hanging out with him, watching television, and building model airplanes in the middle of a school day.

Whenever I was half-awake I saw them, Mom and Dad. I admit it was a comfort. Mom said more than once that she had vowed to the Virgin Mary, right there in the ER, that if the Blessed Virgin would intercede on my behalf she would make sure, absolutely sure, I "got the hell out" of Pico Rivera, out of L.A. altogether. What's more she'll see to it that I go to college; that I escape, even if she has to rob a bank to pay for it. Coming from Mom that was not an idle threat.

—⁓—

The cops, and Mom and Dad, want to know who did this to me. I tell them I don't know, some guys I had never seen jumped me. It was dark, the damned streetlight was out, they tried to rob me. "But you had your wallet in your pocket when you got to home," Mom points out.

"I fought them off," I say. "That's how I broke my hand."

This is not police business, this is my business. I know exactly what I have to do. Ben had that .45 in his trunk with a full mag. He is off somewhere in the service but I'll ask his brother Jorge what happened to it. I'll borrow it, or buy or even steal a gun if I have to, hunt those pussies down and take them out, together or one at a time. I don't care about the consequences. I *will* kill them, that is certain.

Mom is determined to get me out of town, before I "wind up like Ernie." I hear her saying as much to Dad when they think I am asleep. As usual Dad is a harder one to figure. I am in the hospital for about two weeks and, after the crisis passes, either he or Mom is still with me all the time. Once, when we are alone, after Mom has told me how Dad came home and found me, and what he did, I ask him: "How'd you know what to do, like how to stop the bleeding. The doctor said you saved my life." I was 'bleeding out,' my pulse barely detectable when I arrived at the hospital.

Dad mumbles, "I learnt some a dat first aid crap in da Army. Never tought I woulda needed it with youse." He shakes his head.

He has never mentioned the Army before. I know he was in the service, since we have a picture of him in uniform, looking young and handsome, with the photographer's retouched rosy cheeks, sitting in a frame on top of the television in the living room. He has given me an opening – a huge one under the rules we play by – and I take it.

"So, is that where you got them welts on your arm, in the Army? Where were you at?"

Dad looks at me with pain in his tired face, then changes the subject. Like he suddenly realizes that I do in fact need him to open up a little but still he can't do it.

Later Dad is at work and I see Mom alone. "Look, what's up with him? You gotta tell me, why won't he talk to me? Has he always been like this?" I have asked her this before, but never demanded answers, hoping against all reason that I would get them eventually from Dad himself. It isn't just the information I crave but to hear his story, from him, told to me. I have now given up that hope. If he can't talk to me after all of this he never will. This time, maybe because in her eyes I am practically on my deathbed, Mom tries.

"I don't know, honey," she says. "He came back from the war and he was quieter, I mean he was quiet before, but I didn't really know him too good then. We only had a couple of weeks to get to know each other. But I knew even then I would marry him when he came back." She smiles, remembering her first look at Dad. "I told my friend, Lois, when I first saw your Dad, in the park. I says, 'See that guy, he's real good-looking, I'm gonna marry him.' Boy that was a stupid decision!" This last is Mom's usual put-down of Dad; I have heard it so many times before that I ignore it.

"Did he ever tell you about the war?"

"No, not really. I think he drove a truck. That's what he told me before he shipped out, but when he came back he was mum about the whole thing. If I asked him what happened over there, or how he got that scar on his arm, he would start cursing and walk out, so after a while I just dropped it. You know he was gone for more than three goddamned years, the S.O.B., and I waited for him never knowing if he was alive or dead. I waited, even though he never wrote me a single, stinking letter – I knew he wouldn't. Have you ever seen him write anything? His mother would have heard if he'd been killed, so that was how I knew he was still alive. Then one day just like that he was back. No warning, no letter, nothing.

"Did he say why he never wrote?"

"He used to say, 'I wrote you a letter, but it got lost.' But I didn't believe him. Like one letter in three years would have meant something anyway. Then I dropped it. You know, back then they said it was better to forget all that crap they went through, to put it behind them and go ahead and live their lives. I do know he went to a lot of different places and wound up in Germany on V-E Day. Before that I think he was somewhere in Africa. He once said something when we were at the beach. He was complaining about the damned sand getting into the food I brought for our picnic. He said it was like how it got into the food when he was at some place in Africa. Then he clammed up again. That's about it."

XXV

Trucks?

Finally clear of the chaos in town, Sarge led them to a line of Stuart tanks and tank destroyers that were digging in along a shallow depression. They might have been the same tanks they had wandered into when they finally reconnected with the American lines, or the ones they saw heading out from Sbeitla hours earlier, but he couldn't be sure. Sarge spat, rubbed his stubbled cheek with his bloodied hand, and then shifted his helmet on his head. For all the world he looked like a farmer contemplating what to plant this spring as he gazed out over his land. That wasn't far from the truth, because Sarge's family were Minnesota dairy farmers and he liked nothing better than going home on leave to tend the livestock with his brothers. He couldn't stand it like they did, full time, but he loved the feeling of peace and contentment that doing the regular chores gave him. It was a lot like the routine in the peace-time army, and very unlike war.

A very young tanker lieutenant, he could not have been more than twenty-two, walked over to the group. He was the same kid who had tried to salvage the leaking gas in town. "You come to fight or to gawk, Sergeant?" he said with the self-assurance of a West Pointer. Sarge noticed his class ring.

"Where you spectin' them to come from," Sarge answered, pointedly leaving off the customary "sir." As a rule, Sarge found West Pointers to be a pain in the ass.

To his credit the lieutenant took no offense, he was clearly overjoyed to have volunteers for the fight. Several gunshots rang out, the clear crack of M1s. Everyone turned toward the sound, a small enclosure beside a bombed-out farmhouse behind them. "Deserters. They got the JAG organizing a firing squad for anyone found leaving the line without orders."

Russo thought to ask about the hundreds if not thousands of fleeing soldiers they had passed on the road, not a mile from here, but figured only the slow of foot got the firing squad. So now that he was here, he was here to stay.

The lieutenant wore armor insignia on his lapels; he was in charge of the small force digging in. He stood nearly as tall as Sarge, which was something for a tanker. He pointed out along the highway, a ribbon of dust set in a slightly darker landscape also of dust.

"I figure they'll come down the highway, and expect to roll right through town." He turned and pointed to the highway's entrance to the remains of Sbeitla. "My orders are to slow them down, then, when it looks like we've done all we can, get the hell out of Dodge. We'll give the first part of those orders a good airing, but I'm not too sure about how we'll pull off our retreat, we're about out of gas. Care to join us?" He even managed a brief smile.

Sarge looked at the disposition of the tanks and liked what he saw. He also liked the kid's spunk.

Getting no response from Sarge, the lieutenant continued, "Here's the plan. The Krauts come down the road, with scouts out front, but not too far, they don't like to get too far ahead of their main body. We can't take them head on, we know that. Plenty of our guys got burned up in M3's trying to fight a Tiger head on. So we lie low on the side of the road here, in and along this ditch, and take them with enfilade fire as they pass. We can at least immobilize a few, slow them up, before they come after us."

"And then what, sir?" Goldie asked.

"Then we run for it, corporal. The Stuarts don't have enough gas to even try to get them out of here, so we blow them in place. We found four trucks parked back in that enclosure," he pointed to the place where the firing squad had been at work. "I just hope they still run."

"Trucks?" both Russo and Goldie asked at once.

"Sir," Sarge said distinctly, his respect for the kid growing by the moment. "I got two truckers right here. Why don't they take a look, we can at least see what shape they're in. And where do you want my infantry?"

The lieutenant smiled.

—∞—

They found four beat up deuce-and-a-half's parked in the enclosure, as the Lieutenant had promised. They also found the bodies of six infantrymen, arms tied behind their backs, blindfolds partially slipped off their dead faces as they lay in a heap.

"Forget 'em, they're fuckin' dead," Sarge said, "get some of them trucks to run. I doubt we have enough men even now to fill four of 'em, let alone after the next fight. Save what you can, siphon gas, cannibalize 'em, whatever you gotta do, do it. And do it fast, I need you two assholes out on the line when the shootin' starts."

As soon as Sarge left, Goldie told Russo: "And while you're at it, Sarge, why don't you stick a broom up my ass so I can sweep the street at the same time?" Russo was too tired, and too scared, to laugh.

Russo climbed up into the cab of the nearest truck and tried to turn over the engine. Goldie jumped into its neighbor. They tried all four, and sure enough, while they didn't sound all that smooth, three of them at least started. Short on fuel, they siphoned the gas from the dead truck, and another, into the two that seemed the sturdiest, lined up those trucks so they were ready to run, doors open, tailgates down, and then returned to the line. It was all they could do, and those trucks would have to serve.

XXVI

We find the war, like always.

The long column of dust approached Sbeitla for the main assault in mid-morning. As the Lieutenant predicted, only a couple of German scout cars were out in front, with no one placed on the flanks, where they might have seen the sunken ambush waiting for them. The Germans were overconfident, assuming the entire U.S. Army was on the run. As the scouts and then the first tanks rolled by, hatches open, commanders standing tall in the cool air, torsos above the turrets, the Lieutenant gave the command and every tank, tank destroyer, and infantryman in the small detachment opened fire at once.

Russo was on the right end of the line of ambush, closest to the escape trucks, alongside Goldie. He had a clear view of the lead scout car as the firing began. The infantry poured M1 and BAR fire into it from a distance of 100 yards, watching as the car stopped, reversed direction, then burst into smoky fire as its fuel tank was hit by .50 caliber fire from a concealed tank destroyer. The scouts jumped out and fled back in the direction of their tanks, only to be cut down by accurate .30 caliber fire from the concealed infantry.

Three Tigers, including the commander's, judging by the array of antennas, were hit in the first volley of high-explosive tank rounds. The command *panzer* exploded as the on-board ammo ignited, creating a spectacular spray of metal and an enormous fireball that lifted more than a hundred feet into the air before returning to earth in billowing smoke. The two remaining lead Tigers were disabled, mostly tread damage rendering them immobile but not toothless.

Russo had the feeling of having stuck his hand into a wasp's nest and squashed the bug nearest him. He expected the rest of the hive to sting him, and he didn't have long to wait. The main column approaching Sbeitla fielded at least thirty *Panzers* and several now turned toward the ambushers, well hidden but immobile, and began to return fire. The element of surprise, their only real weapon, had been well used, but now it was gone and they were mere sitting ducks.

The Stuart crews held up their end of the fight with amazing courage given that their inability to maneuver against the superior Tigers, which were now coming head on, meant almost certain death. They continued a rapid fire drill, trying to enfilade the turning *Panzers* rather than watch their shells bounce off the Germans' heavily armored fronts. The enemy closed with the ambush line and began to exact revenge. Three Stuarts were incinerated in place and two more Tigers were stopped by tank destroyers whose rounds managed, once again, to damage the Germans' treads, immobilizing them.

After an intense ten-minute firefight the Lieutenant gave the order to withdraw. First the infantry, only a handful of men in addition to Sarge's little platoon, scrambled out of their holes and ran, then provided covering fire from a secondary line fifty yards to the rear of the dug-in tanks. Small arms were largely ineffective against armor but continuous and accurate fire forced the German tankers to remain buttoned-up, their visibility severely limited. This offered some comfort to the Lieutenant's tankers, whose turn to run came next. They began the dangerous process of abandoning their mounts, each tank commander tossing a thermite grenade into the hatch before hopping off and running full speed past the infantry's covering fire.

When the last of the tankers passed the secondary line the Lieutenant gave the order to fall back to the trucks. This was done at a sprint, under heavy German fire. Russo and Goldie flew into their cabs, cranked the engines, and on a hand signal from Sarge, who was with Goldie in the lead truck, pulled out with all the speed they could manage, creating a dust cloud of their own.

The burning Stuarts made an unanticipated but welcome line of defense as the trucks began their escape. Most of the *Panzer* commanders did not want to maneuver too close to the burning American tank line as occasionally a Stuart's ammo load would explode in a colorful and deadly spray of shrapnel. Still, the Germans poured continuous fire from behind the line of Stuarts. As the trucks turned away, still accelerating, a high-explosive round from a Tiger's main gun tore through Goldie's mount, severing it in half so that momentarily he was driving only the cab, and some torn metal from the chassis, which continued its forward momentum, with Goldie and Sarge on board, while the rear half of the truck was utterly destroyed, killing the dozen infantryman and tankers who were clinging to the deck when the round hit.

Goldie's cab, trailing its mutilated rear end in the dirt, abruptly halted a few dozen yards down the road. At the time Goldie's truck was hit Russo was behind him, accelerating, and he plowed right into the suddenly immobile rear half of the lead truck's bed.

The young tanker Lieutenant, seated next to Russo, screamed "Noooo!" but at that moment the laws of physics, and luck, took over.

Upon impact what was left of Goldie's truck bed, a torn wreck of twisted metal, cut through the front of Russo's cab, stopping it like a brick wall. Russo was briefly dazed by his impact with the steering wheel. As he regained his senses he found himself in a tangle of metal and men. The young tanker Lieutenant's decapitated body was slumped on the seat beside him. Impact with the rear of Goldie's truck had forced Russo's truck's massive hood to come loose, slicing like a guillotine through the windshield and into the cab, missing him but not the Lieutenant.

The two trucks were welded into one mass of metal, fire and bodies. Troops from Russo's truck bed had been thrown forward with the impact, one flying over the cab and into the engine compartment. A smashed body was the first thing Russo saw when he opened his eyes: a dead and mangled soldier lying not two feet in front of him. The soldier's flight forward had brought him into contact with the hood, which was slicing back. Blood poured onto the cab's floor. Russo noted that it was Wilson, the Texan.

The dead and dying from the back of Goldie's truck were now mingled with some of Russo's forward-thrown passengers in the engine compartment and cab. The mass of metal was burning, men were screaming, and as Russo regained full consciousness he found that he could not move. A panic set in as he tried with every ounce of strength to extricate himself. The door handle turned but the deformed driver's door would not move, trapped in the truck's bent framing. The headless body of the Lieutenant was at his side. Above him was the corpse of a tanker corporal, spewing blood onto Russo's lap. For as much as he struggled he found no release. No movement was possible, with the steering wheel bent down onto him, the door, his only hope, jammed, and his body pinned by his dead comrades. He screamed as his efforts produced no effect and he felt himself sinking into a mire of gore.

Goldie heard none of this over the din of the ongoing battle but knew his friend was in trouble from one look at the wrecks. He ran from his cab as soon as it stopped skidding. Sarge too jumped from his door and raced back to Russo's truck. Another high-explosive tank round flew overhead, closely missing the fat, immobile target. As machine gun bullets clattered all around, slicing through the twisted steel, Goldie got to Russo. The driver's door would not open but Goldie could see and touch his friend through the open window. And now he could hear his buddy's cries for help.

"Shit, Johnny, what a fuckin' mess!" was the first thing he said. Russo only gaped at him, confounded. He looked like a man recognizing for the first time in his life that he is not alone. Some of the few survivors who were still able to fight were returning fire against the Germans if only to keep them at bay, while Sarge, Goldie, and a couple of others tried to separate the living from the dead, and to move them from the burning trucks.

"We gotta get him out, *now!*" Goldie yelled across the cab to Sarge who had managed to pry open the passenger door with a tire iron and was pulling men, and parts of men, out of the cab onto the ground with more speed than tenderness.

The fire had started with leaking fuel in Russo's engine compartment. It engulfed the front of his truck and the rear of Goldie's, and the smell of the human mound was overpowering. Flames consumed some bodies while the red hot metal burned others. The smoke had a metallic smell, reminiscent of a tea kettle left on the stove too long, with the greasy tinge of burning flesh.

As the cab heated Russo pushed frantically at the door with his back, trying to force the wheel away from him with his arms. The natural expansion of the heated metal finally allowed Goldie to get the door open and yank his friend out. As he did so a steel strut from the wreckage fell onto Russo, who raised his arm in defense. He screamed as the hot metal laid into his bicep, where it stayed for an eternity, as if soldered to him. With Goldie's help he finally scrambled away from the wreck. Gasping for air, they moved upwind out of the billowing smoke.

Russo sat on the ground, shivering with shock and hacking with cough. Lacking anything else Goldie pulled Russo's tattered shirt off and wrapped it around his wound to stop the bleeding, of which he found surprisingly little. The burn had gone deep into his bicep, then largely cauterized itself.

As Goldie rescued Russo a German tanker behind the line of burning Stuarts noted their motion, swiveled his machine gun, and spit a long burst in their direction. Aided by Goldie, Russo ran for cover.

Only a dozen men were still capable of fighting and most of them were wounded. They had gathered on the passenger side of the wrecked trucks keeping the tangle of steel and fire between themselves and the *Panzers*. After the wreck their return fire was minimal so the Germans, emboldened, opening their hatches for a better view, advanced across the American ambush line that had until now kept them at bay. A Tiger approached the positions of two burning Stuarts, pouring machine gun fire into the truck wreck as it approached the defenders huddled behind. At any moment they would be annihilated. When the *Panzer's* advance placed it directly between the two American tanks, one of the burning M3's decided to fight back on its own – its ammo load cooked off, exploding with such fury that the much heavier Tiger was instantly engulfed and destroyed, its own ammo and fuel adding still more explosive power to the conflagration.

This scene gave the rest of the *Panzers* an excuse to break off the costly engagement with an insignificant, dismounted, and defeated enemy outpost, returning to the highway and their main line of attack straight into Sbeitla.

Although the skirmish had ended the noise had hardly abated as burning and exploding vehicles kept up the roar and caustic smoke covered the scene. Sarge looked at his watch and announced to the little group of survivors: "We held them up for about thirty minutes, and we lost about thirty men, I hope to Christ it's worth it."

"What do we do now, Sarge," Russo asked, sitting up against a low stone wall, his face and chest bright red from the heat that had nearly consumed him, his clothes sopping in the blood of his comrades. Goldie lit a cigarette and handed it to his friend, whose hand shook. Then he lit another and another, until each of the little group had a smoke.

"We find the war," Sarge answered quietly, "like always."

Free from enemy fire they made a more thorough check of the wreckage that had been two trucks and located eleven men in and around the bed of Russo's mount who were seriously wounded but still more or less alive. They had no medic, and most of their medical supplies, along with their ammo, food, and water, had been devoured by the fire. So the survivors gathered the worst wounded, men whom they knew were dying, and made them as comfortable as possible. Most contributed a syrette of morphine from their personal medical kits. They administered doses to those who were conscious, wrote the time on their foreheads in grease pencil in the prescribed manner: "M 1145," to prevent accidental overdose in the unlikely event someone came along to provide medical care, and left them.

It was difficult, more difficult than leaving the wounded up on the Dj, because they had no medics and they knew for a fact these brave men would die, alone, right here. The survivors, who were mostly walking wounded themselves, picked up what weapons and ammo they could find and headed back in the direction Sarge had led them in from just hours before. Only now, retracing their steps along the recent route of retreat, they were moving toward the front. The German advance had left them behind the new lines, on the enemy side.

"Goldie, you still got dat paper?" Russo asked as they started walking, his voice shaky.

"What, you need fuckin' toilet paper? Johnny, I don't know about you but I think personally I am never gonna shit again." Goldie was exhausted, scared, and covered in other people's blood, but otherwise, amazingly, unharmed. He still had the BAR he had lifted from the fleeing GI on the way out to the ambush, and it was still the group's heaviest weapon.

"Nah, Goldie, I need dat paper for writin' ta Gina. I tought maybe I'd do dat now."

Goldie recognized that Russo was badly shaken and was grasping at something comforting: the thought of his sweetheart. "OK buddy, tonight when we bunk down we'll write that letter, and tomorrow we'll find a postmaster somewhere and send it off."

XXVII

A real date.

They walked for several hours to outflank the advancing Germans, who had the advantage of being mounted, but were slowed by their decision to stick to the highway, which led through the chaotic town of Sbeitla, where they destroyed what was left of its hasty defenses. All the while they knew that if they succeeded in maneuvering around the column of *Panzers*, all they would accomplish would be getting themselves back in the line of fire once again. They had little choice; remaining behind enemy lines was not an attractive option.

Sarge led them in a wide arc, well clear of the fighting. At dusk they stopped at a small, recently abandoned mud-brick farmhouse just outside of town that was miraculously untouched by the battle. The structure had two rooms, one for sleeping, judging from the straw mats on the floor, and another for cooking, eating, and living. The terrain was mostly flat so from the enclosed barnyard that connected the house with a series of chicken coops they could see flashes from the firefight but they were perhaps a mile from the action. Close enough for now, Russo thought.

Chow consisted of a few canned rations they pooled and some wheat they found in the farmhouse and made into a glutinous porridge. It was sticky, bland, and undercooked but it was hot and they ate every bit of it. Then, true to his word, Goldie produced a sheet of Army-issue writing paper and a pencil, and said to his friend, "OK, last time we tried this we got as far as . . ." he looked at the crumpled sheet. "We got as far as 'Dear Gina.' Then that shit started up on the Dj, remember?"

"What was dat, day before yestaday?" Russo asked.

"Sounds about right, Johnny." Goldie showed the paper to Russo. "So what you wanna say to her, Casanova?"

Russo, as usual, was tongue-tied but with Goldie's prodding he managed to produce a short letter.

February, 1943

Dear Gina,

I am sorry I have not wrote earlier, but the United States Army has kept me pretty busy since we shipped over here. I am sorry too for the dirt on this paper, but out here everything, including me, is just plain filthy. I think about you all the time. I think about walking to the movies and then feeding the pigeons in the park. I remember how one of them landed on your lap and scared the hell out of you. We really laughed at that one, didn't we? We laughed a lot together. Anyhow, I have no way of knowing when this lousy war is going to end, you probably know more about what is going on than I do. But once it's over and I come home, I would like to take you out on a real date, to a nice club for supper and to take in the show. How's that sound?

Very Truly Yours,

John Russo

Goldie even helped him stuff it into its self-envelope leaving it unsealed. The censors would have to read it. Never having written a letter home, Russo didn't know how the censor system worked. He was easily intimidated and confused by new information, a situation which was not helped by his current state of mind, so Goldie, who seemed to know everything, said he would keep the letter and take care of the posting himself. He stuffed it in his breast pocket, buttoned it up and patted the outside to show Russo it was safe.

As they settled down to sleep on the straw mats the farmer's wife must have left strewn over the packed earth floor of the small, windowless sleeping room at the farmhouse Russo's burned arm throbbed. It also reminded him, much as he tried to avoid it, of that burning truck and the guys who were in it with him. His clothes were caked with their dried gore. As he relaxed toward sleep he started to sob. It began quietly, involuntarily, then grew loud enough for Goldie and the others crammed into the farmhouse to hear him. For once, no one wisecracked; they just pretended not to notice. Finally, Goldie put an arm on his friend's shoulder and patted him a couple of times, just to do something.

Russo turned, looking over his shoulder. "Goldie," he sniffed, tears streaming down the dirt and dried blood on his face, "you saved my miserable fuckin' life today."

Goldie nodded in recognition but Russo shook his head emphatically, like Goldie didn't get it. "Goldie, you come and hauled me out." He had no words for the terror he had experienced or for what he felt toward his friend. When we get back home, first ting I'm gonna do, I'm gonna buy you a fuckin' beer."

XXVIII

Dead to me.

As I begin to feel myself again I learn that having someone rip up your
intestines is not in every way a bad experience. For one thing my teachers
cut me some slack so that my grades won't suffer any more than they already
are. For another, if you survive something like this your reputation for being *El
Mero Chingón* only grows. I like that.

Soon after I get out of the hospital I ask around for Ben's .45 but Jorge
says he took it with him when he enlisted. That's Ben: he joins the Marines with
their M16s, assault helicopters, and laser-guided tanks, but he brings his own
weapon. Alright, I know some guys through my study hall contacts who can
get me *un cuete*, all I'll need is money. I have been saving up for college and I'll
use some of that, I have to take care of business. It is my first priority. College,
anyway, is a dream, they'll never take me.

My broken hand is more of a problem. I am not going to be able to fire a
pistol until it gets out of the cast and heals, which is going to be at least another
four weeks, maybe as long as eight. I could try firing right-handed but my aim
will be poor and I am going to have to be good to pull this off. Even with my
left hand healed up I am going to need a small caliber gun, a "woman's piece"
they call it, a .22 caliber or at most a .32, unless I want to wait until my hand
fully regains its strength, months longer. It is just as well that Ben took his old
Army piece with him; the thing weighed a ton and firing a .45 would probably
be enough to re-break something. Still, with a .45 you don't have to be a great
shot. If you hit the guy at all he will likely bleed to death from an entry hole the
size of a nickel and an exit hole, well, huge. With a smaller caliber I'll have to

plan on head shots, from up close. That last thought reminds me of how Ernie got dropped: two small caliber rounds to the face, the gun close enough to leave powder burns. I wonder for the millionth time who he pissed off badly enough to do that? Or was it only business, a drug deal like the cops said?

In the midst of these plans I get the packet from UC San Diego. Not the thin envelope that says "No," but the thick packet filled with enrollment forms that lets you know before you even open it that you have been admitted. The *Chicano* recruiters were as good as their word – almost. My terrible grades and minimal S.A.T. scores are overlooked. I am being admitted, but the promise of "the man" paying for everything falls quite a bit short.

Despite the expense Mom is still determined that I go. We sit down and count our pennies. Tuition is $1,200 a year. With living expenses make it two thousand. The U estimates $100 a quarter for books but I figure I can steal those from the college bookstore. Mom thinks she can come up with $500 over the first year, by raiding the money she has been skimming from the register at the shoe store. She also thinks she and Dad can send me something every month by tightening their belts a bit further. "Besides, we won't have you to feed here at home, and you eat a lot," Mom says with noticeable pain in her voice as she imagines my absence from the dinner table.

I may be the only kid at UC San Diego who plans to finance his education through a larcenous conspiracy with his mother. I tell her I think I can increase my hours at work over the summer. I don't mention my plan to blow some cash buying a piece to waste Art Bolero and the others who jumped me. We'll make it work, Mom says.

With each passing day of planning for college, looking at the courses offered in the catalogue they sent, and Mom's unbending determination that I go, the idea of buying the gun slowly fades. I don't understand a lot of what they say these courses are about, but topics like "Existentialism," "Satire," "Psychology," and "Creative Writing," pique my interest all the same. If you had asked me, I would have said I was still planning to do it, to kill them, once my hand healed, before I left in the fall, but I never do. My focus slowly shifts from recovery and revenge to the possibility of escape. I know, much as I want to deny it, that finding out what those courses are all about and killing those guys cannot both happen in the same lifetime. I also know, on some level, which is the better choice. I am torn between what I know, the code I live by, which demands revenge, and the first stirrings of a world out there beyond L.A., a world where throwing good *chingazos* is not the greatest achievement in a guy's life.

Several of my classmates were also at the recruitment meeting for UCSD but very few of them apply. Some don't want to leave the neighborhood. Others say I must be crazy to sign up for more school just when we're finally about to get the fuck out. Still others say that they want to get a good job and make some money so they can move out of their parents' house. Some are getting married or have a kid on the way and need money. Some like Ben have decided on the service, usually the Marines. I agree with all of them and with all of their reasons. Yet somehow the idea of going to college appeals to me. I don't know why. I don't know what I am expecting. I don't know where it comes from. But I now *want* to be a student. Fucking incredible.

Of course that transformation is easier said than done. At school everyone knows what happened to me and is expecting me to retaliate. It's *la vida*. Guys who already have it in for the Pico Boys offer to help. In the parking lot one afternoon a kid I barely know, Ysidro, hands me a brown paper bag and walks away. I get into my car before opening the gift, already knowing what I will find. It's a Smith and Wesson snub nose .38, a sweet little piece that only has a chance of hitting anything if you are real close. I stuff it in my jacket's right side pocket, given my cast, and forget about it. It's a light piece and easy to stash. If I had run into Art or any of his friends while carrying this revolver I honestly don't know what I would have done. But I don't see Art Bolero or his friends after that night under the burned out street lamp, not ever again. Eventually I hear CYA stories: he was sent up for attempted murder, he got beaten senseless by some guys at the youth camps and has brain damage, but by that time I just don't care anymore. They can lock him up or not, kill him or not, it's all the same to me. And in that way maybe I have killed him: he is dead to me. I am leaving, getting out. For a time the cast on my arm and my slow walking pace are enough to convince people that I am waiting to get stronger before I go after them. But eventually the whole thing fades from collective memory, replaced by more recent dramas, attacks, deaths.

———∿∿∿∿———

I am leaving. Maybe.

It is June, final grades are in and I learn that I have failed Chemistry, as expected. I never put an ounce of effort into that class and on the final exam I randomly marked boxes and walked out after ten minutes dropping the answer sheet on the teacher's desk with a flourish that said it all. Still I manage somehow to graduate, even with three F's on my record: English, Geometry, and now Chemistry. Maybe someone feels sorry for me or maybe they want to make sure I actually leave – God forbid I should decide to stick around and enroll for a second senior year.

The bar of academic expectations at my high school was set very low. Earlier in senior year the principal informed our class that as a group we scored second worst statewide on the new California achievement tests.

I barely manage to hang on for graduation. I am initially barred from participating in the ceremony due to my 'poor citizenship." That's fine with me. Like my father before me, I cannot wait to get away from high school. But when I see how much my participation in the ceremony matters to Mom I promise to behave myself for the last two weeks of the school year and the authorities relent. When I walk out onto the stage to accept my diploma, wearing that deep blue cap and gown, Mom cries. I don't know what Dad thought, and Grandpa and Gramma stayed at home.

I am the first person in that long line of Sicilian peasants and laborers to receive a high school diploma. I get the degree but not the benefits of the education that was supposed to go with it. I cannot remember reading a single book cover-to-cover prior to my eighteenth birthday.

In the middle of the summer I get another letter from UCSD, and this is a thin one. It says reasonably enough that my admission was based on the assumption that I would complete all my coursework with passing grades during this final semester. Since I have not complied I am no longer admitted.

I show the form letter to Mom. "It's no biggie," I tell her. "I'll join the Marines like I been wanting to anyhow." Then, "damn chemistry."

She says: "The Marines? Like hell you will! When you were in the hospital I swore to the Blessed Virgin that if you lived I would get your ass the hell outta here and into college and godammit that's what I'm gonna do. You call them up at that college and you tell them you ain't gonna be no chemist and they still gotta let you in."

There is no arguing with Mom when she is in *that* mood, so I make the call.

"I am sorry," the admissions lady says in an officious manner that lets you know she really couldn't give a shit. "The University's rule is that admitted students must pass all their remaining classes in spring term and you have not." The way she says "University's rule" makes me want to puke, like she said "God's law," something sacred and inviolable.

"Tell 'em about being an EOP student," Mom says, chiming in from the background when it sounds to her like it is not going well.

For a moment it's a toss-up between that and telling the woman to go fuck herself but with Mom breathing down my neck I say the magic words: "I am part of the Educational Opportunity Program." It feels like I have just declared myself as a retard. I don't know what she is going to say.

To my surprise, the woman's attitude changes. "Is that right? Just a moment, let me look at your file," she says. Then, after a long pause, "Oh, you're an EOP student? Yes, it's right here. It's OK, you can ignore that letter."

And that is it – I'm still in. I am still leaving.

XXIX

A nice deep hole in the Pacific.

T he only other kid from school who goes to UCSD is Joe Fleming, a bright, oddball guy. He is both the only Black kid at school and the only surfer. I have known him since kindergarten; he lives next door to my cousin Linia, from whom he hears my college plans. One day he calls up and asks if I am going to UCSD. Then he asks, "Want to room together?"

It turns out to be an inspired decision. We are quite different from most of the kids we meet at UCSD. A lot are either Jewish, or from rich-kid places I have never visited or in some cases even heard of like Westwood, Santa Monica, Brentwood, Beverly Hills, Palo Alto, Los Altos. Many are both Jewish *and* rich. Joe and I are roommates but not best friends, which is ideal. We provide a familiar and friendly face for each other in the dorm. Sometimes at night we lie in our beds and try to figure out the new people we have met. It helps us both with the transition.

Joe finds a network of Black, Filipino, and *Latino* kids on campus, which they call "Lumumba-Zapata College," and we start hanging out. I never knew how oppressed I had been growing up until I met these kids. Jesus! They have a huge political agenda and philosophies that include Marxism, Maoism, and Trotskyism, all of which are new and confusing to me. I don't even really understand democracy.

They explain how the factory workers, the "proletariat," will rise up when they realize the raw deal they have been getting. I tell them that if they showed up at my Dad's job and started talking to the paint factory proletariat like this they would get their asses kicked. Still, they are not deterred from bringing the revolution to the masses, at least to those privileged masses living here on campus, so I sign up. Aside from the politics I meet some really amazing girls involved in this movement. They are devoted to revolution, which means to breaking all the rules. So I become a Maoist.

I do well academically. It's amazing what studying does for your grades. Still I have this feeling that I don't belong here except when I am around the Brown and Black kids. But even most of them are middle class, they didn't grow up like Joe and me, and many have fathers who are lawyers or doctors, so the affiliation is only skin deep. I continue to wonder if I belong as I learn about concepts like "class" and "race." I wear creased khakis, white T-shirts, and biker shades. I sit in the back of the room and seldom speak.

In my Introductory Religious Studies class the professor, Terry Lindberg, takes an interest in me. He is also the U's Episcopal chaplain so maybe I am a mark for his pastoral work. Anyway, he says soon we'll be doing a session on existentialism and he doesn't have it worked out so would I be willing to co-teach it with him? Existentialism. Here it is, that long, seductive word, just like in the course catalog. I am suspicious. What do I know about Existentialism? I am also flattered. He uses this as a way in, a way to reach me, and over the next month we meet and talk, literally about the meaning of life. That is what Existentialism is all about, it turns out. When the session finally comes I show up dressed in wrinkled jeans like all the other kids and I have lost the shades. Although Professor Lindberg carries the session he gives me an opportunity to try myself out and it is fun.

One evening a couple weeks later I open my bottom desk drawer in the dorm room Joe and I share and take out a brown paper bag. I hop on my motorcycle – I had to sell my croaking Mustang to help pay tuition – and ride down to the La Jolla cove. This is my favorite spot in the new, larger world: rugged, beautiful, mysterious, and by moonless night as dark as the place under the burned-out street light back home. I walk out on the rocks and stare down into the darkening, luminescent sea. It is the most powerful thing I know, but that power doesn't scare me. The ocean is somehow reassuring, although I still don't know how to swim.

No one is around. I remove the .38, shake out the handful of bullets, and toss them seaward in a wide arc. Then I slide the cylinder out, feel its weight in my hand, and send it also arcing out and into the ocean. Finally I heft the pistol itself, off balance without its cylinder, and point it out to sea, taking aim at the dark horizon. I pull the trigger just for the feel of it then walk to the very edge of the rocks and drop it into a nice deep hole in the Pacific.

—⁂—

As I struggled to get over the shock of being in a safe environment that is dedicated to learning not driven by an insanely competitive *machismo*, a place where I didn't have to be on guard, *cholo* game-face on, every time I left my room, I dug deeply into what was offered at UCSD. I knew that I was there by accident. I didn't kid myself that I was a scholar. I didn't belong. I was not *Chicano*, and I certainly didn't get in on merit. I was there for one reason only – dumb luck. But it was luck that could change my family's course if I took advantage of it. Just as Grandpa killing Lampare and then escaping to New York improved the succeeding generations' lives this move, my move, getting an education, could propel us forward again if I didn't waste it. I wouldn't.

EOP was designed for kids like me who had not gotten much out of high school. Tutors helped me through the required math and science courses, for which I had no real aptitude or interest. Through Professor Lindberg I met the Marxist Herbert Marcuse. I was drawn to the philosophy, history, religion, psychology, and literature courses, anything that required thinking. Against my fears, I did reasonably well. I might not have really belonged there, but I no longer belonged on the streets back home either.

The feeling that haunted me throughout my college years, and long afterward, was that sooner or later, "they" would find out I did not belong and would kick me out: out of school, out of restaurants or shops, out of society. Snooty rich kids from Westwood in the dorms, intellectual snobs in classes that were way over my head, and absolute poverty that had me at one point during my sophomore year working two jobs and living in a friend's VW van, all intensified that feeling of being outside, of sneaking in where I didn't belong. But even in my first months away I had changed sufficiently that I no longer fit in back home. For a time I was stuck uncomfortably between Pico Rivera and UCSD, belonging to neither.

—⁂—

After our freshman year Joe dropped out, moving to Hawaii with plans to spend the rest of his life surfing. Most of my friends from childhood did not turn out so well as that. After Ben joined the Marines I never saw him or talked to him again. Two decades later Mom ran into him on the street and he told her he got into trouble while in the service. Once again it was in a pool hall and once again Gentle Ben whacked a guy with the fat end of a pool cue. This time it was a noncommissioned officer, an Anglo who made the mistake of exchanging words with Ben, and he went down with a skull fracture. Ben drew a long sentence for assault.

Mario also took the military path. He joined the Marines right after graduation and managed to be on one of the last rotations over to Vietnam, in 1973. Afterward he knocked around and for a time I lost track of him. He eventually fell into a job installing carpets. He and his girlfriend had a baby. Then one night, coming out of a bar drunk, he walked into the street and was killed by a passing truck.

Gilberto didn't appear much in my story because while he was always around he was usually too high to contribute much to the action. Still we had been friends and neighbors since kindergarten. After school he went on an impressive twenty-year run as an alcoholic, drug user and sometime dealer, and he was homeless on and off. Then, approaching forty, he met a good woman, got clean, and went to work as a community organizer in a nonprofit in town. Today he holds a responsible job with the school district.

The Truly Bad Kids from my study hall days ended up, without exception, either in jail or dead. The three I spent the most time with – Steve, Arturo, and Billy – I think of them as one person, since they were always together – two out of three did not make it to their twentieth birthdays. Steve OD'd on heroin, possibly a bad batch, possibly on purpose; Arturo died in a replay of Ernie's murder – a car, a drug deal, bullets at close range – and Billy, the only Russian among my crowd, went to prison for a long time after killing a guy over a girl in a bar fight, with his bare hands.

I was lucky to get out of L.A., and to stay out. I mostly heard news of my friends from Mom, who tried to keep me distant from it all while she kept up with the guys and their moms. For example, she didn't tell me about Arturo's death until after the funeral. When I complained that I would have wanted to come home for it she said, "That's why I didn't tell you. I went but not you. You need to stay the hell away."

XXX

Gone.

The Army was still retreating and it occurred to Russo that if this kept up they would soon be all the way back where they started, in Oran. Hearing this, Goldie said, "Great, then we can get back on them transports and sail home again, like none of this ever happened." For nearly a week now the Army – beaten, humbled, and then beaten some more – continued to fall back.

"You still got that letter of Russo's with you, Goldie?" Sarge asked as they walked up a steep embankment into the latest position Division was trying to secure against the next anticipated German advance.

"Sure do, Sarge," said Goldie with a smile, patting his pocket. "I keep looking for a censor and a postmaster, ain't seen neither yet."

"You think maybe they know somethin' we don't?" Mac chimed in.

Goldie looked over at Russo, his friend, who he knew was still badly shaken by the crash and fire. Turning to Mac, but intending his words for Russo, he simply said: "I won't rest until I find them lazy fuckers and get Johnny's letter mailed home to his girl."

The little group of survivors from the ambush, who were once defined by such roles as infantryman, truck driver, and tanker, were now joined as foot soldiers in the unending retreat. After the night at the farmhouse they had simply walked up to the nearest American position they encountered and just like that rejoined the battle. They had stumbled onto an OP whose occupants, three disheveled and dispirited teenagers with a radio, had pointed them in the right direction and told them to get on their way before a corresponding Kraut OP noticed the little gathering and called fire on their position – which they seemed to be capable of doing at will. It was good advice for everyone, which Sarge heeded.

As they made their way toward Division's new front line they were joined by other men from a mixed bag of units who were all headed in the same direction, with no more cohesion or order, and no larger authority, than what each little group of survivors could impose on itself. With no officers in evidence, Sarge took control. The German offensive had continued in fits and starts rather than with an overpowering final blow which could have crushed the American Army in its current state. But the *coup de main* never came either because of German commanders with different plans, poor intelligence regarding the Americans' degraded fighting condition, or most likely, an inability to keep the frontline units supplied with enough fuel, food, and ammo to press the attack. The offensive was probably going better than their logistics people had planned. If an army marches on its stomach a mechanized army rolls on gas, lots of it. Tanks are rated on gallons per mile, not miles per gallon.

Since the ambush they had laid for the *Panzer* column outside of Sbeitla, Sarge and his men had seen nothing that would give them the slightest cause to believe the situation was about to turn around. They just kept going because that is what soldiers do.

"Incoming!"

They were nearing the ridge, currently the American frontline, still trudging up the sandy embankment when the Germans opened up again with 105's. Sarge's little group was exposed on the slope facing the incoming artillery with nothing to do but hunker down, hug the sand, and wait. They had all experienced enough artillery fire by this point in the campaign to know that trying to flee toward the ridge would be suicidal. They made themselves flat and waited it out.

The only place for a soldier during an artillery barrage was hugging dirt. Since the target of the barrage was probably the ridge and the American lines concealed just behind it, had they tried to advance farther they would only have walked right into the teeth of it. Nonetheless, their current position was anything but comforting. Artillery fired from a distance of several miles was not terribly accurate, so being only fifty yards from the ridge they were well within the German's margin of error; they were in the kill zone.

The barrage continued for at least thirty minutes, which sounds like a long time but is in fact an eternity. The ground convulses, the air is full of sand, cordite, shrapnel, and a very fine dust; hearing is obliterated, coherent thought is all but impossible. Shock waves travel across the area taking the wind, and sometimes the very consciousness, from men left unprotected.

Russo remembered viewing the German artillery assault on Dj Ksaira. He and Goldie had witnessed it with a mixture of terror, sympathy for the poor bastards under attack, and relief that for the moment at least they themselves were not. That was what, maybe five days ago? Now all he knew was that he hurt: with every breath, with every shaking of the ground he clung to, he hurt.

Then, as suddenly as it had begun, it ended. The pause could be momentary, perhaps allowing for more ammunition to be brought up to the guns, or it could be timed to coincide with a ground assault by armored units. Or it could simply be a harassing attack, nothing more than an attempt to terrorize the defenders, to keep them off balance, and to inflict damage. They had no way of knowing.

Slowly, the dazed men arose, studied themselves for injuries, dusted themselves off, swished water in their eyes and mouths to clear the dust and, as their hearing returned, listened for the cries of anyone needing help. The German 105MM artillery piece was a fearsome weapon and any wounds inflicted tended to be catastrophic. After a 105 barrage you were either alive and shaken but unhurt or dead and dismembered. Russo heard screams from somewhere nearby, a crater excavated by a shell. He ran toward the sound and found a corporal whose left leg was completely severed at the knee. He tied a tourniquet, offered soothing words, and yelled for a medic. The man was screaming for his mother in the most pitiful way, and shivering like he was having an epileptic fit, but Russo's training told him not to administer morphine to a traumatically wounded man until he was assessed by a medic; the morphine would intensify the effects of shock and could kill him.

The medics came down from the ridge along with stretcher parties to evacuate the wounded. Sarge pulled Russo out of the hole, telling him he had done all he could. Russo kept looking back at the screaming man while Sarge called for those present to sound off. They formed up to quickly move the last distance up the slope and over the ridge.

In addition to the wounded corporal, two others did not respond to Mac's reading of the muster list Sarge had insisted he keep up to date even as the composition of his little command regularly changed. Both Allen and Goldstein failed to respond to repeated calls.

Russo noted Goldstein's absence immediately and began a frantic search across the sandy slope for his friend. Others joined in. The dead body of Private Allen, without any visible wounds or marks, was soon discovered. He appeared to be sleeping peacefully. "Poor SOB was killed by blast concussion, musta crushed his innards," Sarge mumbled to those gathered around the body. "Get his tags and let's move." Mac jumped into the hole and pulled Allen's dog tags loose. Sarge added them to a bulging collection in his blouse pocket.

They continued the search for Goldstein, calling his name, but got no response. "OK," Sarge called out. "We've spent all the time we can here. Let's move it up and over the ridge before them 105's open up again."

"What, and leave Goldie out here?" Russo screamed. "He could be hurt, he needs help." His eyes darted, and he continued a desperate search. But he found nothing.

Then one of the last surviving tankers called, "Over here!" Russo beat the rest of them to the spot, where he encountered the tanker standing in a shell hole holding up, quite gingerly, a BAR whose wooden stock was shattered and long barrel bent sideways nearly 45 degrees. Sarge and several others arrived. For a moment they all stared in silence at the strangely deformed weapon.

"Where'd you find it?" Sarge asked softly.

"Right here," the tanker pointed to the open depression in which he stood.

"Goldstein was the only man out here carrying a BAR, wasn't he?" Sarge asked. Several men nodded, as he knew they would. They looked around the area for a couple of minutes but found nothing, not a drop of blood, not a shred of clothing, not a scrap of paper from what had once been his buddy's letter to his girl, nothing. Then Sarge quietly ordered, "OK, move out, over the ridge."

Russo started to protest, began digging in the sand of the shell hole where the BAR had been found, muttering that Goldie could be buried alive. Sarge reached down, grabbed him by the shoulder, and physically shoved him all the way up the hill.

Walking behind him, Sarge explained, "Direct hit from a 105. Never knew what hit him. That's how we should all be lucky enough to go."

Russo couldn't accept it, "But how do we know he's gone. All we have is his fuckin' weapon. He could be. . ." his voice trailed off as he stuttered to find an alternative, then gave up.

"I don't think there's much chance Goldie decided to drop his weapon and go AWOL during that barrage, do you, Russo?" Sarge said gently. "Unless you think maybe he did, then it was a direct hit, and he's gone, just fuckin' gone."

XXXI

I'm his son.

I am back for Thanksgiving break a few months after leaving for my freshman year at UCSD and a few days after I dropped the .38 in the ocean at La Jolla. In the short time that has passed since I was last here a space has begun to open, making it strange to be at home. I hang out with some of the guys, The Truly Bad Kids, but it already feels like I am an outsider, a visitor. I don't want to cruise the boulevard, break into a house, or get wasted so they think I have gotten stuck-up and start calling me "college boy."

I see Linda, my old girlfriend, whom I took up with again just before leaving for college. Her parents are away so I spend the night, and in the morning I tell her very clearly that it is not going to work to keep seeing her, with me living in San Diego. This is something that in honesty I have needed to say to her for months. Maybe I should have said it before sleeping with her one last time, just broke it off on the phone, but I didn't. I still feel that great peace with her like in the early days, and selfishly I wanted to experience it again.

I visit with Linia, who has gotten married and is pregnant. As always, she wants to know about my love life, and, for once I have something to tell, stories about all those pretty Maoist girls from exotic Westwood and faraway Palo Alto in their flowered skirts, long straight hair, funny glasses, and, of course, no bras. Linia loves it, but wonders if I have anyone special. I don't have to mention Teresita's name for her to know I don't. I make no mention of Linda.

Roberto Arrias, our mailman for the past decade, arrives on Saturday while I am in the living room. He asks about college and we exchange small talk. One envelope stands out. It appears to be from the Army, or on closer inspection from an association of Army World War II veterans. They are putting on a reunion to mark the thirtieth anniversary of the Battle of Kasserine Pass. It is addressed to Dad. I hand it to him, but he only gives it a disgusted don't-bother-me look, throws it into the kitchen trash, and walks away. I fish it out and take it back to school with me the next day.

In the University library, a concrete monstrosity resembling an upside-down pyramid, I find a book on World War II. It turns out The Battle of Kasserine Pass was one of the worst defeats of American arms in any war, and at the time was the low point for the American offensive against the Nazis. Kasserine Pass is in North Africa, so this must be the place Mom was talking about back when I was in the hospital. She said that Dad had served "some place in Africa." The reunion will be held in only three months, in February, the anniversary month of the actual battle. By some incredible coincidence it is going to take place at the Del Coronado, the fanciest hotel in San Diego. I send in the registration form and beg for a free pass based on "financial necessity," mine, not Dad's. I say nothing about any of this to him.

As the date approaches I read everything I can find about the North Africa campaign and its role in the bigger war. Much is written about the strategy, the politics, and the doings of the great generals, German, British, and American, but not much at all about the men who actually fought the war. I half-hope to find a mention of Dad in the history books.

On the day of the reunion, I shave my Maoist beard clean off, comb my wild hair back as best I can, and put on the most respectable clothing I can find. I realize, with the anti-Vietnam War protests in full swing, that I may not receive the warmest of welcomes from these old guys, who answered the call for their war, while we keep "griping" about ours. But still I have to go. I am hoping that at their age they will be more interested in reliving the battles of the past than in fighting new ones with me. I hope at least to learn something about this battle he participated in, and maybe get lucky and meet someone who knew him. So I ride my motorcycle down to Coronado Island. When I find the ballroom I check in and discover, as I should have guessed, that I am the only person under fifty in the room. A couple of months ago I voted for the first time. I am also pretty sure that I am the only person in the room who voted for McGovern. I tell the registration lady, the wife of one of the vet-organizers, that I am here representing my father. She gives me a sympathetic look. Maybe she thinks he's dead and I am honoring his memory, which in a sense would not be far from the truth.

The hotel is opulent, a word I have only recently learned. I like to use it, it sounds so, well, opulent. The ballroom is huge and impressive, definitely not the Los Nietos veteran's hall. I walk around watching the vets drink beer or scotch on the rocks, but now that I am here I realize that I have no real plan. I spend a moment considering how to connect with the thousand or so old guys, most of whom are wearing VFW caps, old Army floppy caps, or their own Army jackets, proud if they still fit. Then I see a huge bulletin board running along one wall and covered with notices. The vets are using this wall to reconnect with old buddies. I take a sheet of the paper provided beside the wall and write, in the biggest letters I can manage: JOHN RUSSO: ANYONE REMEMBER ME? I post it high up on the wall and then stand under it and wait.

Everyone seems to file by the bulletin board wall at some point during the reception. A guy reads a name and room number and then, with tears streaming down his cheeks, runs off to use the house phone. An older vet who gets around pretty well given he has a fake leg takes a paper and writes his name and a strange code: "Dog 1/3, chow 0700, cafeteria."

I ask anybody who glances at me, or who hangs around too long in front of the wall, if he knows John Russo. They are mostly friendly, if not very helpful.

"What unit was he with?"

"I don't know, I'm his son."

"Sorry kid, I don't remember him."

This same conversation is repeated over and over. After I have been at it for nearly two hours a very tall, muscular, nearly bald man in his sixties, with the broad shoulders of a former linebacker, walks up and scans the wall while I scan him. The old guy is still impressive. Even today no one would mess with him. He has "bad ass" written all over him. Suddenly his eyes widen in recognition. He looks around the room with a smile, then bellows, "Russo, you sonovabitch! Where the hell are you?"

I am shocked both by the fact that he is calling for Dad and by the sheer power of his voice. It booms over the hubbub made by a thousand or more vets engaged in hundreds of animated conversations. "Right here," I answer, sounding like a mouse. His gaze, following my small voice, slowly descends from the heights and finds me standing right in front of him. In response to his confusion I say, "I'm his son, did you know John Russo?"

—⋙—

This is how I met the man who in 1943 was Staff Sergeant Chuck Magnussen from Minnesota. He survived the war, twice wounded, and stayed in the Army for thirty years retiring a Command Sergeant Major. "That's the best you can do as an enlisted man," he tells me matter-of-factly. Then, "Call me Sarge," he says. He can't spend the whole evening with me, he has lots of guys to catch up with, but he agrees to meet for breakfast the next morning.

I return to the hotel first thing. Over eggs, bacon, toast, and coffee Sarge spends the morning telling me about the Battle of Kasserine Pass, which he calls "a classic fuck-up." I can tell he is going to give me a history lesson, not the low-down on my father, but that's OK for now. I want to hear about his war, especially the parts of it that he spent with Dad. He is impressed that I know something about this particular battle, which took place early in the war, resulted in a resounding American defeat, and for that reason alone is usually overlooked amid the stories of more successful American operations in places like Sicily, Anzio, Guadalcanal, Okinawa, Normandy and Bastogne. "You've done your homework, kid," is, I suspect, quite a compliment from this man.

It is not a one-way conversation. He wants to know how Dad is, what he's doing for a living, where he lives, and all the rest. He specifically asks if Mom's name is Gina and is relieved when he hears that it is. Then he asks if she received any letters from Dad during the war and looks disappointed when I relate that Mom says she never did. I fill him in on the few facts I know but I also tell him that Dad won't ever speak of the war, wouldn't come to the reunion, and is like a person who is not there most of the time.

"He just works and eats and sleeps," I tell him with pain. "I can't help thinking it has something to do with that scar on his arm and that he must have gotten it in the war."

"You mean he never told you how he got that fucking burn?"

"Nothing," I confirm. "I didn't even know it was a burn."

"Shit," he mutters. He nods knowingly as I press him for details, peppering him with questions, memories of anything that might help me to understand my father. Eventually, I realize that he is no longer answering, has stopped listening, is thinking about something else, remembering something.

"What?" I ask.

"Looking at you, and imagining you without all that damn hair, I can see him as he was at your age, kid," Sarge says with a big sigh.

—∿—

Sarge told me most of the story I have just recounted about Dad's experiences during the war in North Africa. The basic story, but there were still huge gaps I had to fill in on my own, imagining what might have been. He added a bit more before we parted.

"After Kasserine we were all pretty beat up. Your Dad had that nasty burn, and he had lost his best friend in the world. We all loved Goldstein, the wise ass, but Russo and him, they were like brothers. When things calmed down they gave us a week or so to pull ourselves together. You know: eat, sleep, shower, fresh uniforms, that sort of thing. At first, Russo slept like the rest of us but as the days wore on he stayed in his tent and only came out for meals. I figured he had done enough wallowing over Goldie – don't get me wrong, he was a great guy, but we had thousands of Goldie's, kid, let me tell you. When we got relieved I handed over to the graves registration people a pocketful of their dog tags.

"You couldn't let all the death get to you or you would stop functioning. And there was still a lot of war left to fight. So I told him to get his goldbrickin' ass outta the tent. He did as he was told, but he was not right. It was like he was still back in that shithole Sbeitla.

"Finally they pulled up some trucks and told us to climb aboard, we were going somewhere. The usual Army bullshit. Russo looks at the truck we are assigned to, a deuce-and-a-half like he used to drive, and he starts crying, balling his eyes out right in the company street. I tried to help him into the back but he started screaming and fighting me and he pulled away from it. He said he was never going to get in one of those 'deathtraps' ever again.

"Well, they put it down to combat fatigue. That was obvious, but it's nothing to be ashamed of about your ol' man. He was not the only one to fall apart after a tough fight, I can tell you that. Your Dad fought honorably, bravely, but it all got to him. Goldie's death got to him.

"The standard treatment when this happened was a few weeks rest away from the guns, so we moved on without him. I didn't see him again until near the end, in Germany two years later. I was with that SOB Patton by then. He took over Third Army and we had fought our way from France through Belgium, and on into The Goddamned Fatherland over the Rhine.

"My infantry company was waiting with a long stream of armor for the engineers to finish throwing a pontoon bridge across some little waterway we had to cross. They brought up another company that for some reason the pow-ers-that-be decided needed to cross before my company. Like I said, the usual Army crap. While they were waiting alongside us for the engineers to finish their work I spotted a familiar guy: your Dad. He recognized me right off too, smiled and shook my hand. He seemed almost back to normal except without Goldie around he had much less to say.

"I said, 'Russo, you dumbass, you volunteered for the infantry?' After all he had been through in Tunisia, having the deuce-and-a-half shot out from under him, then the crash at Sbeitla, sure enough your father decided he was through with driving.

"'I'd rather walk than drive' he said. He looked thin and tired, no different from anyone else. We were winning the war, that much we knew, but the Krauts fought us every inch of the way. And the closer we got to Germany the harder they fought, you had to give 'em that. So it was still taking a toll on men and machines. Russo had that thousand-yard stare guys got when they had been at it too long – we all had it, I guess, by that point. It was almost over, you could feel it, but we all wondered if we would make it to the finish or catch a bullet on the last day of fighting.

"You know he wasn't ever much of a talker, but I got out of him that he had been in Sicily in '43 and went with Patton all the way to Messina. Your family's from Sicily, right kid? Patton was on a tear to beat the Brits across the island. Your Dad said he just kept his head down and did what he was told. We must have been in the same fights a couple of times, in Sicily or France or Belgium, but it was a big war. Anyway, we had never seen each other 'til then, just a few weeks before it ended. An hour later the bridgehead was opened.

Russo shook my hand again, but. . .I don't know. That was that, I never seen him again."

—◊◊◊—

Over the next few weeks I peppered Sarge with letters and on one occasion a long distance phone call to Minnesota, filling in gaps in the story. I made up other missing pieces, things Sarge didn't know, and imagined what Dad felt or what he and Goldie might have said when they were alone and scared. The story now feels complete. Through it I came to see how the war, the whole lousy war, but especially losing Goldie, just overwhelmed Dad's limited ability to make sense of things. When he got overwhelmed he shut down, and he never really opened up again, with me or, it seems, with anyone. Not with his brothers. Not even with Mom. I had my story but I was still not sure if any of this would matter. That depended on Dad.

XXXII

Didya see any of da guys?

The question is what to do with all the information I have gathered. I can't just drop these sheets in his lap, or start at the beginning and tell him what I know, what I guessed, what I just made up, can I? I try to picture the conversation but I just can't imagine how he would react. Easter break is approaching and I have plans to go home for a week. This is my opportunity but I am not clear on how best to use it. I talk to Mom on the phone a couple of times, filling her in on most of what I have learned from Sarge.

"This explains a lot, a whole lot," she says. "So that's why I never got a letter from him for three damn years," she says when I finish telling about Goldie's disappearance – with Dad's letter to her in his pocket. "And he's been holding it all in for thirty years, Jesus Christ."

I decide to approach him on Palm Sunday, 1973. I see it as my own personal D-Day. I even call it that to myself, "Dad-Day," Palm Sunday, the day on which Jesus rode into Jerusalem on the back of an ass, doing his Father's work less than a week before they killed him. I will confront him after Mass. I just want him to acknowledge something: the war, Goldie, that he served and suffered, I don't know what. Maybe I really just want him to acknowledge me, that I am here, his son, that I have done all of this work to try to understand him. He'll never read this story. He doesn't read anything. But maybe he'll listen to me if I tell him what I know.

It is early afternoon and Dad is sitting out on the front porch stoop enjoying a warm breeze and a cigarette. It is still only April, but this is L.A. "Dad, look at this," I say as calmly as I can, plopping down beside him. I hand him a brochure for a vets' organization that I picked up at the reunion and I wait for a reaction.

"Where'd ya get dis, at dat college?" he asks, reasonably enough.

"No, not the college Dad. I went to that reunion back in February." Seeing his blank look, I quickly add, "The one for guys who fought at Kasserine Pass." Now he looks over at me, but what is he feeling? "Remember, I showed you the invitation and you tossed it? But I went. I went for you."

This has got to get a reaction out of him, doesn't it? He is going to yell at me, tell me to mind my own damn business, right? He can't ignore what I have said, can he?

"Didya see any of da guys?" he asks, finally. So now he wants to know about "the guys," whose existence he has never up until this moment acknowledged? The familiarity of it, what makes him think I would know who his particular "guys" were, even if I did run into them?

But of course I did run into one of them. "Yeah, I met Sergeant Magnussen. He asked about you."

"Jesus Christ, you met Sarge?" he warms a bit, smiling to himself and turning toward me. I describe how I met him, his initial reaction to my note, his booming voice, and my general impression of the man. "Dat's him, sure as shit, da big Swede," Dad says with a nod when I finish. "So he stayed in for da full tirty years?" He shakes his head, either in wonder, disgust, or admiration, I can't tell which.

"Dad," I venture, since this is going so well. "I. . .Sarge told me everything. About the battle, about the ambush you guys laid for those German tanks, about the truck wreck, how your arm got burned." I pause, "and about Goldie."

Dad's face doesn't change. He has never had a very expressive face. You can never read his moods, if he has any, by his expression. But I sense a moment of recognition, maybe a connection of my words to buried memories kept underground only by great and continuous effort. He says nothing, just nods again, taking it in, acknowledging what I have said.

I am about to continue. But suddenly he raises his hand, shakes his head, and mutters for me to stop. He starts to get up off the stoop, like he is going to walk away and leave it at that. Maybe I pushed him too far. But then eighteen years of frustration come out of me.

"Dammit Dad, I lost my best friend too, remember. He lived right over there," I gesture across the street toward Ernie's house. "We grew up together and then he was killed too, like Goldie, and I lost him right when I needed him worst. When I got jumped he wasn't around. He was gone; dead and buried."

Dad sits back down, but looks away from me, down at his Sunday dress shoes, which he has left on from Mass this morning, spit polished and gleaming as always. "So, maybe you're not the only one suffering around here, maybe other people. . ." but then I lose it. Despite my best efforts to hold it in, I cannot continue this. I don't know if it is talking about Ernie, or about getting jumped, or because of failing once again with my father, but whatever it is I get up and walk into the house, leaving him looking toward the empty spot I vacated. As I leave the stoop I notice that Mom is standing behind us and has probably overheard the whole thing.

Now I am in the living room looking out through the screen door as Mom goes over and takes my place on the stoop. She puts her arm around Dad's shoulders, laying her fingers gently on top of his scarred arm with a tenderness I have never before seen her show toward him.

Epilogue

Is that what Dad was?

M y father died on another Palm Sunday, in 2004, thirty-one years after I attended the veterans' reunion and tried for the last time to connect with him. He had experienced several years of slow decline, during which he refused to see a doctor unless I dragged him, and a "final illness" as they called it, lasting two weeks. He was nearly ninety. I was with him when he died, in a hospital bed we had set up where the dining table usually stood. Finally the pain he had refused to acknowledge for weeks became unavoidable, like death itself, and equally apparent. The hospice nurse said that his time was running out so I gave him morphine from the supply she provided and he settled into a sleep. I thought about the army, about writing "M 1200" on his forehead for noon, the time I dosed him, but no medic was going to come along to read it.

His breathing became irregular: for long minutes he took no breath at all and we would think it was over. Then, suddenly, he would gulp down a ragged breath and start the irregular rhythm again. I spent those last two weeks living with my parents, helping Mom to care for him. I had not spent so much time with them in thirty years.

One morning I was in their kitchen staring at a piece of toast when I felt a sudden, overpowering need to go to him. I went back into the dining area where he lay. Just as I entered the room he took one of those long gulping breaths and then ceased, as he had done so many times before. But somehow I knew this time was different.

"Come here!"

Mom hurried into the room and stood across the bed from me.

"You think?" she asked faintly.

I nodded, unwilling to meet her eye.

We stayed at his side, each of us with a hand on his emaciated chest. By this point he weighed only eighty-five pounds and his skin was drawn tight across a carcass of bones and little else. When his breathing did not start up again we accepted that he was gone. Although we knew it was coming and had watched him dying over the past weeks it was still a shock that he was now actually gone. We stayed there, in physical contact with him, our hands on his skin, unwilling to leave him, as his body cooled. We cried. I ran my fingers over the scar on his shrunken, once muscular arm, red and angry as ever. We told him it was OK to go, to leave us. We thanked God we had been with him; I told myself he would not have wanted to die alone.

The workers from the Neptune Society came at my call, bringing a black body bag that made a disturbingly crisp sound as it was unfolded on the gurney they rolled up to his bed. One of the workers was middle aged. His jet-black hair is the only feature I can recall. The younger one I do not remember even that much about – he was just younger. The whole process struck me as undignified and inhuman, despite their forced, businesslike respectfulness, something they had been trained for, but training cannot replace actual caring. Their routine reminded me of opening a new plastic bag to line the kitchen can.

They easily lifted Dad's insubstantial body onto the gurney and closed him into the bag. As his face disappeared beneath the zipper Mom screamed and fell back onto the sofa. I understood: they were suffocating him. I wanted to stop them, to tell them that he would not be able to breathe. The mortuary workers glanced at us and in their look I read that this happened all the time, it was the part people dreaded most, the zipping up.

The older of the two approached, smelling of a cigarette he must have extinguished just before walking in to collect my father's body. He showed me a small, heavy piece of metal with a hole punched through one end and a number etched onto it. Next he produced, with great solemnity, a small piece of paper with the same number printed on it. He held them side by side so that I could be certain the numbers were identical. Then he attached the metal tag to a grommet on the body bag and handed me the paper to keep. They took Dad's body away to their van, parked at the curb. When the older one returned, alone, Mom and I were sitting on the sofa, numb.

"This," he said, pointing to the piece of paper I was still holding in my hand. "This here number matches the number we attached to the remains. Like you seen."

When my look told him I had missed the reason for this practice, he tried to reassure me, "This way you can be certain that the cremains you get back from us will be your loved one's, without a doubt."

Loved one, I thought. *Is that what Dad was?*

"Cremains?" Mom said, "What the hell is that?"

When I still seemed not to grasp what he was saying, he added, helpfully, "The numbers will be the same, on the card I gave you, and on the cre. . . the cremated remains you will get back." He looked at me questioningly, wanting to be sure I understood.

I thanked him sincerely, eager to convince him that my deepest concern was mistakenly receiving a pile of ash that had once been someone other than my father. Then they left, with Dad in a black plastic bag riding in the rear of a black Ford van on his way to an incinerator. I was still holding the little piece of paper with the number printed on it, a receipt for Dad's body.

We held the funeral service mid-Holy Week, before the annual communion ban, which would continue until Easter, an ancient practice intended to remind us that without the Resurrection we would find no eternal life and so, no bread of life. I did not need to be reminded that Dad would not return; that the Easter Resurrection would not bring him back; that for him there would be no more bread, and no more life; least of all did I need reminding that our relationship was over, the unresolved in our lives together remaining forever unresolved.

Afterward I began to see him in my sleep. I had seldom dreamed of him before this but now he came to me night after night for weeks. One of these dreams stands out. I was on trial for some offense, standing in front of a group of faceless, formally-dressed, unknown people who were seated at a high and massive oak table. It was long, with microphones set at intervals, the kind of table a congressional committee or panel of judges might use. I was being asked difficult questions about a matter I did not understand and I was stumbling with every attempt to answer. I felt panic rising. Then I noticed Dad, seated among that impressive group, with the sleeves of his plaid work shirt rolled up and his elbows propped on the imposing table top. He was younger, maybe fifty, and quite hearty. I wondered what he was doing seated on such a panel, out of place in his worn work clothes among all those judges or senators. He just looked at me steadily and, saying nothing, conveyed his assurance that I would get through this, that I would be alright, that I would get off.

D avid La Piana is the author of six non-fiction books on topics in non-profit strategy and management. This is his first novel. He lives in the San Francisco Bay Area.

CPSIA information can be obtained at www.ICGtesting.com
Printed in the USA
LVOW09s2035260814

401019LV00029B/1077/P